Death in the Dark

I was cat footing across the prairie when I should have been thinking about Samson in particular, and Ty and Clell. I was forgetting the rules that had kept me alive for so long, rules I had made myself. I came on a gully I hadn't known was there, stumbled down the slope, and collided with someone slinking along the shadows at the bottom. The next instant, iron fingers like a vise clamped onto my throat.

In the dark above me loomed Clell Butcher. I seized his wrist and sought to wrench his hand from my throat, but he was strong as a bull. His other hand locked on my right wrist even as his knee gouged into my gut, and he slowly bent me backward into a bow. All the while, his fingers dug deeper into my flesh.

I could not break his hold. I could not throw him off. My lungs started to ache for air. . . .

Ralph Compton

A Wolf in the Fold

A Ralph Compton Novel
by David Robbins

A SIGNET BOOK

SIGNET
Published by New American Library, a division of
Penguin Group (USA) Inc., 375 Hudson Street,
New York, New York 10014, USA
Penguin Group (Canada), 10 Alcorn Avenue, Toronto,
Ontario M4V 3B2, Canada (a division of Pearson Penguin Canada Inc.)
Penguin Books Ltd., 80 Strand, London WC2R 0RL, England
Penguin Ireland, 25 St. Stephen's Green, Dublin 2,
Ireland (a division of Penguin Books Ltd.)
Penguin Group (Australia), 250 Camberwell Road, Camberwell, Victoria 3124,
Australia (a division of Pearson Australia Group Pty. Ltd.)
Penguin Books India Pvt. Ltd., 11 Community Centre, Panchsheel Park,
New Delhi - 110 017, India
Penguin Group (NZ), cnr Airborne and Rosedale Roads, Albany,
Auckland 1310, New Zealand (a division of Pearson New Zealand Ltd.)
Penguin Books (South Africa) (Pty.) Ltd., 24 Sturdee Avenue,
Rosebank, Johannesburg 2196, South Africa

Penguin Books Ltd., Registered Offices:
80 Strand, London WC2R 0RL, England

First published by Signet, an imprint of New American Library,
a division of Penguin Group (USA) Inc.

First Printing, February 2007
10 9 8 7 6 5 4 3

Copyright © The Estate of Ralph Compton, 2007
All rights reserved

THE IMMORTAL COWBOY

This is respectfully dedicated to the "American Cowboy." His was the saga sparked by the turmoil that followed the Civil War, and the passing of more than a century has by no means diminished the flame.

True, the old days and the old ways are but treasured memories, and the old trails have grown dim with the ravages of time, but the spirit of the cowboy lives on.

In my travels—to Texas, Oklahoma, Kansas, Nebraska, Colorado, Wyoming, New Mexico, and Arizona—I always find something that reminds me of the Old West. While I am walking these plains and mountains for the first time, there is this feeling that a part of me is eternal, that I have known these old trails before. I believe it is the undying spirit of the frontier calling, allowing me, through the mind's eye, to step back into time. What is the appeal of the Old West of the American frontier?

It has been epitomized by some as the dark and bloody period in American history. Its heroes—Crockett, Bowie, Hickok, Earp—have been reviled and criticized. Yet the Old West lives on, larger than life.

It has become a symbol of freedom, when there was always another mountain to climb and another river to cross; when a dispute between two men was settled not with expensive lawyers, but with fists, knives, or guns. Barbaric? Maybe. But some things never change. When the cowboy rode into the pages of American history, he left behind a legacy that lives within the hearts of us all.

—*Ralph Compton*

Prologue

They didn't hear me, which was how I wanted it. I slipped into the canyon well before the moon rose above the east rim and worked my way down to their shack. Gruff voices and an occasional laugh told me they were there. In the corral were the thirty head they had stolen.

I firmed my grip on the scattergun and stalked to within a pebble's toss of a side window, which was covered by a piece of hide. No one could see in, and no one could see out either, unless they moved the hide. Training both barrels on the square of light, I cat footed to the corner.

So far, so good. But in my profession it's the yet-to-do that can do you in. I crept toward the front door. With any luck I could kick it in and let them have both barrels before they so much as blinked.

I'm partial to shotguns for close-in work. Mine was a double-barreled twelve-gauge made by an outfit in England. I'd sawed off all but six inches of barrel and whittled down the stock to a stub so I could carry it under my slicker, or, for that matter, under my vest, with no one the wiser. All I had to do was loop a piece of rawhide over my shoulder so the scattergun hung free and easy, and I was in business.

I was maybe two steps from the door when I thumbed back the first hammer. With the noise they were making, I figured they wouldn't hear. What I didn't count on was Ned Wheatley having to heed nature's call. Light spilled into the night, catching me in its glare, and it was hard to say who was more surprised, the old rustler or me.

To his credit Wheatley didn't panic. He kept his wits about him and clawed for his Smith & Wesson, bawling over his shoulder, "It's him, boys! Lucifer himself!"

I've been called a lot of things but never that, although when you think about it, it fits. The flattery aside, I let Ned Wheatley have the right barrel full in the gut, which had the same effect as cutting loose on a cantaloupe at that range. Wheatley was lifted off his feet and flew backward, his innards exploding every which way. I truly believe he was dead before he smashed into the table and upended it and a couple of chairs, besides.

The other three were caught with cards or glasses in their hands. Spike Thompson recovered first and snaked a hand for his Colt. I gave him the second barrel square, as much for the splatter as for the fact that Spike was the one who bragged in town that no so-called miserable excuse for a Regulator would ever make worm food of him. A person should be careful what they say.

Some of the gore caught Festus Blish in the face

and Festus instinctively jerked away. It slowed his draw. My Remington cleared leather before his revolver. I shot him in the chest and he started to melt, but I was already spinning toward the last rustler.

Pettigrew was on his feet. He favored a cross-draw and he was pretty slick at it, too, but in his haste he snagged his long-barreled Whitney on the table. I shot him between the eyes, then crouched to finish off those that needed finishing, but they were all down and would stay down this side of evermore.

Folks say I'm a cold-blooded cuss, but with all the body parts and brains and whatnot lying about, I needed a drink as much as the next man. I leaned against the jamb, took out my flask, and treated myself to a healthy swig. The coffin varnish burned clear down to my toes.

I smacked my lips in satisfaction at a job well done. Of course, it doesn't do to put the cart before the horse, and I had a lot of work left to do before I could collect. There's another gent in the same business who likes to put rocks under the heads of those he kills, but me, I take their ears. That way I've got proof, yet I don't have to tote the bodies all over creation. I shucked my boot knife and set to work, and soon my pouch bulged with eight ears.

I didn't bury the deceased. Hell, why should I? It wasn't likely anyone would pay their shack a visit before all the flesh rotted from their bones, so I let them be. That, and I'm as lazy as the next man.

Brisco was where I had left him. The roan knew

better than to run off. The last time he pulled that stunt, I staked him out under the hot sun for three days without water. Nothing like a powerful thirst to teach a horse to mind its betters.

I headed for the Tyler spread. I admit I was feeling pretty good. Soon my nest egg would grow. But once again I was mixing my carts and my horses. Until you have the money in hand, never spend it in your head.

Judging by the North Star, midnight came and went by the time I drew rein in front of the main house. I was bone tired after a week on the stalk, so I wasn't as alert as I should be. Which explains why the *click* of the hammer took me unawares. Naturally, I hiked my hands and said, "Hold on, hoss. Your boss is expecting me."

I reckoned it was one of the hands. But no, it was the big sugar himself, Bryce Tyler, who strode out of the shadows into the moonlight, a level Winchester at his hip. "Am I, now?" he said with a grin.

I relaxed and started to lower my hands.

"Keep reaching for the sky," Tyler said.

"What is this?" I was mighty confused.

"Is it done?"

"Of course it's done," I snapped, annoyed by his treatment. "And I'm here to collect the rest of my fee."

"Five hundred in advance and five hundred after," Tyler quoted our agreement, his bald pate bobbing. "Did you bring them?"

I started to reach under my vest for the pouch but thought better of the notion. "The ears? Yes."

"Are you sure you're not part Apache?"

"Whatever gave you that notion?"

"How else can you do the things you do? What does this make? Twenty-nine? And you without ever so much as a scratch."

I couldn't decide if he was serious or poking fun.

"Then there's this business with the ears. What kind of depraved human being mutilates folks like that? What sort of man are you, Lucius Stark? How is it you're so fond of killing?"

Forgetting myself, I shrugged. "It's a job. I do what I have to. Now, suppose I give you the ears and you give me the rest of the money I'm due, and we part company and go our separate ways?"

That was how it should be. When we first met, we shook hands, sealing our word. Nine times out of ten those who hire me prove trustworthy. But there is always that tenth time, that tenth hombre, who thinks that giving his word to a Regulator is not really giving his word at all.

"I've been thinking," Tyler said.

I swore.

"Now, now. Let's keep a civil tongue. Five hundred is more than enough for four measly rustlers."

"We agreed to a thousand."

"Yes, we did, but that was before I sat down and talked it over with my wife."

There it was. He had come right out and admitted it. "We also agreed no one else was to know you hired me. It was one of the conditions I set. Remember?"

Tyler took another step, the Winchester's muzzle pointed at my head. "Conditions change. I didn't feel right not telling her. She has as much of a stake in this ranch as I do."

"You gave your word," I reminded him. I always reminded them. Not that it ever did any good.

"Don't lecture me, assassin," Tyler spat. "Just take the five hundred and go. Take the ears, too, because I sure as hell don't want them."

By then I was good and mad. If there is anything I hate worse than a no-account who goes back on his word, I have yet to come across it. "What about your missus?"

The question caused him to blink. "What about her?"

"Maybe your wife wants the ears to hang over the mantel. Trophies of the time you hired a Regulator and made a damn fool out of him by cheating him and sending him skulking away with his tail between his legs."

"I don't much like your tone," Tyler said. "And I'll thank you not to speak ill of my wife. She is the salt of the earth, my Mildred. It was her brainstorm to hire you in the first place."

I was flabbergasted. He had lied all along. He and the missus had planned the whole thing, including their swindle of me. I gave him one last chance, though. Folks say I don't have a shred of decency in me, but they don't have to put up with the nitwits I have to put up with. Like the Tylers. "Please. I'm asking you nicely. Give me my money and I'll be out of your hair."

"Haven't you been listening? Five hundred is all you are going to get." He wagged the Winchester. "Were I you, I'd light a shuck while I still can."

"Do you have any sprouts?"

Tyler cocked his head as if he was not quite sure he had heard the question right. "Do you mean children? No, we don't." Then he added, lowering the rifle an inch or so, "Not for a lack of trying. We've been to the doc and tried a few patent medicines, but nothing seems to work." He paused. "Why did you want to know, anyway?"

"Because I don't shoot kids." I snapped my left wrist out and down and the derringer slid into my palm as neatly as you please. The shot wasn't that loud. He stood there a full thirty seconds before it occurred to his brain that his forehead had a hole in it. Buckling at the knees, he sprawled at my feet.

I swung down and was across the porch in a twinkling. Sure enough, Mildred had been listening just inside. When I yanked the door open, she recoiled in horror with a hand to her throat.

"You shot him!"

"I damn sure did." I held out my left hand. "The rest of the thousand, lady, and you can bury him come morning." I admit her red hair got to me, the way it shimmered so; otherwise I would not have been so charitable.

Mildred sputtered and made sounds that reminded me of the time I strangled a cat. Then she poked a finger at my chest and lit into me in female fury. "I'll see you hang! The whole countryside will be after you! Find a hole and crawl into it, but it won't help. Your days are numbered!"

"The money, lady." I was losing my patience.

Mildred made the mistake of glancing at the

ceiling. Then she poked me again and said, "All I have to do is holler and our hands will rush to my aid."

The bunkhouse was a hundred yards or more from the main house. Odds were, the cowpokes had not heard the derringer, but a woman's scream was something else. "Are you going to give me what's due me or not?"

Mildred drew herself up to her full height. "You can go to hell, sir."

"Damned contrary critters." I jammed the derringer against her chest about where her heart should be, and shot her. She collapsed in a tidy heap without another sound. Eventually folks would tie the dead rustlers to me and me to the Tylers, and the newspapers would brand me as vicious and vile, as they always did, and demand that something be done about the notorious Lucius Stark. They had been demanding it for quite a spell, but so far no one had been able to oblige them.

I went up the stairs three at a bound. The bedroom was directly over the parlor. I looked in the jewelry box and the closet and opened every drawer but did not find the money. I tried under the bed and in the pillowcases and under the mattress and was about to give up when I noticed a pair of boots between the night table and the bed. Her boots, not his, boots so new, I doubted she'd ever worn them. I shook each and upended the second and out tumbled a roll. Evidently the Tylers did not trust banks and Mildred had not trusted Bryce to hold on to their savings. I stopped counting at four thousand, rolled the money back up, and slid the roll into my pocket. It made a nice bulge.

Mildred was still alive. As I stepped over her she stirred and moaned, so I placed my boot on her throat until she was still.

About to climb on Brisco, I heard a sound from the direction of the bunkhouse. A lamp had been hit and figures were spilling outside.

"Mr. Tyler?" a cowboy called out. "Is that you?"

"Yes," I answered, reining Brisco around.

"It doesn't sound like you!"

"I have a cold." I gigged Brisco. Shouts broke out. By the time the cowboys reached the main house I was safely shrouded in darkness. Some of the lunkheads began shooting at the sound of the hoofbeats, and some of their slugs came uncomfortably close. Bending low over the saddle, I lashed Brisco into a gallop.

All in all, it hadn't been a bad night. The job got done, I got paid, and the son of a bitch and his conniving wife who intended to cheat me got their due.

Then other hooves drummed. Tyler's hands were after me. I tried to recollect the lay of the land, but I had only been over it once. There was a creek to the north sprinkled with stands of trees. It wasn't much cover, but it was all that was to be had.

I reined Brisco north, and to add sugar to the pie, I let out with a whoop that the cowboys were bound to hear.

Excited yells greeted my outcry. They reckoned I was heading for the creek, exactly as I wanted. But I only went a short way before I cut to the west and slowed Brisco to a walk. After a hundred yards I drew rein and slid down. I did not have much time. Gripping the bridle, I tugged on Brisco's mane. It had taken me the better part of a month to teach him this trick back when he was knee-high to the stallion that sired him, and on more than one occasion it had saved my hide.

Brisco sank onto his side and I shucked my rifle from the saddle scabbard and hunkered behind him, just in case. The thunder of pursuit grew louder and louder, and soon I saw them, eight or nine, riding hell bent for leather. They passed within fifty or sixty feet of me and did not spot me. As soon as the night swallowed them, I shoved the rifle back into the scabbard, brought Brisco up off the ground, and cantered south.

Ten days later I reached Denver. I took my usual room. Several letters were waiting for me. One was a job offer from Kansas. A sodbuster wanted some Indians killed. They had taken his milk cow, and he offered me a hundred dollars to wipe out the whole blamed tribe. I tore his letter up. My fee was a thousand dollars. Everyone knew that.

The next offer was from Utah. A Mormon gent was upset that another Mormon gent married all three of his sisters and promised me a thousand plus one of his sisters if I would fill the other Mormon gent with more holes than a sieve. I liked the idea of the sister and set the letter aside.

The third letter interested me more, though.

I decided to give myself two days to rest up and then head out. The plain truth is, a Regulator's work is never done.

Chapter 1

When most folks think of Texas they imagine the lowland along the Gulf Coast or the heavy brush of longhorn country or even the vast inland prairies. Few think of mountains, yet in west Texas there are more mountains than you can shake a stick at. Fact is, Guadalupe Peak, the highest in the state at over eight thousand feet, is part of the chain of Rocky Mountains that runs clear down into Mexico.

I had been there before and loved the country. Something about it appealed to me. Particularly what they call the lost mountains. Peaks that are not part of the chain but exist like islands in an ocean of grass. Mix in the gorges that crisscross the region and you have as rugged and pretty a chunk of landscape as anywhere in this here United States of America. I should know. Since the end of the war I've been most everywhere and seen most everything.

Whiskey Flats had sprouted on a plain between two lost mountains. To the east rose the Fair Sister, a bald mountain with a rocky peak that gleamed in bright sunshine and lent the mountain its name. Miles west of Whiskey Flats reared the Dark Sister, a wooded mountain laced by ravines and canyons. The Dark Sister was a notorious haunt of badmen and beasts and was shunned by most decent folk.

I rode into Whiskey Flats on a Sunday morning. That was fitting, all things considered. My getup attracted a lot of attention as I rode down the main and only street to a hitch rail in front of the saloon. Out of habit I almost reined up, then thought better of it and gigged Brisco to the livery. As I dismounted an old geezer with a limp came hobbling to take the reins.

"How do, mister. Planning to put your horse up? It will cost you—" The old man stopped and his lower jaw dropped. He had seen the Bible and the collar. "Land sakes! Are you a parson?"

"No, I'm a Comanche," I said with a poker face.

The old coot cackled and slapped his bad leg. "A parson with a sense of humor! Now I've done seen everything." He offered his hand. "They call me Billy No-Knee on account I lost part of mine to a Yankee cannon." He thumped the side of his leg about where his knee would be. "Hear that? It's a wood brace I have to wear every minute of every day or I fall flat on my face. Damned stinking Yankees." Catching himself, he said sheepishly, "Sorry about that, Parson. I know we're supposed to turn the other cheek, but it's hard to forgive folks who lob cannonballs at you."

"We all have our burdens to bear." I wiped dust from the Bible with my sleeve, pushed my hat back, and lied. "I had no idea there was a town in these parts, Brother Billy."

"If you can call it that," No-Knee responded. "As towns go, it's a mite puny. Hell, if it was a flea, the dog wouldn't hardly notice." Again he caught himself. "Sorry about my language, but I ain't used to gabbing with a Bible-thumper."

"Indeed." I like that word. It sounded as if I was smarter than I am.

Billy coughed and pointed at the only two-story building Whiskey Flats boasted. "That there is the hotel. It's also the only place to get eats. The gal who runs it, Miss Modine, is as pretty a filly as you'll find on either side of the Rio Grande." He coughed again. "Not that parsons think about such things, I reckon."

"Ever read this?" I asked, tapping the Good Book.

"No, sir, can't say as I have. I never had me much schooling. Oh, I can wrestle with a menu if I have to, but reading and writing give me headaches."

The one and only thing I was grateful to my ma for was her teaching me to read. Since the only book we owned was the Bible, she made me read from it every night from the time I was six until I was twelve. I got to know it pretty well. Well enough that I can fake knowing it better than I do. "Then you have never read the Song of Solomon?" I opened the Bible and flipped the pages to the part I wanted. " 'Your lips are like a strand of scarlet, and your mouth is lovely.' " I picked another part. " 'Your two breasts are like two fawns, twins of a gazelle.' "

His eyes about popped from their sockets. "It says *that* in *there*?"

"And much more," I assured him.

"I'll be switched. And here I thought it was all about begatting and blessing." Billy shook his head in wonderment. "How is it I never heard a parson talk about breasts and lips and such at church?"

"And be tarred and feathered and run out on a rail?"

Billy snorted and grinned. "That's what would happen, sure enough. The prim and proper don't like to be reminded that under their clothes they're the same as the rest of us."

I took a liking to him. "I'd be obliged if you would see to my horse." Handing him the reins, I turned to go.

"Fixing to stay long, if you don't mind my askin'?"

"I'm just passing through."

"Too bad. We don't have a church. About a year ago a traveling preacher stayed a week and held meetings every night. He'd bellow at us about fire and brimstone, then pass around a plate. I didn't mind being called a worthless sinner, but I wasn't about to pay for the privilege."

I liked the old coot more by the minute. "Blessed are the meek," I said. I knew snatches here and there, but I couldn't recite an entire passage if my life depended on it.

"Exactly," Billy said. "And that preacher was anything but. Oh well." He shrugged. "I can't hardly cast stones. I have too many sins to my credit."

"The Almighty forgives all," I intoned, and proceeded down the street. The half-dozen or so people out and about stopped to stare, and faces peered out of windows. I did some staring of my own at the sign above the restaurant. *The Calamity House*, it read. I went on in.

After the glare and heat of the sun, the dimly lit room was a welcome relief. I waited to let my eyes adjust, then moved to an empty table. Only four customers were present. To my left was a pretty mother with a girl of ten or so, indulging in slices of pie. To my right were two scruffy men in need of a wash and a shave.

I had hardly sat down when a door at the back burst open and in bustled as handsome a female as I ever set eyes on. Billy had called her pretty, but that didn't hardly do her justice. She had lustrous brunette hair that cascaded in curls past her shoulders, full cheeks a chipmunk would envy, the reddest lips this side of cherries, and flashing green eyes that sliced into me like twin sabers. I was smitten at first sight, and mighty upset with myself for picking to play a parson instead of a patent medicine salesman.

"Be right with you," the vision said as she carried a tray to the two men and set plates heaped high with food in front of them. "Here you go, boys. But why you want to eat my cooking when your ma is the best cook in these parts is beyond me."

The pair were not much over twenty, if that. The

youngest had cropped sandy hair and enough freckles to fill a whiskey jug. He showed his buck teeth in a wide smile and answered, "I'll tell her you said that, Miss Calista. She'll be flattered."

"Just call me Calista, Sam. How many times have I asked you?"

The other one had black hair and a surly disposition. "Took you long enough," he grumbled, picking up a fork and holding it like he was fixing to stab someone.

"Patience is a virtue, Carson," the woman said.

"Don't lecture me. I get enough of that from Ma." Carson speared a potato and shoved it into his mouth. Chomping hungrily, he declared, "Not bad. I guess it was worth the wait."

The woman turned and gave me a smile that would melt wax. "And what may I do for you, sir?" Those green eyes narrowed, then widened. "Oh my. A parson? A warm welcome to you, sir. Whiskey Flats is in dire need of spiritual succor."

My, but she had a fancy vocabulary. I squared my shoulders and leaned back to impress her with my chest. "How would that be, my good woman?"

"Calista. Calista Modine." She glanced at the two scruffy specimens, then said softly, "Let's just say there is a lot of ill will in our fair community."

"Do I call you Miss Calista or Miss Modine?"

"Either is fine," she answered. Then, as if unsure whether I had heard her, she stressed, "Yes, sir, a lot of ill will. If things keep up as they are, it won't be long before men shoot each other right out in the street."

"Is that so?" The bare essentials were in the letter I had been sent, but here was a chance to learn more from someone not directly involved. "Care to explain, my dear?" Inwardly, I chuckled. Being a parson had its benefits, such as calling a pretty woman I barely knew "dear" and getting away with it.

"It's the usual," Calista said. "A falling out over cattle. The LT Ranch has been losing cows and its owners blame a certain family who deny they have had anything to do with it."

Metal rang on china as Carson slammed his fork down. "I heard that! Why don't you come right out and tell him? The Tanners blame us. The Butchers. They've made that plain enough."

The younger one, Sam, looked up. "We haven't taken any of their mangy cows, Miss Calista. Honest we haven't."

"I believe you, Sam."

Carson speared another potato and waved it in the air. "Then you're about the only one who does. We've seen how people look at us. We've heard the whispers behind our backs." He glared at the mother and her daughter. "Town folks. A bunch of biddy hens is what they are."

"Behave," Calista cautioned. "I won't have you mistreat my customers." She smiled at the pretty mother. "Please forgive him, Mrs. Almont. He didn't mean to insult you."

Carson grumbled something I couldn't quite catch.

"That's quite enough out of you," Calista warned

him, then faced me. "Now then. What would you like?"

"I hear tell you rent rooms."

She brightened and set down the tray. "That I do. I have eight boarders in five rooms at the moment, with two rooms empty."

"It is a bit off the beaten path," I allowed. Removing my hat, I placed it on the table. I had shaved and greased my hair. It felt strange not to have a woolly caterpillar on my upper lip and not to have hair hanging down my brow. "I could do with a cup of coffee. Hot and black, if you please."

"Right away." Calista took several steps, and paused. "I didn't catch your name, Parson."

"Luke Storm, ma'am." I always picked names with the same first letters as my own. It made them easier to recollect.

"Reverend Storm," she said. "It's a pleasure to make your acquaintance. How long will you be staying?"

"I'm not rightly sure," I replied. It depended on how long it took to finish the job.

"I hope you will conduct a few services while you are with us. I'll even let you hold them here, if you want."

"That's mighty gracious," I praised her.

"Be right back with that coffee." Calista gave a little curtsy and whisked out of the room.

I liked how her dress clung to her long legs, but since it wouldn't do for a parson to ogle a pretty woman, I tore my gaze from her and acknowledged the presence of the Butcher boys with a nod. "Would you attend services if I held them?"

Sam was sawing at a hunk of beef. "Most likely we wouldn't have any choice, Parson. Our ma would drag us by the ears."

I grinned, and he misunderstood.

"Don't get me wrong. She's the best ma anyone ever had, but she doesn't abide sass. When she wants us to do something, we do it or else."

Carson glumly forked a carrot. "That's all I need. I've got better things to do with my time than have religion crammed down my throat."

"I try not to cram if I can help it," I remarked.

"Even so. No offense, Parson, but all that 'do unto others' stuff is just a bunch of bunkum to me."

Sam glanced at the front door. "Be careful, brother! If ma should walk in and hear you, she'd take a board to your backside."

The image of a grown man being spanked brought another grin. "You're a little old for that, aren't you?"

"Ma likes to say that we're never too old to have some sense beat into us," Sam said.

"And she beats it into us every chance she gets," Carson amended.

"Is she religious, your ma?" I inquired. When pretending to be a preacher, it's smart to find out who might know more about the subject.

"Is she ever!" Sam exclaimed. "She reads from the Bible every evening right after supper. And she's always going on about how the Good Book says this and the Good Book says that."

"A woman after my own heart."

Carson nearly choked on the carrot. "You wouldn't say that if you had to live with her. Don't get me wrong, mister. I love my ma. But she can be a powerful nuisance at times."

"Tarnation!" Sam chided. "You shouldn't talk about her that way."

"Well, she is," Carson sulked, and focused on me. "He's the youngest, so he tends to overlook her faults. He'll change when he's older. We all do."

Calista returned bearing a tray with a cup and saucer and the coffeepot. As she bent over my table I felt a puff of warm air and heard spurs jangle.

Two men had entered. Cowboys, wearing high-crowned hats and all the trimmings, including six-guns in holsters on their hips. If they saw me they gave no sign but walked straight over to the Butchers. The tallest, a rangy, bowlegged cuss who swaggered like he was God's gift to creation, hooked his thumbs in his gun belt and asked in a gravelly tone, "What do we have here?"

"We're not hankering after trouble, Hank," Sam said.

"That's too bad, boy, because Skeeter and me have a bone to pick with you and your brother. This morning four LT cows were found with their throats slit and their tongues cut out."

Predictably, Carson bristled. "Are you accusing us?"

"That, and then some." Hank rested his hand on his Colt. "Your cow-killing days are over."

Chapter 2

Carson came out of his chair as if it were on fire. He did not wear a holster but had a revolver tucked under his belt. A Prescott, unless I was mistaken, an older model with well-worn grips.

"Here now!" Calista Modine yelled. "There will be none of that! If you gentlemen insist on being foolish, do so outside."

The mother had risen and dashed around the table to her daughter. She held the girl close, and they hastily departed.

Calista angrily stamped a foot. "Look at what you've done! Gone and scared off my customers!"

I was content to sit there and let them have at it, but Calista looked at me in heartfelt appeal. Since it was a rare minister who would permit blood to be shed in his presence if he could help it, I stood up and stepped between Carson Butcher and Hank. "Have a care, brothers. The lady is right. This is hardly the right time or place."

Hank put a hand on my shoulder. "Who in hell are you to butt in, mister?" he growled.

The other cowboy, Skeeter, grabbed Hank's

wrist. "Are you plumb blind, pard? That's a preacher you're shoving." He was of middling size and build and had the bushiest eyebrows I ever came across.

"What?" Hank stepped back and raked me up and down. "Damn. You're right. Sorry, Parson. I was so mad, I didn't notice."

"That's quite all right," I said civilly. "But I must ask you to calm yourself. If you have a complaint against these gentlemen, find the marshal and charge them."

"Whiskey Flats doesn't have a lawdog," Skeeter said.

"We don't need one," Hank declared. "A man steps out of line, we treat him to a strangulation jig." He cast meaningful glances at Carson and Sam.

"But we didn't kill your stupid cows!" the youngest Butcher objected.

Hank was offended. "That's my livelihood you're insulting, boy. But I'll let you walk out as a favor to the reverend."

"We're not leaving until we're done our meal," Carson informed him. "And no flea-ridden cow nurses are scaring us off, neither."

His jaw muscles twitching, Hank looked at Calista and then at me. It was plain he was in the mood for a scrape, but he swallowed his resentment and touched his hat brim. "Sorry to have barged in like this, ma'am. I trust you won't speak ill of me to Lloyd and Gerty." Glowering at the Butchers, he backed out. Skeeter opened the door for him and they were gone.

Calista let out a long breath. "See what I meant about ill will?" she asked me. "I shudder to think what would have happened if you weren't here."

"Glad I could be of help." I reclaimed my seat and went to pour coffee, but she snatched the coffeepot and did the honors.

"Permit me, Reverend Storm. After you finish, give a yell and I will show you to your room."

"Why not join me?" I requested, indicating an empty chair. "I would very much enjoy the pleasure of your company." Sometimes I surprised myself at how polite I could be.

"Well, perhaps for a minute or two." Calista fussed with her hair and smoothed her dress, and sat. "Normally I wouldn't, but I'll make an exception in your case."

"I'm honored." I was also admiring the swell of her bosom, and once again had to tear my gaze away.

"I must say, Reverend, that you are not at all what I would expect," Calista commented. "You're different from most parsons."

I couldn't have that. In order to do what I was sent for, I must remain above suspicion. "In what regard?"

"You don't look like someone who spends most of their time indoors with their nose buried in Scripture," Calista answered. "You're as dark as an Indian. If I didn't know better, I would take you for a cowboy or a scout or a mountain man."

"I travel a lot, my dear, and am often out under the sun," I said, hoping to explain my bronzed hide.

"There's more to it. The way you move, the way

you carry yourself, the way you fill out your coat."
Calista appraised me like I was a racehorse and she
was a buyer. "I'm just not used to a parson being
so"—she seemed to search for the right word and
came out with—"manly."

Make of that what you will. I made it out to be
that she found me attractive, which isn't as far-
fetched as it sounds. My wife must have thought I
was halfway handsome or she never would have
married me. That our marriage did not end well is
irrelevant. The thought caused me to grimace.

"Are you all right? You appeared to be in pain
there for a moment?"

"Just a twinge." I was quick to change the subject. She was too observant, this one. "Tell me
more about the bad blood between the LT and
the Butchers." It always paid to hear other points
of view.

Calista placed her elbows on the table and her
chin in her hands. "The LT is run by Lloyd Tanner.
He owns practically all the land between the two
Sisters. About twenty hands ride for his brand, and
as you just saw, they are a salty bunch. His wife,
Gerty, is a friend of mine. They have a son named
Phil who recently came home from back East,
where he went to school."

"And the Butchers?"

"Hannah and Everett Butcher moved here from
Tennessee about five years ago. They staked a
claim to land up on the Dark Sister. Everyone
thought they were loco, but the Butchers are hill
folk, and used to living by themselves."

Out of the corner of my eye I saw that Carson and Sam had stopped eating and were listening.

"Eight months ago or so, Everett disappeared. Indians, everyone figured, although the Comanches haven't acted up in a coon's age."

"It weren't no danged Comanche!" Carson Butcher interrupted. "Pa was too savvy to be caught by any mangy redskins."

"Be that as it may," Calista said skeptically. "Now Hannah runs the clan. Sam is the baby of the bunch. Next oldest is Carson, there. After him is Kip. Then there is Jordy, Clell, and Ty. The two girls are Daisy and Sissy."

I had been counting them off on my fingers under the table. "Eight in all. That's some brood."

"There was a ninth," Sam mentioned. "But he died a few days after he was born. Something to do with his heart, the doc said. Ma wouldn't leave her bed for two weeks, she was so sad."

I finally got around to the reason I had been sent for. "When did the trouble over the cows start?"

"During the spring roundup," Calista revealed. "A tally showed the LT was fifty head short. They scoured the countryside and someone found a hide with the LT brand up on Dark Sister. Since only the Butchers live up there . . ." She did not finish. She did not need to.

Carson did it for her. "Since only my family lives up there, naturally everyone blames us. But we had nothing to do with that hide, and we sure as blazes didn't steal no fifty head."

"So far it's been a lot of finger-pointing," Calista

said. "But it won't be long before lead starts to fly." She extended an arm across the table and lightly clasped mine. "Your arrival is a godsend."

"In what way?"

"Isn't it obvious? You can do what no one else can. That collar gives you the right. You can stop the bloodshed before it begins."

Little did she realize I was there to do the opposite. "Blessed are the peacemakers." I was rather proud of that one. There was more to the quote, but I'd be dipped in gold if I could remember it.

Calista warmly squeezed my hand. "I knew you would understand. Now if you will excuse me, I have breakfast dishes to attend to."

I pondered the situation over my coffee. The letter had been short and to the point, merely stating that I was needed to regulate rustlers. My standard fee of a thousand dollars was acceptable, half on arrival, half when the job was done.

I often marveled at how far and wide word of my services had spread. I did not advertise. I did not mail flyers. I couldn't. In some jurisdictions what I did was out and out illegal and would earn me the privilege of being the guest of honor at a hemp social as quick as you can spit. In others, such as the recent business in Wyoming, Regulators were tolerated so long as they did not make a spectacle of themselves. Secrecy was my byword.

Yet despite that, word spread. From town to town and territory to territory, until now there probably wasn't a soul anywhere west of the Mississippi who had not heard of Lucius Stark the Regulator. That might be an exaggeration but not by much.

I knew I was playing with fire. Those who lived by the gun died by the gun. Eventually, if I stayed at it, someone would put a slug in my back or prove quicker or cleverer. But I didn't intend to stay at it forever. I had a plan. Or rather, a dream.

I saved nearly all the money I made. To date I had over twenty thousand dollars. That might not sound like a lot, but I was almost halfway to my goal. As soon as I had fifty thousand, I aimed to call the regulating quits. I would take my money and buy a small but comfortable place in New Mexico and spend the rest of my days lazing on a rocking chair.

I admit I was growing impatient. I wanted that fifty thousand. I wanted my life of ease right that second. So I was taking jobs as fast as they were thrown at me, with little regard for anything other than how fast I could get each job done and be paid.

This one looked to be no different from the rest. Cattle were being rustled. The letter had not pointed the finger of blame, but apparently the Butchers were believed to be the culprits. Without their being aware, I studied the two brothers. Carson was a hothead, that was for sure, but he had sounded sincere when he claimed his family had nothing to do with the missing cattle. And there was no doubting Sam's honesty. The boy was hardly an accomplished liar.

I shrugged and drained my cup in two gulps. It

wasn't for me to decide guilt or innocence. I was paid to do a job and I always did it.

Just then the front door opened and in swirled a stiff-backed woman dressed in the height of fashion. Her hat, her dress, everything looked as if she had just bought it, and paid top dollar. She had a sharp, flinty face, and dark, brooding eyes that flicked over me and then fixed on the Butcher boys. Without hesitation she strode up to their table and snapped in a voice as hard as her features, "You have your nerve."

Sam rose and doffed his hat, saying nervously, "Mrs. Tanner! This is a pleasure."

So here was Gertrude Tanner, wife of Lloyd Tanner, Gerty, as Calista called her. She impressed me as being the kind of woman who would never stoop to nagging a man to death. She would not nag, she would command. She would *tell* her man what to do, and he had damn well better do it.

"Don't patronize me," Gertrude rasped. "The gall! Showing yourselves in public after killing more of my cattle."

Carson wiped a sleeve across his mouth and jabbed a finger at her. "A couple of your cowboys were in here a while ago accusing us of the same thing, and I'll say to you what I said to them." He paused. "We didn't do it. We've never killed any of your stinking cows, never stole a single head."

"So you claim."

"Now look, lady," Carson said. "My family is sick and tired of you blaming us if one of your cows so much as comes up lame."

"We're not rustlers, ma'am," Sam added.

"Spare me your shammed innocence. I was not born yesterday. Of course you deny it. Your ilk always do."

Sam glanced at Carson. "What's an ilk?"

"I reckon she means an elk. But that makes no kind of sense. We don't have antlers or four legs."

Gertrude stood with her hands folded and her chin high and sheer scorn on her features, as a queen might regard disloyal subjects. "Have your fun. But we won't abide your shenanigans forever. My husband has reached the end of his tether."

"Send him over to talk to Ma," Sam proposed. "She would love to sit down with him and hash this out."

"That will be the day," Gertrude replied. "I will not have my husband associate with the likes of you or that liquor-guzzling mother of yours."

"Be careful, lady," Carson said.

"No, *you* be careful. You and your entire wretched family. If you do not cease and desist, I will not be held accountable for the consequences. Consider this your final warning."

"I don't much like being threatened, even by a female."

"And I don't much care what you like or do not like. As for my gender, don't let that hamper you. I am the equal of anything in britches."

I had met some tough women, but this one was at the top of the ladder. She could whittle most men down to size with her tongue alone.

Carson was plunking coins on the table. "Let's head out. I can't take much more of this shrew."

"Be nice," Sam said.

"To her?"

Carson shouldered past Gertrude, and I swear she almost took a swing at him. Sam smiled and bowed and said, "Sorry about the misunderstanding, ma'am. I sure do wish we could be friends."

"When hell freezes over, boy."

They left, and Gertrude Tanner turned. The change that came over her was something to see. She went from hard to soft in the blink of an eye, from a fierce she-cat to a kitten. "Do my eyes deceive me, or are you a man of the cloth?"

"Reverend Storm, ma'am," I said, rising. We were alone, so I felt safe in revealing the truth. "Or Lucius Stark, although you might to keep that to yourself. We need to sit down and hash things over. Your letter didn't give a whole lot of details."

Gertrude did not hide her surprise. "Can it be? You're him? I must say, you chose a marvelous disguise." Lowering her voice, she leaned toward me. "Yes, by all means, we must talk. But not here. Later." She smiled thinly. "Then you can start the killing."

Chapter 3

The Tanner ranch was in the shadow of the Fair Sister. Besides the main house, there was a bunkhouse, a cookhouse, a blacksmith shop, the stable, a chicken coop, six or seven sheds, and the inevitable outhouse. Make that two. Gertrude Tanner insisted on having her own, and as I had guessed, whatever Gertrude Tanner wanted, Gertrude Tanner got.

Supper was to be served at seven. I arrived at six in a buckboard I rented from the livery in Whiskey Flats. I had to be careful to keep my black coat buttoned. Otherwise, someone might wonder why a parson wore a shoulder holster. The Remington was the same model as my hip iron except I'd had the barrel sawed down to two inches and the ejector rod removed so it was less likely to snag.

Calista Modine wore a Sunday-go-to-meeting dress that clung to her in all the places a dress should cling. It was all I could do not to let my appreciation show. Fortunately, she didn't notice me squirm and fidget. At least, I don't think she did.

The buildings were in sight when she straightened and commented, "It was nice of Gerty to invite us, don't you think?"

I forgot myself and grunted. Calista had not said much on the way out. Whether she was shy because I was supposed to be a parson or shy around men or just plain shy, I couldn't say.

"Don't let her manner put you off. She can be brusque, but deep down she has a heart of gold."

I tried to imagine Gertrude Tanner as kindly and considerate. It was like trying to imagine a wolf on a leash.

"It hasn't been easy for her," Calista went on. "Running a ranch is hard work. And don't let anyone tell you she doesn't do her share. Fact is, I'd wager she does more of the actual running than her husband."

"Lloyd is timid, is he?" I played my part.

"Gracious, no. He has enough sand for five men. But he doesn't boss her around like some husbands do. He lets her have an equal say in everything." Calista winked. "Or more than an equal say."

"How is it there isn't a man in your life?"

Calista flushed and looked away. "Some questions, Parson, are too personal. They should never be asked."

"I was curious, is all," I said, justifying the snooping.

Calista was quiet a while. Her shawl had slipped from her shoulders, but she did not pull it back up. "Gertrude says I'm too finicky. That I'll never meet the man of my dreams because I set my sights too high."

"We are none of us perfect," I remembered a real parson saying once.

"True. And if I have set my standards too high, it's only because I've seen what happens to women who set their standards too low."

Before I could stop myself, I heard my mouth spout, "My own ma set her sights too low. My pa was lazy and worthless and came home most nights drunk. On good nights he fell into bed and passed out. On bad nights he slapped her around. She would cry and beg him not to, but he would go on beating her anyway."

"How terrible," Calista said. "Did he beat you, too?"

"No. Only my ma. I almost wish he had, to spare her some misery. How she put up with it, I will never know."

"Are they still together?"

"My pa died when I was twelve. He was on his way home one night, drunk as usual, and someone stabbed him to death in the alley behind our house. Stabbed him twenty-seven times."

"Mercy me. Did they catch who did it?"

"No." If they had, I wouldn't be sitting there. I'd warned him to leave Ma lone. I'd told him that I could not stand him hurting her. And what did he do? Pa had ruffled my hair and said I had it backwards, that kids did not tell their parents what to do, that the parents tell the kids. He went on and on about how I was too young to understand, and how I should not meddle in what grown-ups did. The very next night, he beat her. The worst beating ever. He split her ear and broke her nose and knocked a tooth out. Afterward, I could hear him snore, and her cry and cry and cry until she cried herself to sleep. I made myself a promise it would never happen again.

Pa always came by the alley. His favorite watering hole was at the end of the block, and he would cut through to our back door. I had taken the big carving knife from our kitchen and waited for him behind some barrels. He came staggering along, muttering to himself. When I jumped out, it startled him. "I don't have any money!" he cried. Then he saw it was me.

"What the hell are you doing out here, boy?"

"You're not to hurt Ma anymore" was my reply. I can still remember the smooth feel of the knife handle, and how the blood roared in my veins.

"We've been all through that. Get home." Pa lumbered forward and swatted at me with the back of his hand.

Skipping aside, I crouched and held the knife out. "Stop where you are, Pa."

"What's that you've got there?" he demanded. In his befuddled state it was a few seconds before he swore and snarled, "You dare pull a knife on me? On your own flesh and blood?"

"One of these days you could kill her."

Pa's cheeks puffed out and he sputtered, "She put you up to this, didn't she? Sending my own son against me."

"It was my idea, not hers."

But Pa was not listening. He was working himself

into a rage. "It's just like her. The bitch! I try and try, but all she does is nag and gripe and wear me down. But even that's not enough."

"She didn't send me, Pa."

"Don't lie. It won't do any good trying to protect her. You think I've hurt her before? You haven't seen nothing yet."

"Don't talk that way. Please."

Pa swatted at me again, but I was too nimble. "Stand still, you blamed grasshopper. Take your medicine like a man."

"I mean it, Pa."

"Out of my way, I say!"

I skipped backward and tripped over my own feet. The next I knew, he had me by the front of the shirt and shook me so hard, my teeth crunched. He cast me down like a used rag and stepped over me, his big fists clenched.

"Now for your ma."

To this day I do not remember jumping on his back. I vaguely recollect having one arm around his neck and stabbing with the other, again and again and again and again, until I was so exhausted I could not lift my arm. I became aware of him on his belly, of me on top, of the damp, sticky feel of his blood on my hands and my clothes. I don't recall how I got home. Ma undressed me and threw my clothes in the fireplace; that part I do remember. I remember her putting me in bed, and later, the knock on the door and the voices.

Ma knew. She had to know. But she did not tell them. At the funeral she held me close, her fingers digging into my shoulders. Thereafter, late at night, I would hear her sob and sniffle. I thought she was crying for my pa, but maybe she wasn't. She became sad all the time. She never smiled. She would not eat. Gradually she wasted away until winter felled her with chills and fever, and by spring I did not have any parents at all.

"Reverend Storm? Are you listening?"

I snapped back to the here and now and realized we were near the ranch. I had not thought about my pa in a long time. I try not to. It's hell when the first man you ever killed is your own father. "Sorry, ma'am. My mind wandered."

"I inquired as to which denomination you belong to."

Damn me for a fool. No one ever asked that before. "Denomination?" I stalled.

"Yes. Are you Baptist, Methodist, Lutheran, what? Not that it makes much difference. Their beliefs are a lot alike, aren't they? Although I do hear that some denominations let their ministers marry and some don't."

I looked at her. No, it couldn't be, I told myself. But she had me in a pickle if I picked one she knew more about than I did, which wouldn't take much knowing. Then I remembered a real parson I met once. "I'm Presbyterian, Miss Modine."

"What a coincidence! So am I."

I wanted to rip out my tongue and stomp it to death. "You don't say."

"Which group do you belong to?"

This was getting worse by the second. I clutched

at a straw she had unwittingly offered. "Does it make much of a difference?"

"No, I guess it really doesn't. Not to me, anyway. But the Old School and New School have been at odds with each other since before the Civil War. I never have approved of slavery, so I must be New School."

I was foundering in water over my head. The best I could do was say, "It's a shame we can't all live in peace and harmony."

Calista put her hand on my arm and smiled the sweetest of smiles. "If only everyone believed as you do, this world would be a wonderful place."

I had wriggled off the hook, but I was wary as I guided the team past a corral and stable to the broad porch that fronted the main house. Our dust had been seen from a ways off, so our hosts were out to greet us.

Gertrude Tanner wore another splendid dress and had done things with her hair that softened the hard lines of her face. But she could not do anything about her eyes, which were the eyes of a bird of prey.

Lloyd Tanner was not what I expected. He was short, for one thing, with shoulders that drooped, a wispy mustache, and lackluster blue eyes. Shaking his hand was like shaking a towel. He had no more vitality than a corpse.

The son was another matter. Phil Tanner was as tall as his mother and had the same hard features. His mouth was not so much a mouth as a slit. When he shook my hand he tried to crush my fingers, but

I gave as good as I got and he looked down in surprise. Right then I took a dislike to him, but I reminded myself that business was one thing and my personal likes another and I must not mix the two.

"Reverend Storm, you honor us," Gertrude sparkled, linking her arm with mine. "You must be thirsty after your long ride. Come inside. I will have the maid bring refreshments."

Not many ranchers' wives had maids. As a general rule, the wives are usually as hardy as their husbands and do the cooking and housework themselves. That Gertrude did not said a lot about Gertrude.

The house was not what I expected, either. Most ranchers were content with enough creature comforts to get by. The Tanners smothered themselves in plush carpet, mahogany furniture, crystal lamps, and the like. Walking into their home was like walking into the finest mansion. They had spared no expense. It made me wonder where the money came from. Savvy ranchers could reap high profits, but Tanner would need a spread five times the size of his to account for so lavish a spending spree.

The parlor was as grand as that of a fancy sporting house I had been to last year in Denver. I practically sank into the cushions on the settee. I remembered to remove my hat and balanced it on my knee.

Gertrude roosted in a straight-backed chair across from me. She gestured, and a maid came out of nowhere, a homely thing in her middle years who stood at attention as if she were a soldier in the army. Gertrude fired off several commands. The maid nodded and hastened out.

Lloyd crossed his legs, then uncrossed them, then crossed them again. "I must say it is an honor to have you," he said mildly. "The last preacher who passed through was ages ago and he didn't stay long."

Phil Tanner broke his silence. Unlike the mousy squeak of his sire, his voice was the boom of a bull elk. "I doubt the collections plates were to his liking, Father."

"Now, now, son," Lloyd said. "We shouldn't speak ill of a minister."

"Why not? He uses the outhouse like everyone else."

Gertrude laughed merrily. "You must excuse my son, Reverend Storm. He always speaks his mind, but he does not mean anything by it."

"Oh?" was all I could think of to say.

Phil frowned in annoyance. "I most certainly did, Mother, or I would not say it." He smiled at me, as cold a smile as I ever received. "You must excuse her, Parson. Like most mothers, she thinks she knows everything."

"Phillip!" Lloyd exclaimed. "I will ask you to show more respect. Apologize for that unseemly remark."

The true state of the Tanner household was betrayed by Gertrude's next remark. "Don't make more out of it than there was. Phil adores me. He would never intentionally insult me."

"Of course not," Phil agreed.

"I still think it was rude," Lloyd said meekly.

Both mother and son regarded him as if he were a bug they would dearly love to squash, and Gertrude responded, "If I say he wasn't, then he wasn't. Honestly. I'm sure the parson did not come all this way to listen to us squabble."

She was bear fat and axle grease rolled into one, that woman. I smiled and said, "Never fear, Mr. Tanner. I expect to stay in these parts a week or two. There seems to be a great need for spiritual guidance."

"Oh?" Phil said with a hint of mockery.

Calista defended me. "There was an incident in my restaurant today. Two of your cowboys confronted two of the Butchers."

"Which of my hands?" Lloyd asked. "I have given specific instructions that they are not to cause trouble. I will see to it they are punished."

Gertrude motioned with displeasure. "No, you will not. I commend them for having the gumption to stand up to those miserable cow thieves. And now the Butchers are killing our cows out of spite."

"We can't prove they are to blame," Lloyd said.

"Who needs proof?" This from Phil. Evidently the mother and the son liked to combine their assaults on the father, the better to keep him in his place. "Were it up to me, I would wipe out every last member of that thieving family."

"Who knows, son? You might just get your wish." Gertrude had icy twinkles in her eyes as she added, "The Lord works in mysterious ways." She bestowed those twinkles on me.

Chapter 4

The meal was fit for kings and queens.

We started out with a brandy toddy. I didn't finish mine. Whoever made it added too much sugar and it was much too sweet. As I was to discover, that was deliberate. Gertrude Tanner had a hankering for sweets and favored foods that suited her craving. As we sat sipping and chatting at the long table in the dining room, she mentioned that after the meal she would like to show me around the ranch. I answered that would be fine.

Next came fish chowder. The fish were from a stream that watered the LT. I can't say as I cared for it either. I seldom ate fish growing up and never have had a taste for it. It didn't help that they mixed in pieces of corn. The chowder smelled awful and looked like vomit.

My appetite was about spoiled when they came to the main course. Or should I say courses? You wouldn't guess it to look at them, but the Tanners ate like hogs. There were slabs of beef. There was chicken with all the fixings. There was pigeon. I was partial to the calf's head. Whoever boiled it had remembered to leave the wind-pipe sticking out. The brains were downright delicious. They had been mashed and mixed with bits of bread and sage.

There were dodgers. There was coleslaw. There were vegetables. There was even a bowl of macaroni, which I found I liked a lot. There was pudding. There was sweet potato pie. Thankfully, there was piping hot coffee by the gallon to wash the food down.

I overdid it. When I finally pushed the last plate back, I was fit to burst and feeling as sluggish as a snail in winter. I told the maid to relay my praise to the cook, and Gertrude mentioned that they had imported him from New Orleans. That was supposed to impress me, and it did with how much she loved money and the trappings that came with having a lot of it. Once again, though, I had to wonder how they could afford feeds like this. The LT wasn't *that* big. I knew of other spreads in Texas that ran many thousands more head, yet the owners did not live in the grand style to which the Tanners were accustomed.

Lloyd and Phil clipped and lit cigars. That was when Gertrude rose and invited me to take a stroll. Her husband did not seem to mind. Calista, though, gave me a strange glance.

The air felt nice after the stuffiness. I stretched and allowed as how I could sleep for a week.

"Sleep on your own time," Gertrude said sharply. "I am not paying you to lollygag. I want them exterminated as quickly as it can be done."

"By them you mean the Butcher clan?"

"Who else? They are rustling our cattle and I will not stand for it."

I leaned against a post and folded my arms. Horses were milling over in the corral, and at the cookhouse the cowboys were indulging in a noisy supper. "The two Butchers I met today claim they have had nothing to do with your missing cattle."

"Have you ever yet met a guilty man who didn't profess his innocence?" was her counter.

She had a point. It was a rare badman who admitted to being bad. Lynching bees are not all that popular with those being lynched. "There are women involved."

Gertrude gave me that pointed stare of hers. "So? You have killed women before, I understand."

"Once or twice," I admitted.

"Then what is the problem?"

"I always like to be sure with women."

"I must say, I never expected you to be so particular," Gertrude sniffed. "Killing is killing."

"If you think it's so easy, do it yourself. Or have your husband and son do it. Or your cowhands."

"Be serious. The finger of blame must not point at the LT. Word might reach the Rangers and I wouldn't want that."

She had another point. The Texas Rangers were a salty bunch. I would as soon be dropped in a pit of alligators as tangle with a company of Texas's finest.

"How soon can you get it done?"

I looked at her. "Understand something. I don't rush. Ever. Rush leads to sloppy and sloppy leads to dead. I will take as long as I need to take and not a minute less or a minute more."

She pursed her lips as if she had just sucked on a lemon and begrudgingly said, "Very well. Just don't take too long. There are factors involved of which you are unaware."

"Then make me aware of them," I said.

"Personal factors. All that should concern you is the job and the money."

Among my peeves is being told what I should and should not be concerned about. "Speaking of which, I want five hundred dollars before I leave tonight or you can hire someone else. The rest is due after they are all dead."

"I will fetch your money shortly." Gertrude placed her hand on my arm. "How long *will* it take? I hate to press you, but it is important."

I shrugged. "Two weeks, at the most."

"Surely not."

"There are nine of them," I reminded her.

"Couldn't you just catch them when they are all in their cabin and blow them up?" Gertrude asked.

And folks accuse *me* of being bloodthirsty. "I could if you want it to be in every newspaper in Texas. As it is, word is bound to spread. But I'll be long gone, my trail so cold, not even the Rangers could track me down."

"I suppose you know best," Gertrude said, but she did not sound as if she believed I did. "Is there anything you need?"

"Just half of the money."

"Wait here."

I sat on the rail and pondered. Something about the job didn't sit right with me, but I could not put my finger on what. Sure, Gertrude was pushy, but it was not unusual for those who hired me to want the job done quickly. Some even tried to tell me when and where I should do the killing. No, this was something else. I chalked it up to the fact I didn't much like the Tanners. The husband was a lump of clay, the son thought he walked on water, and as for Gerty, she was tougher than most men. Maybe that was it. I generally like females more on the dainty side.

As if that were a stage cue, out the door came Calista Modine. She wrapped her shawl about her slim shoulders and stood beside me, smiling. "I hope you don't mind my joining you."

I was thinking of the five hundred. "Not at all," I lied.

"It's the cigar smoke. I could do with fresh air." Calista inhaled, her bosom swelling under the shawl. "It's pretty here, isn't it? The setting sun makes the Fair Sister look like a volcano."

The top of the mountain was bright with color. "Seen a lot of volcanoes, have you?" I joked.

"Nary a one, Reverend Storm," Calista replied. "But I have an imagination. Don't you?"

I couldn't quite savvy why she was so testy with me. "Not much of one, no, I'm afraid. I like pretty things, but half the time I can't say why I think they're pretty. They just are." Now what made me say that?

"Did you enjoy the meal?"

"If I ate that much every night, I'd be fit company for pigs," I said, patting my gut.

Calista had a nice laugh. "I wouldn't want that to happen. But perhaps tomorrow night you will do me the honor of dining with me?"

It never fails. Put on a parson's rig and you become as popular as gold. I should have told her no. I had a job to do. "I would like nothing better."

We were grinning at each other like idiots when out stepped Gertrude Tanner. She had a poke in her hand, which she quickly slipped behind her back before Calista noticed. "Calista, my dear. When did you come out?"

"A few minutes ago. The sunset is spectacular. I envy you so, living amid such beauty."

Gertrude followed Calista's gaze. "To tell you the truth, I hardly ever notice. If you have seen one sunset, you have seen them all."

"A sunset doesn't stir you?"

"Not as much as a new dress. Or fine china. Or a gold necklace. Things I can touch and admire to my heart's content. Things of lasting value."

"If that's the case, I feel sorry for you, Gerty," Calista said. "Man-made wonders can't begin to compare to natural ones."

"That's a matter of opinion, is it not? Some people regard, say, the Grand Canyon as a marvel. But to me it's just a hole in the ground."

"You're joshing."

"No, my dear, I am not. I do not fawn over waterfalls. I am not impressed by rainbows. The stars in the night sky do not make me feel romantic because they are, after all, just stars."

"I had no idea," Calista said rather sadly.

"Oh, please. You make it sound as if I should be pitied. But I assure you that I would rather be as I am than compose sonnets to the moon." Gertrude shook with silent mirth.

For some reason I resented her smug treatment of Calista. I wouldn't know a sonnet from a horseshoe, but I butted in with, "If everyone thought like you did, this world would be a poorer place."

Gertrude was surprised, and I can't say I blame her. I was a bit surprised myself. "Don't tell me that you, of all people, admire sunsets and the like?"

"Why do you say that?" Calista came to my defense. "Why can't a parson appreciate beauty?"

Gertrude had blundered. When she said "of all people," she was referring to my true profession. But she recovered nicely. "He's a man first, a parson second, and the only beauty men care about is the kind they find under a woman's petticoats."

"Gerty!" Calista exclaimed, scandalized.

"Well, it's true, and I'll warrant our parson, here, will agree." Gertrude looked at me as if daring me to dispute her.

"You both made good points," I said.

Calista used that as a footstool to say, "I have another point to bring up. But it has nothing to do with what we have been talking about, and everything to do with averting bloodshed."

"Not this again," Gertrude said. "It's the Butchers, I take it?"

"Yes. I have had an excellent idea." Calista bobbed her chin at me. "Why not have Reverend

Storm intervene? He could sit down with both par-
ties and work things out."

"Are you suggesting I am incapable of working
it out on my own?" Gertrude demanded.

"Don't put words in my mouth. After what happened in my restaurant today, I am worried that
sooner or later one side or the other will pull a gun
and go on pulling until one side or the other is six
feet under."

"And what would be wrong with that?"

Calista was shocked. "You can't mean that,
Gerty. The Butchers are not bad people. A little
wild, yes. But not bad."

"A little wild?" Gertrude repeated scornfully.
"Have you forgotten the last time the three older
boys came to town? They got drunk and started a
fight with several of our hands."

"Ty, Clell, and Jordy were only having a good
time. They had a few drinks and got a little rowdy."

"You know them so well, you are on a first-name
basis, is that it?" Gertrude carped. "Reckless is one
thing, disregard for the law another. How you can
stand there and side with them when you know
as well as I do that they are rustling LT stock, is
beyond me."

"I don't know anything of the sort."

"Who else could it be? Have any strangers been
seen? By anyone? I tell you in all honesty, Calista,
that the tracks of the rustled cattle always lead to
the Dark Sister, but our trackers lose them in the
canyons. Those Butchers know all kinds of tricks,
I would imagine."

"I still refuse to believe they are to blame."

"Only because you are too kindhearted," Gertrude said. "But I do not have your tender nature. Even so, you must admit I have been patient with them. I have warned Hannah on several occasions to control her wild brood or suffer the consequences."

Again she had blundered. I wanted to kick her.

"What consequences?" Calista asked.

"The next time LT cattle are stolen or slaughtered, I will send for a federal marshal or the Rangers and formally charge the Butchers. Nothing would please me more than to see each and every one of them swing at the end of a rope."

Calista said softly, "Oh, Gerty." Shaking her head, she made for the door. "If you will excuse me."

We were alone. I stared at Gertrude without saying anything.

"What's the matter? Why are you looking at me like that?" She brought her hand from behind her back and held out the poke. "Here you go. Half in advance, exactly as you require."

"I'll count it later," I said, slipping the poke under my black jacket.

Gertrude snickered in amusement. "You don't trust me?"

"I don't trust anyone."

"Ordinarily I would be insulted. But we will let it pass." Gertrude put her hand on my arm again and I almost slapped it off. "I expect you to start earning that money, Mr. Stark. And remember. All

nine of them, or I won't pay you another dollar."
Gertrude patted my cheek and went in.

She would never know how close she came. I
had my hand on the butt of the Remington, but I
did not draw. Instead, I admired the fading glory
of the setting sun, and wished to hell I made my
living some other way.

Chapter 5

The Dark Sister had a fitting name. From afar, the peak resembled a giant fist thrust skyward. A dark fist, due to a mantle of forest that covered the mountain from the crown to the base.

A rutted track led toward it across the grassland. The buckboard rattled and creaked without cease. I never had liked riding in a wagon; I liked it even less by the time the buckboard clattered up an emerald foothill to its grassy crest. There, I brought the team to a stop.

According to the directions Calista had given me, I had miles to go yet to reach the Butcher homestead. It would take most of the morning. I started to reach under my jacket to ensure my short-barreled Remington was snug in my shoulder holster, then elected not to. Some of the Butchers might be watching. I must not do anything to kindle suspicion.

On the seat beside me was the Bible. I picked it up and held it in plain sight and thumbed the pages as if searching for a particular passage. When I stopped thumbing, I moved my lips to give the im-

pression I was reading. Then I set the Bible on the
seat and creaked and clattered on.

I was alert for not only the Butchers, but for
signs of cattle. All the hoofprints I had seen so far
were of shod horses. Nor did I come across cow
droppings. But that did not necessarily mean the
Butchers were innocent. They could easily hide the
rustled critters in any of the many ravines and canyons that poked outward from Dark Sister like the
spokes on a wagon wheel.

Hours went by. Then a bend appeared, flanked by
thick forest. I don't know what I expected to see when
I went around it, but it certainly wasn't a sprightly girl
of fifteen or sixteen skipping along with the sun playing off her straw hair and her bare feet. She heard the
buckboard and turned. I figured she would run off,
but she stood there as bold as brass with a smile
that would warm harder hearts than mine.

I stopped next to her and smiled my friendliest
smile. "Should I pinch myself or are you real?"

"I'm real, and you can pinch me instead." She
had a voice like honey and eyes that brought to
mind a high country lake.

"That's no way to talk to a parson, young lady."

She giggled and brazenly devoured me with those
blue eyes. "You're no minister, mister."

I was speechless.

"At least, you're not like any minister I've ever
seen. Usually they're fat or bald or both. You have
all your hair and you're right handsome."

Pure delight pulsed through me. But I was supposed to be a parson, so I said jokingly, "I am
going to tell your ma on you, young lady."

At that, she outright laughed. "Why, Parson, would you have me dragged out to the woodshed and switched until my backside is black and blue? My ma would blister me so bad, I couldn't sit for a month of Sundays." To stress her point, she rubbed her backside, then laughed louder.

"Might you be a Butcher?" I doubted she was a town girl up here on a lark, but with females you never know.

"Daisy Mae. But most folks just call me Daisy." She arched a fine eyebrow. "You're fixing to visit my ma, I take it?"

"If she is to home, yes."

"She's nearly always there," Daisy said. "Except for once a month or so when she goes into town for her medicine and whatnot." She gripped the edge of the seat. "Mind if I ride along? My feet are tired."

I did not believe that for a second, but I moved over to make room and in a lithe bound she planted herself next to me. A flick of the reins and we were in motion. "Is it safe for you to be traipsing about by your lonesome?"

"Why wouldn't it be? I can outrun most anyone or anything hereabouts. And I know this mountain like you know the back of your hand."

"Just the same, I gather there's a lot of ill will toward your family. You should take precautions. Never go anywhere without a revolver or a rifle." Now why in God's name was I telling her that? When she was on the list?

"I've never shot another living thing and I don't reckon to start," Daisy informed me.

"But you're a country girl, aren't you?"

"Oh. I get it. That means I must kill rabbits for breakfast and squirrels for dinner and deer for supper."

"And chipmunks to nibble on between meals and elk for special occasions," I bantered.

"Sorry to disappoint you, Parson, but my brothers do all the hunting. Me, I like to plant flowers and heal things."

Daisy had such an honest face, it made me wince inside to look at her. "Do your brothers kill the cattle they steal?"

I nearly lost an eye. She swiped her nails at me and would have clawed my eye to ribbons had I not caught her wrist.

"You've been talking to that mean Gertrude Tanner, haven't you? She's wrong, Parson. My ma doesn't have any truck with stealing." Daisy crooked her neck to study me. "Is that why you're paying us a visit?"

I let go and clucked to the team. "I'm making it a point to get to know everyone in these parts."

"You're saving Ma a trip. She was fixing to come see you."

"Any particular reason?"

"I should let her tell you."

I glanced up and down the track. We had it to ourselves. My palms itched, but I could not shake the feeling that other Butchers might be watching. Better, I thought, to continue to playact.

"So tell me, preacher man," Daisy said, "are you married to the Good Book or are you like the rest of us?"

Her frankness was unsettling in more ways than one. "That's not the kind of question a girl asks a man of the cloth."

In typical female fashion, she ignored me. "Most preachers are so attached to it, they won't look at a gal unless she wears the Bible around her neck as proof she has virtue."

I could not stop myself. I laughed.

"Do you always turn the other cheek, Parson?"

"It's what the Bible says to do," I hedged, thinking of my wife and the night I came home to find her in bed with another man. I didn't turn the other cheek then. I used a shotgun on him and my bare hands on her, and I've never been more ashamed of anything in my life.

"So my ma keeps reminding us. But we can't let that awful woman go on accusing us of things we didn't do. My brothers Ty and Clell and Jordy are for paying the LT a visit, but Ma won't hear of it."

"Your mother is wise." Several hundred yards ahead the track ended at a broad clearing. I saw a cabin but no sign of life except for half a dozen horses and a dog. "Is that your place?"

Daisy poked me with her elbow. "Whose else would it be? No one but us dares live up here. They're too afraid."

"Of your family?"

"No, silly. Of Injuns and outlaws and such. But we haven't had a lick of trouble except for the Tanners."

I glimpsed movement in the trees to my right and then to my left. A young man with a rifle appeared. He grinned as if he were playing a game.

My instincts told me he had been shadowing the buckboard for some time. He had the shoulders of a bull and a sloping forehead, and pointed a Henry rifle at me, saying, "Bang. You're dead."

"That's Jordy." Daisy grinned. "He sure is a caution."

I brought the buckboard into the clearing in a half circle so that the team was pointed toward the track in case I had to get out of there in a hurry. The dog, a large speckled mongrel, barked its fool head off until Daisy yelled at it to shut up. It contented itself with baring its fangs and growling at me.

More Butchers came out of the woods. Carson and Sam, I recognized. Another young man about the same age I took to be Kip.

From the cabin emerged more. First was the older sister, Sissy, I believe she was called. She had blond hair that was not quite as lustrous as Daisy's. She also had the same blue eyes, only paler.

The two oldest boys were enough alike to be twins, although it was my understanding they were born a year apart. They were big boned, with anvils for jaws, and held matching Winchesters. I remembered Calista saying one was Ty, the other was Clell.

Last to step out was the matriarch, as Gertrude had referred to her. Hannah Butcher was as broad as she was tall, and she was not much over five feet, a stout wall of a woman with a wide face and a wide mouth that curled in a smile as she held out a hand as big as mine. "So you're the new parson.

I'm right pleased to meet you. I'm Hannah, as if you couldn't guess."

"How do you do?" Her grip put Lloyd Tanner's to shame.

Her offspring had formed a ring around the buckboard and me. Every single one except Daisy had a rifle, and the boys wore pistols, as well, tucked under their belts. Their clothes were homespun. Only Hannah wore store-bought shoes. Sissy, like Daisy, was barefoot. The males had on moccasins. But not Indian moccasins. These they had made themselves.

"What are you doing here, mister?" one demanded.

"Now, now, Tyrel," Hannah said. "Keep a civil tongue. He is our guest and we will treat him cordial. The rest of you, lower those rifles. Sistine, fetch a fresh bucket of water from the stream. Kip, you go with her."

"I don't need guarding, Ma," Sissy said. "I can take care of myself."

"What with all the goings-on around here lately, you'll do as I say," Hannah commanded. She had an air of calm assurance about her. Here was a woman who had lived a hard life. You could see it in the lines in her face. Raising several children, living in the wild, having to fend for herself since her husband vanished, she had to be as tough as rawhide.

"That is part of the reason I'm here," I said. "To talk about setting things right with the Tanners."

"You've got it backwards, Reverend Storm,"

Hannah said. "They're at fault, not us." She motioned. "But come inside. No need to stand out in the sun unless you want to."

I figured to find a mess, but I'd underestimated them. No slovenliness here. Everything was as clean and as tidy as at the LT. Hannah ushered me to a high-backed chair. "This was my Everett's favorite, God rest his soul."

"I was told he disappeared."

Hannah's features clouded. "Murdered, is more like it. My Everett would never leave me so long as he had breath in his body. They got rid of him first to put the fear of dying into us and drive us off, but it didn't work."

"They?"

"The Tanners. Who else? They have it out for us, Reverend." Hannah eased into a chair opposite me.

Her boys and Daisy had filed in after us. Most chose to sit on the floor, their rifles across their laps. Daisy perched on the stones that framed the hearth, her legs drawn up, her chin on her knees.

"They say your family has been stealing and killing their cattle," I brought up.

"Lies, Reverend. All lies." Hannah appeared more hurt than mad. "But where are my manners? Would you care for refreshments? We have milk, berry juice, or coffee. Goat's milk, I should mention. Not all folks are partial to it."

"You don't own a cow?"

"We have no need of one. Cows are just big

dumb brutes. Goats don't take up as much space or need as much feed. We have twenty in a pen out back. I usually let them have the run of the place, but I want them where I can keep an eye on them in case the Tanners try something."

"You're afraid the Tanners will massacre your goats?"

"Grin if you want. But they blame us for their cows, don't they? And our goats mean as much to us." Hannah crooked a finger at Daisy, who rose to do her bidding. "So what will it be, Reverend?"

"Coffee, if it is not too much bother."

One of the twins who were not twins cleared his throat. "Want Tyrel and me to drop a deer for supper, Ma?"

"That's up to our guest, Clell," Hannah said. "How late will you be staying?" she asked me.

I had reckoned on only a few hours. But the better I got to know them, the easier the job would be. "I appreciate the invite. I haven't had venison in a coon's age."

Hannah seemed extremely pleased. "Good. I've been hoping you and me can get well acquainted. I do need your help."

"How so?"

"You said it yourself, Reverend. The Tanners. I want them to leave us be. I want them to stop accusing us of things we haven't done. If not, worse will happen than already has, and losing my Everett was terrible enough. I can't bear the thought of losing my younguns as well."

"I will do all I can." The lie nearly caught in my

throat, which jarred me considerable. The Butchers were nothing to me.

"Bless you, Reverend," Hannah said. "You are a godsend."

I could not look her in the eyes, so I watched Daisy put a coffeepot on to brew. But that proved just as unsettling if in a different way, so I switched to the window and pretended to be interested in the woods.

Hannah was as sharp as my razor. She had not missed my reaction. "I'm sorry, Reverend. Does it make you uncomfortable, my talking like that?"

"Not at all."

"I love my kids, Reverend. Love them more than I have ever cared for anyone, and that includes Everett. Maybe you have to be a mother to understand. But I am scared as scared can be that the Tanners mean us harm." She bent toward me. "You are the only hope I have of smoothing things over. Will you help us? Can I count on you?"

When you have told a thousand lies in your lifetime, what is one more? "Of course you can, my dear woman."

Chapter 6

For the second evening in a row, I was treated to a feast.

Compared to the Tanners, the Butcher clan were simple folk who lived by simple means. But they more than got by, thanks to the bounty the Dark Sister supplied. The virgin forest teemed with wildlife.

In addition to the venison, served roasted and boiled, the meal included squirrel soup and rabbit on a spit. Corn pone served for bread. They devoured hominy from a giant pot, but I can't say I shared their enthusiasm. Brown betty was our dessert. The coffee would float an anvil, it was so thick. I ate until I had food coming out my ears and drank more coffee than any of them. Pushing back my chair, I put a hand on my stomach. If this kept up, I would become the fattest Regulator west of the Mississippi River.

The notion reminded me of why I was there. "I could use to walk some of this off," I commented, hoping one of them would take the bait.

The Butchers were still eating. Hannah looked

up from her third helping of hominy and said, "Daisy, why don't you show the parson around?"

"Sure thing, Ma."

As I followed the girl out, I wondered why Hannah chose her out of all the children. It made more sense for Hannah to pick one of the boys. Had she noticed what I had tried to hide? It was hard, as pretty as the girl was, and given the way she moved and carried herself. But it could be I was fretting over nothing. Maybe Hannah just thought I would be more comfortable with one of the girls and picked the one I had ridden in with.

For Daisy's part, she was all smiles. The moment we stepped through the door, their mongrel commenced yapping at me, and she went over and kicked it. That quieted him. She led me around back to show off their goats and their garden, nearly a full acre planted with all kinds of vegetables arranged in neat rows. Gardens took a lot of work. It, and the tidiness of their cabin, put the lie to the claim that they were a bunch of lazy no-accounts. They took pride in themselves and their home. A large part of that was probably Hannah, but still, they were not the slobs Gertrude Tanner painted them. But what did that matter to me? I had a job to do. What they did, how they lived, should be of no interest except for how it bore on my work.

"You sure are a quiet one," Daisy remarked as we stood at the corral rails watching a frisky mare. "The last preacher I met talked my ears off about sin and the like."

"Did he, now?"

She bobbed her blond head. "He sure did. About the only thing I recollect is him saying that we're all of us trapped between heaven and hell, and where we end up depends on the life we live here and now."

Since I couldn't think of a suitable quote, I simply said, "He was right."

"It must be nice being you. Knowing that the day you die, you'll stroll through the pearly gates without a worry in creation."

"You'll stroll through those pearly gates, too."

Daisy averted her gaze. "That's kind of you, Parson, but I know better. I'm as much of a sinner as the next person."

"They say that confession is good for the soul." I had heard that somewhere once. It almost sounded like I knew what I was talking about.

"Oh, no, Reverend. I would be too ashamed. The things I've done would curl your toes."

Suddenly she did not seem nearly as sweet. The fancies I had built up in my head came crashing down. "Don't be so rough on yourself. We all have things we're ashamed of." My pa came to mind. And my wife.

"You too? I thought men of the cloth always live clean and honest?"

"They try." I had slipped up, but she didn't notice.

"Would you like to see my favorite spot in all the world?"

I nodded, and Daisy clasped my hand and hur-

ried us around the corral and along a path through
the woods. In a hundred yards we came to a hollow
so closely rimmed by vegetation that had she not
shown it to me, I could have passed within ten feet
of it and not realized it was there. A stream flowed
through the center.

On a spur of grass Daisy hunkered and dipped
a finger in the clear water. "It's so peaceful and
restful here. I often come and just sit for hours."

I chose a log for my seat. The peak of Dark
Sister hid the setting sun, but enough light re-
mained to cast a golden sheen over everything. The
buzz of insects and the croak of frogs were a lullaby
that lulled me to drowsiness.

"You're not falling asleep, are you?" Daisy
teased.

"I might," I admitted, mentally vowing that I had
eaten my last big meal until the job was done.

"We have us a fine life here," Daisy commented.
"The best we've ever had. I don't want it to ever
end." She shifted toward me. "Why do the Tanners
hate us so?"

"They claim you rustle their beef."

"But we don't. Honest to God, we don't. Can't
you convince them we're telling the truth?"

"I will try." I felt awful after saying that. More
awful than I had any right feeling.

"It's Gertrude," Daisy said. "She's the mean
one. It's her who is always talking about us behind
our backs. The townsfolk have told us as much.
She won't rest until she's driven us off or wiped us
out, and we won't be driven off."

"I will do what I can."

Daisy leaned back, unconscious of how her dress clung and shifted. "Ma thinks they killed Pa. She can't prove it, but she feels it in her bones."

I had a thought. "Did the Tanners accuse your family of rustling before your pa disappeared?"

Her smooth brow and her full lips puckered. "Not that I remember, no. They didn't start in on us until after he vanished."

"How were they before that?"

"Polite enough, I suppose. They would say 'howdy' in town. But that Gertrude always said it like she had a mouth full of nails."

"Some people are born with too much acid in their system."

"Ain't that the truth."

We sat in silence, the shadows lengthening around us, the birds and the insects and the frogs providing a sort of music. It made me wish we could sit there forever, but presently I sensed we were not alone and I shifted to find Ty and Clell with their rifles.

I was becoming downright sloppy. I never heard them come up. It would do well for me to keep in mind that I was dealing with a bunch of back-woodsmen with as much wilderness savvy as Indians.

"Ma wants you and him back at the cabin," Ty said to Daisy.

"You shouldn't have come out here without a gun," Clell scolded her. "It's not safe."

I didn't like the glance he shot at me. Rising, I held out my hand and Daisy took it.

"Don't fret about me, big brother. I can take

care of myself. I heard you two clomping through the brush like a pair of half-blind bulls."

"Like hell," Ty said.

Grinning, Daisy skipped past them, pulling me after her. "I'm not a little girl anymore, big brother. The sooner you own up to it, the sooner you can rest easy when I'm off by himself."

"So long as the Tanners are out for our hides, I can't ever rest easy" was Ty's reply.

So far I had not seen any sign of cattle, alive or otherwise. I reasoned that if the Butchers were lying—and they had to be—then they must keep the cattle off in a canyon somewhere.

Hannah was in a rocking chair under the overhang. Another chair had been set beside it for me. "I like to sit out here and admire the sunsets," she said as I sank down. "They're always so pretty."

The Dark Sister was silhouetted against a sky painted bright hues of red and orange, laced with traces of pink. "That they are," I allowed.

Daisy had roosted nearby. Ty and Clell were listening with their arms folded. Out of the cabin filed Sissy, Jordy, Kip, and Sam. There was no sign of Carson.

"We need to talk, Reverend. We need to work out what to do about the Tanners."

"I promise to do what I can."

Hannah nodded. "And I'm grateful. But how do you intend to go about it, exactly? How can we get it through Gertrude Tanner's thick head that me and mine don't steal her cows?"

"I will talk to them—" I began.

"No offense, Reverend, but talking hasn't done us much good. I sent word to Gertrude through Calista that I would welcome the chance to sit down with her and hash it out, but Calista says all Gertrude did was laugh."

"Now there is a bitch if ever there was one," Sissy remarked.

Hannah grew as stern as a riled schoolmaster. "That will be quite enough cussing in front of our guest! You are a lady and you will act like one. Never forget you're not too old for a tanning."

"Switch my backside all you want," Sissy said. "It won't change the truth."

Tapping her fingers on the rocker's arm, Hannah said, "Do you see what I have to put up with, Reverend? I never gave my ma sass like they sass me."

Sissy snorted. "Since when is saying our mind sass? You've always told us to be honest with you, haven't you? Or would you rather we wear gags all day? If so, I want a pink one. You'll have to go into town and buy a bolt of pink cloth or I'll just keep on speaking my piece."

"We don't have the money for a scrap of cloth, let alone a bolt," Hannah said good-naturedly, "so flap your gums all you want."

They grinned and chuckled and laughed, and I was struck by how much they cared for one another. Genuinely and truly cared. It put me in a funk. I kept forgetting who I was and why I was there. This had never happened to me before. I never let myself have feelings for those I was to exterminate for the same reason you never became too fond of a cow or a hog or chicken you might have to eat. Yet here I was, entertaining preposterous notions about Daisy and feeling sympathy for the rest of her family.

I needed a drink. I needed a drink bad. I needed to get drunk and stay drunk for a week, but I had the job to do. The damned, stinking job.

Suddenly I became aware they were all staring at me.

"You all right?" Hannah asked. "Do I bore you so much that you're not paying attention?"

"Sorry, my dear woman," I said. "I was racking my brain for a way to get Gertrude to listen to reason."

"You would have to be a miracle worker," Hannah said. "But I reckon that's your line of work."

I had seen all I needed to. I had the lay of their homestead worked out, and a fair notion of how best to go about the chore that would earn me the thousand dollars. But I could not bring myself to leave. I sat there admiring the sunset and liking them, and hating myself for it. Twilight shrouded the Dark Sister when I stirred and commented, "I better be on my way. I have a long ride in that buckboard ahead of me."

"You're welcome to stay the night," Hannah kindly offered.

Lord, I was tempted. But I was being foolish. "Thank you, no. I have an early appointment in Whiskey Flats I must keep." Rising, I stretched.

Ty hefted his rifle. "Keep your eyes skinned for cowboys on the way down the mountain. We've seen them skulking about a lot of late."

"They're probably searching for their missing cattle," I guessed.

"If they are, they're going about it mighty peculiar," Ty said. "Clell and me caught sight of a bunch of them the other day riding out of a canyon on the south side of the mountain."

"What is so peculiar about that?"

"The canyon doesn't have a lick of water or graze," Ty said. "It's nothing but rocks and boulders. No one would hide cows in there unless they wanted the cows to die of thirst or hunger."

"Maybe the cowhands didn't know that," I suggested.

"Except that it was the second time we saw them there in the past couple of weeks," Ty enlightened me.

"I'll ask the Tanners about it." Yet another lie. The antics of their cowboys were of no interest to me. I thanked Hannah for a fine time, shook her hand, and shook Daisy's hand, then climbed on the buckboard and lifted the reins.

"Remember," Hannah said, "we're counting on you. Any help you need from me, you have only to ask."

"It will all work out. You'll see." I clucked to the team and did not look back. My mood was as black as the night. It didn't help that there was no moon and twice I nearly blundered off the track.

Dark Sister was half a mile behind me when hooves drummed to my rear. I twisted in the seat, half expecting to find some of the Butchers. But the four riders who came up alongside the buckboard, a pair on either side, were cowboys. Two I recognized from the restaurant: Hank and Skeeter. The former had his hand on his Colt and started to snarl something when he recoiled as if I had smacked him.

"It's the parson!"

The others appeared mad more than anything. Skeeter had his revolver partway out but shoved it back into his holster. "What in tarnation are you doing this far out from town?"

I wondered how much Gertrude had told them. She was not supposed to say a word to anyone about who I was or why I was there.

"Making the rounds," I said.

Skeeter scratched his chin, then declared as if it were the world's greatest hunch, "He's been to visit the Butchers, that's where he's been!"

"You shouldn't ought to do that, Preacher," Hank declared. "Who knows what you might have seen?"

I remembered what Ty had said, and fished for information. "Like you and these others coming out of a canyon on the south side of the Dark Sister?"

Suddenly one of the other cowboys reined in close, grabbed hold of the traces, and brought the buckboard to a stop. I opened my mouth to protest just as he palmed his six-shooter. The *click* of the hammer seemed unnaturally loud.

"This varmint knows too much," he growled. "The only way to be safe is to buck him out in gore."

Bewildered, I got out. "Can't we talk about this, gentlemen?"

"No, we can't." The cowboy took deliberate aim.

Chapter 7

I don't know what made me do it. Instinct, I reckon. Self-preservation, folks call it. I never have liked having guns pointed at me, and when that cowboy pointed his with the intent of shooting me, I did what I always do when that happens. Instead of sitting there calmly and trying to talk the cowboy out of blowing my brains out, as a real preacher would, I dived off the buckboard, drawing my Colt from my shoulder rig as I did. Fortunately I had unbuttoned my jacket after leaving the Butchers, and could get at it quick-like.

Maybe the sight of a parson whipping out a revolver startled him. He was a shade slow in squeezing the trigger. I fired first. My slug caught him high in the forehead and did to his skull what he had been about to do to mine.

I rolled up into a crouch. The other three were too stunned to do anything. Evidently it did not occur to them that I could not leave witnesses.

Skeeter was reaching for his revolver when I shot him square in the face. Pivoting, I sent a slug into Hank. It cored his chest and he flopped backward off his saddle as if kicked by a mule. That left number four, who had his Colt almost clear of leather when I shot him. A hole appeared where his left eye had been and the rear of his cranium exploded.

Two of their mounts bolted. The buckboard's team shied and would have run off, but I got hold of them.

The first thing I did was reload. The second thing I did was go from cowboy to cowboy and go through their pockets and then through their saddlebags. They did not have much, barely thirty dollars. The third thing was to smack the remaining mounts on the rump, but only after untying the two bedrolls. I unrolled them and spread them out over the buckboard's bed, then hoisted each body up and in. I had to be careful not to get blood on my clothes. Fortunately, only one bled much, and only for a little while.

I could not leave the bodies lying there in the open. Come daylight, buzzards would gather. It would arouse interest should anyone spot them.

Wheeling the wagon, I headed back toward the Dark Sister. Along about then, what I had done sank in. I just killed four men who worked for the woman who had hired me. She might not take too kindly to the loss.

Their horses would show up at the LT by afternoon. The Tanners would start a search. Since it was likely they knew that the cowboys had been in the vicinity of the Dark Sister, that was where the search would start.

I had been hasty in running off the horses. I could use them now. But I had two strong legs, and while I didn't much like it, I carried the bodies a couple of hundred yards and hid them in a ravine. I gathered up rocks and what boulders I could lift to cover them. It took hours. It was well past midnight when I wearily climbed back on the buckboard and rolled toward town.

Whiskey Flats was as dead as a cemetery. The saloon had closed, and the streets were deserted. I had rented the buckboard for the day, so I was obliged to take it direct to the livery. I figured to leave it parked out front and take the team into the corral, but no sooner had I brought it to a stop than one of the big double doors opened and out limped the livery owner.

I figured he would be mad. "Sorry it's so late," I apologized. "I lost my way in the dark."

Anyone else, he likely would have lit into like an angry rooster. But to me he said, "That's all right, Parson. I won't hold it against you."

Just like that, he took it off my hands and I was free to head for Calista's. She gave all her boarders a key, so soon I was in my room on the second floor, lying on my bed and wondering what in hell I was going to do if the finger of guilt was pointed at me. I could still finish the job, but there would be complications.

I fell asleep fully dressed. My last thoughts were of the Butchers, and how nice they were, and of Daisy.

I awoke at eight, famished. I used the outhouse,

then went around front to the restaurant. The buzz of talk stopped when I entered. Right away I looked down at myself, afraid I had blood on my clothes and did not know it, but no, my clothes were fine. I smiled and nodded at the townspeople and a pair of cowboys as I angled to a corner table and sat with my back to the wall.

"How did your visit go?" Calista was as fresh and as pretty as a rose in full bloom and smelled just as nice.

"It went fine. Hannah asked me to have a word with the Tanners on her family's behalf."

"That's fine. I'm sure you can nip this in the bud. I like Hannah and Gerty, both, and it would be a shame to have them at each other's throats."

For breakfast I had six eggs, four sizzling strips of bacon, toast smothered in jam, and enough coffee to drown a moose. I took my time. As I was draining my last cup, several cowboys came in, spoke in soft tones to the pair already there, and all five hurried out.

So Hank and his friends were already missed.

I paid and strolled about town, smiling and doffing my hat to the ladies. In the afternoon I played billiards. I kept an eye to the west, but the cowboys did not return.

It was pushing six o'clock, and I had just sat down in the restaurant to have my supper, when a commotion drew me and everyone else outside.

The five cowboys were back, four of them with bodies wrapped in blankets over the backs of their horses. They had not dismounted.

"Who did it?" I heard a townsman ask.

"How did it happen, George?" asked another.

The cowpoke he had addressed was grinding his teeth in anger. "Who do you reckon is to blame?" he snapped. "Who else but those stinking, no-good, cattle-rustling trash, the Butchers!"

"Do you have proof?" a woman wanted to know.

George pointed at a body. "What more proof do you need? Mrs. Tanner sent Hank and these others to hunt for missing cows on the Dark Sister. The Butchers live there, don't they?"

"What about Injuns?" someone suggested.

"Would Injuns have covered the bodies with rocks? Would Injuns have left the scalps?"

George had an answer for everything, and I could see he was convincing most of the crowd. I had not counted on this. It could be a lynch party would form, and they would ride out to the Butcher place and decorate the woods with human fruit. In which case I would not be paid.

Raising my arms, I moved out into the street. "Brothers! Sisters! I beg you, judge not! We must not be rash."

"Stay out of this, Parson," George said.

"That's no way to talk to a man of the Lord," a woman objected, and received support from others.

I put my hand on George's boot. "I understand your anger, brother. I understand your grief."

He balled his fists, but did not strike me. "Then you won't hold it against us if we ride to the LT, gather up the rest of the hands, and do to the Butchers what should have been done months ago."

"Now, now," I said. "By all means, take the bodies to the ranch. But there will be no vigilante justice. Not while I am here."

"This doesn't concern you," George said.

" 'Thou shalt not kill,' " I quoted. "I have a right to speak on the Lord's behalf to save you from perdition."

"Oh, hell," George said.

The other cowboys grumbled, but I was having an effect. I pressed on. "Advise Mr. and Mrs. Tanner that I will be out to the LT tomorrow at noon to conduct services. I expect everyone on the ranch to attend."

I pumped the hand of each cowboy in a show of brotherliness. As they rode off, Calista's shoulder brushed mine.

"That was a good thing you just did. Hanging the Butchers would be wrong."

"Someone should ride out and warn them." Even as I said it, I was plotting ahead. Luck had placed a fine opportunity in my lap.

"I would go, but I have no one to look after things," Calista said.

Neither could I. Not and be back in time for the funeral at the LT. I mentioned as much.

"I know a boy I can hire to ride out."

That settled, I ate supper. The restaurant filled, and all anyone talked about was the murders. Whiskey Flats had not seen this much excitement since the town was founded.

I was in good spirits. Another twenty-four hours and I could start doing what I was being paid to do. I went for a walk and put on quite a show; I had a pleasant greeting for everyone I met. The townsfolk were right friendly. It occurred to me that I could start up a church if I was of a mind to and live out the rest of my days in ease and peace. I wouldn't ever get rich, but I wouldn't die of lead poisoning, either, a not-so-rare fate for Regulators.

Yes, sir, I was feeling downright capital, as those gents from London say, when I returned to my room. I planned to turn in early and head out to the LT in the morning. But I wasn't counting on finding someone perched in the chair by the window.

"I hope you don't mind," Daisy Butcher said. "Calista let me in. *Snuck* me in, is more like it, since I didn't dare let myself be seen. My family isn't exactly popular right now."

"You've heard about the four cowboys who were shot?"

Daisy nodded and rose, careful now to let herself be glimpsed from below. "Calista told me. But I will swear on the Bible, if you want, that me and mine had nothing to do with it."

"Everyone else thinks otherwise."

"It's not right, them accusing us of something we didn't do," Daisy said sadly. "They'd blame us for flies and measles and gout if they could."

I was about to take her in my arms and console her when I noticed my bedroll and saddlebags poking from under the end of the bed. Yet I distinctly recalled sliding them all the way under. Despite the lingering heat of the day, a chill seized me. "How long have you been waiting?"

"No more than fifteen minutes." The top of her head came only as high as my chin, and she had to tilt her head back to look me in the eyes. "Ma sent me with a message. Me and Tyrel and Clell."

Disappointed, I asked, "Where are they?"

"Over behind the livery. The man who owns it is our friend. It was him who warned us when we rode in that we were in danger of being strung up on sight."

My fingers tingling, I sat on the edge of the bed. "What is so important your ma couldn't wait?"

"It's about the meeting with the Tanners. She wants it to be the day after tomorrow at one in the afternoon, right here in town." Daisy bit her lower lip in thought. "But I reckon that can't be now, can it?"

"I doubt Gertrude would accept the invite." I went to the window and peered toward the livery but could not spot her brothers. "The best thing for you to do is ride like the wind and warn your loved ones they might be gurgling at the end of ropes if they let down their guard."

"The townsfolk wouldn't!" Daisy declared. "Not without a trial!"

I went into my preacher act. "Hate makes folks do crazy things. Look at Cain and Abel. Brother slew brother out of pure mean hate. And that pharaoh who hated Moses on account of the plagues of frogs and bugs."

"But we're innocent!"

"I believe you, my dear. But most folks here believe differently. To say nothing of the LT cowhands."

Daisy began to pace. "This is terrible. We should make ourselves scarce. Pack our effects and skedaddle someplace where we will be accepted for who we are and not judged to be trash just because we don't live like everyone else or have much money."

I didn't want the thousand dollars slipping through my fingers, so I said, "No need to go to that extreme. I'm on your side. So is Calista. Give us a few days to calm everyone down."

"Oh, Reverend," Daisy gushed, and threw her arms around my neck in gratitude.

My skin grew warm and prickly. I held her loosely, afraid to pull her close for fear of how my body would react. " 'Blessed are the peacemakers,' " I mumbled.

Daisy kissed me. Not a chaste kiss, either, but the kind of kiss a woman gives a man when she has a certain kind of hunger deep inside her.

Damn me for being human. Double damn me for not having any more willpower than any other man.

"I'll take your advice," Daisy said huskily in due course. "Ty and Clell and me will sneak off and tell Ma to wait until we hear from you."

It was dark enough that they should be able to slip out of Whiskey Flats undetected, but I insisted on going ahead and having her follow me, signaling when it was safe with a wave of my hand. In that way we made it down the hall and down the stairs and out the back door. Once we reached the street, I had her walk on the inside, her shoulder to mine, her head bowed.

Ty and Clell came out of deep shadow to meet us.

"We were getting worried," the oldest said. "Another ten minutes and we'd have torn this town apart looking for you."

Daisy relayed my promise to help, which prompted Ty into grasping my hand in both of his and pumping my arm as if he were dying of thirst and I were a water pump.

"We're counting on you, Parson. Ma says without your help, this whole mess will get worse."

"She's right," I said.

"You are our only hope of avoiding bloodshed," Clell said.

Daisy nodded. "We trust you, Parson. You inspire confidence." She touched my cheek, then climbed on her mount.

I smiled and watched them fade into the dark, thinking to myself, *The poor, pitiful fools.*

Chapter 8

The four cowboys were buried on a hill in the shadow of the Fair Sister. I liked doing funerals. I did not have to make up sermons. All I did was read from the Bible and say a few words about how the dear departed were the salt of the earth and how much their friends would miss them.

The Tanners were there, of course, along with every last puncher on the spread. I counted sixteen plus the cook. Four servants Gerty employed and half a dozen townsfolk rounded out the mourners.

Calista Modine came. After the bodies had been planted and everyone was standing around looking sorrowful or pretending to look sorrowful, I remarked that it was a shame more of Whiskey Flats's good citizens had not shown up.

Calista glanced around, then leaned close and said so only I could hear, "The LT outfit is not all that popular in some quarters."

"Care to explain?"

Tugging gently on my sleeve, she drew me out of earshot. "For one thing, Gerty is not well liked. She is too high-handed with everyone."

"Imagine that."

"She behaves like she is a queen and the people are her subjects, and they rightfully resent it."

At that moment the lady in question was scolding one of the cowboys filling in one of the holes for flinging dirt recklessly with his shovel and getting some on her new shoes.

"The other thing is that the LT's hands tend to become rowdy when they come to town on Friday and Saturday nights. They shoot out windows and lamps, make people dance to a six-shooter serenade, that sort of nonsense."

"Gerty permits that?"

"The owner of the general store and some others have complained to her time and again. She always says how sorry she is, but men will be men, and there is only so much she can do."

"When should we talk to her about the Butchers?" I asked.

"The sooner, the better."

The mourners, such as they were, began drifting down the hill. Townsfolk climbed into their buggies. Cowboys swung onto their horses. The Tanners lingered. Lloyd and Phil were arguing in hushed voices while Gerty waited in disgust.

I nudged Calista and went over. "Miss Modine and I would like a few words with you, if we may."

"Save your breath," Gertrude said.

"But, Gerty—" Calista began.

"But nothing. Do you think I don't know what you're going to say? That I must not be hasty. I must not jump to conclusions. There is no evidence the Butchers were involved. I should hold my men in check and not exact revenge."

"You missed one," I said. "Let the law handle it."

"Texans don't run crying to a badge every time someone steps on their toes," Gertrude declared. "We handle our own problems, and the Butchers are mine."

I was proud of myself for the quote I remembered. "Have you not heard, sister? 'Vengeance is mine, sayeth the Lord.' "

"The Almighty can take his vengeance whenever He wants. I'll take mine when I want."

There was no reasoning with her, as I knew there would not be. But a real parson would not give up, so neither did I. "You will be damned for all eternity."

Gertrude looked at me and grinned. "I already am, Reverend Storm. So I might as well make the most of the time I have left."

"Oh, Gerty," Calista said.

"Don't 'Oh, Gerty' me. If you had my responsibilities, you would do the same as I am doing."

Calista shook her head. "I would never kill. Nor would I ever give orders to have someone killed. And that's what you intend to do, isn't it? Unleash your cowpokes on the Butchers?"

"Justice demands they hang."

"*All* of them?" Calista was appalled. "Even Hannah and the two girls?"

"When you find rats in your house, you don't

kill one or two. You kill them all," Gertrude said harshly.

"We are talking about human lives. I warn you here and now, I won't stand for it, and I have taken a step to prevent it."

"Excuse me?"

I was as surprised as Gertrude. Calista had not said anything to me about it. "What sort of step?"

"I have sent for the Texas Rangers."

Have you ever wanted to bash someone over the head with a rock? I think both Gertrude and I shared the same sentiment, because she turned as purple as a beet and balled her fists.

"You did *what*?"

"Last night. I've sent Horace to the Rangers with a letter I wrote detailing everything that has happened, from Everett Butcher going missing to the rustling and now the killings. Everything."

The last thing I wanted, the absolute last thing of all the things that could be, was to have the Texas Rangers involved. My head swirled with the problems her Good Samaritan impulse presented.

Gertrude was carved from granite for a bit. Then, stirring, she said in a tone as cold as ice, "Please tell me you are making that up. Please tell me you are only trying to scare me into not harming your friends."

"As God is my witness," Calista said.

"Do you have any idea what you have done?" Gertrude was shaking with barely contained rage. "Do you have any idea what your meddling will cause?"

Calista squared her shoulders. "I have stopped you from doing something you would regret."

"You stupid, stupid bitch."

Shocked, Calista took a step back. "You don't mean that."

"I have never meant anything more," Gertrude assured her. "You have stuck your nose in where it does not belong. I will never forgive you."

"No one has the right to lynch whosoever they please," Calista said flatly. "Not even you."

Gertrude gazed toward the Fair Sister, then looked down at herself and plucked a dust mote from her dress. "Our friendship is ended."

"What?"

"You heard me. You are no longer welcome at the LT. When I am in town, do me the courtesy of not speaking to me." Gertrude started down the hill, but Calista caught her by the wrist.

"Gerty, you can't mean that. It's your anger speaking. We have been friends for years."

"No longer." Gertrude stared at Calista's hand until Calista removed it. Smoothing her sleeve, Gertrude said quietly, "Friends do not interfere in matters that do not concern them. Friends do not stab friends in the back. I would never presume to tell you how to run your restaurant or your boardinghouse, yet you presume to tell me how to run my ranch."

Not "our" ranch, as in hers and Lloyd's, I noticed. But "my" ranch, as in hers and hers alone.

"Waging war on the Butchers is not part of running your ranch," Calista argued.

"I beg to differ. LT cattle have been rustled and mutilated. LT hands have been killed. That makes it very much ranch business. Despite what you might think, it gives me the right to do as I please. But now you have interfered. You have taken the right to deal with the problem away from me. You have set yourself up over me, and it is an insult I will not bear."

"I just don't want the Butchers hurt."

"How noble of you." Gertrude dripped sarcasm. "How virtuous. Be sure to polish your halo when you get back to town."

"Please," Calista said.

"Our friendship is ended," Gertrude repeated. "You are never again to set foot on the LT." Wheeling, she strode toward the Tanner buggy.

Calista's eyes moistened and she made as if to follow, but I caught hold of her sleeve and said, "Let me talk to her for you." Calista motioned, and I quickly caught up to my employer. "Is our deal still on?"

"Of course it is," Gertrude growled out of the side of her mouth. "I've paid half the money, haven't I?"

"What about the Rangers?"

"What about them? It will be a week or more before they can get here. That gives you plenty of time to wipe out the Butchers and make yourself scarce."

"I wanted to be sure," I said. "I'll start today."

"It's taken you long enough," Gertrude grumbled. "As soon as you are done, come see me and you will receive the rest of the money. No matter what hour of the day or night."

"Your husband might wonder why I'm on your doorstep at four in the morning," I remarked.

"Who said anything about coming to the door? My bedroom is the second window from the left as you face the rear of our house."

"But, Lloyd—"

"Didn't you hear me? I have my own bedroom. He has his own. I only sleep with him when I am in the mood and I am hardly ever in the mood, which irks him no end."

I could see where a husband might object to being barred from his wife's embraces. "I can't blame him."

Gertrude stopped and faced me. "Haven't you realized by now that I am accustomed to getting my own way? No one tells me how to live. Especially not my husband. I do what I want, when I want."

The more I learned about her, the more formidable she became. "A lot of men wouldn't stand for it."

"Nonsense. Most men have the spines of jellyfish. Lloyd has no gumption at all. It's why I married him."

"You picked a puny man on purpose?"

"Weak men are easy to control. Strong men are not. I chose someone I could wrap around my finger and keep him wrapped from the 'I do' until I plant him. I haven't ever told anyone this, and I trust you will keep it to yourself."

It was with mixed feelings that I watched the Tanners leave. Lloyd had climbed up without a word, but the son had paused.

"Nice eulogy, Parson. Short and to the point. You're not a windbag like some preachers I've come across." Phil had winked at me. "Some people are never what you take them for, are they?"

That had me wondering. Had Gertrude confided in him about me? I hoped not. If she had broken her word, she was in for a nasty surprise when I was done with the Butchers.

Calista was waiting by the buckboard. I helped her up, mounted to the seat, and turned the buckboard around. Clouds of dust from those who preceded us caused her to cough and cover her nose and mouth with her hand. The LT was well behind us when she lowered it and commented, "All these years I thought Gerty was my friend."

"She is upset about the killings."

"That's no excuse for severing our friendship." Calista removed her hat and set it in her lap. The play of sun on her hair and face was quite appealing. "A true friend does not cast you aside like an old hat."

"She will come to her senses in time and say she is sorry." I did not believe that for a second, but I was such an accomplished liar by now, the lies spilled out without me having to think them up.

"You know better. Gerty never admits she is wrong. She never apologizes. Why should she, when in her eyes she never makes mistakes?"

"It must be nice to be perfect."

Calista smiled and fluffed her hair. "She would

say we judge her unfairly. But the truth is, she sees only what she wants to see when she looks in the mirror."

"Don't we all?" I rarely used mirrors. My reflection only reminded me of what I had become. Yet I had no hankering to change. Wasn't that odd?

"True," Calista said. "I just wish I knew what Gerty was up to. It might explain her attitude."

"You've lost me," I admitted.

"For months she has not been herself. Oh, she has always been a cold fish, and always looked down her nose at the rest of humanity. But something more is going on. She isn't like she used to be."

"You've still lost me."

"How can I explain?" Calista asked herself aloud. "It's little things you wouldn't recognize because you haven't known her as long as I have. She's changed. Become more withdrawn. More secretive."

"Maybe it is your imagination," I suggested. It would not do to have her link Gertrude's strange behavior to my arrival and the soon-to-be-departed Butchers.

"No. There can be no mistake. She changed about when Everett Butcher vanished. Although what those two could have in common is beyond me."

I silently exhaled in relief. But I was also puzzled. Was I the one not seeing a link? What did Gertrude have to do with Everett? "Didn't he disappear before the rustling commenced?"

"Long before," Calista confirmed.

If Gerty was involved, her motive was a mystery. It was of no importance to me, anyhow. All that mattered was the job. Always, the job.

We made small talk and in due course I let her off in front of her place and took the buckboard to the livery. I checked on Brisco in his stall, then went to my room and sat on the edge of the bed to wait for the sun to set. Tonight was the night. At long last I could get to doing what I do best.

Chapter 9

I told the livery owner that Brisco had been cooped up too long. Not that I needed an excuse to ride my own horse, but it might seem a smidgen strange, me going for a ride at night. I allowed as how I would ride toward the Fair Sister and if I got back late, I'd tie Brisco to the hitch rail in front of Calista's and bring him to the stable in the morning.

The livery owner thought I was mighty considerate. "Most folks bring in their nags any hour of the night they feel like it," he complained. "It never occurs to them I need my rest the same as everybody else."

Brisco champed at the bit. He really had been cooped up too long. I headed east at a walk, but once I was out of sight of Whiskey Flats I reined in a wide loop and soon was cantering west toward the Dark Sister.

I admit I felt a few twinges. My conscience came out of hibernation. For the first time since I strangled my wife, I felt guilt.

I liked the Butchers. They were a caring, close-knit family. Maybe they were rustlers, maybe they weren't. A court of law was the proper place to decide that. Me, I was a court of death, and sentence had been passed. Once I was paid to do a job, I always saw it through. Always. Without exception. It was part of why people sought me out to do their killing. They knew they could count on me to get it done.

In all the years I had been at this business, I never once considered whether those I was hired to remove deserved to be turned into maggot bait. It simply did not enter into the scheme of things. The same as when someone swats a fly or a spider. You never stop to ask yourself whether the fly or the spider deserves it.

I always prided myself on keeping my emotions under control. There are some who say I don't have any, but that's not true. I have feelings the same as everyone else. I just lock them away and don't let them out because I can't afford to.

But tonight I was in turmoil. By the time I reached the Dark Sister, I was a mess. I wanted to turn around and go back. I kept asking myself stupid questions, such as did I really want to kill these people? Which was stupid. "Want" had nothing to do with anything. It shows what can happen when you think too much. I've noticed that those who do the most thinking are the ones who are the most confused about what is important in life and what isn't.

I drew rein. There I was, a quarter of a mile from the Butcher homestead, and I was fighting a battle with myself inside my head instead of paying attention to my surroundings. Mad at my silliness, I gigged Brisco into the trees and dismounted.

I slipped out of my jacket and laid it over my saddle. I opened one of my saddlebags, removed my gun belt with the long-barreled Remington snug in its holster, and strapped it on. From my other saddlebag I took a box of shotgun shells and crammed a handful into my pocket. The scattergun was hidden in my bedroll. I broke it open, inserted two loads of buckshot, and was ready to commence.

Light glowed in the cabin window. It was likely some of them were still up, but that was all right. I would kick in the door and cut loose with both barrels, then finish off the rest with the Remingtons and my boot knife.

I crept toward the clearing. I did not see their mongrel and reckoned it was indoors.

Daisy's face seemed to float before me in the air. I tried to tell myself that she meant nothing to me, and gave an angry toss of my head to be shed of her image. Not much movement on my part, but suddenly the night exploded with gunfire. I dived flat. The shooters missed but not by much. There were two of them, off to my left, vague shapes in the night, and they had rifles, which gave them greater range. I had to get close for the shotgun to be effective. But that would not be easy, them being backwoodsmen and all.

I laid still a while, thinking they might work toward me, but I never heard so much as a leaf rustle. Along about then I saw that the light had gone out in the cabin, and that the cabin door was open. Someone was peering out, but I could not tell who. They did not make the mistake of calling out to the pair in the woods. Hannah's doing, no doubt. She was a savvy one, that gal.

I started to crawl to my right. But no sooner did I move an arm and a leg than the dark was shattered by more gun blasts. Only this time the two with the rifles were closer. I saw the muzzle flash of one in front of me, and the slug kicked up dirt in my face. I let the shooter have both barrels, then rolled behind a tree and rose onto my knees to reload.

Figures were gliding across the clearing from the cabin. They were coming after me, all of them. This was not good. I was one against nine and that was too much of an advantage for them.

I had to get out of there. I turned and ran. A rifle barked, then another. Fickle fate favored me and they missed. But I made enough noise that they had an inkling where I was. It sounded like they all fired at once. The trunks, branches, and leaves around me were peppered.

I poured on speed, but they were hard after me and impossible to shake. I willed my legs to their utmost in order to reach Brisco ahead of them, and in that I succeeded. I was in the saddle and reining to the east when someone—I think it was Clell—hollered, "There he is!"

Rifles and revolvers boomed like mad. For one of the few times in my life, I was scared. Not for me but for Brisco. He was a big target and I did not want to lose him. I slapped my legs, wishing I had spurs on. Bent low, I rode for my life.

The trees saved me. There were so many of them, so close together, the Butchers could not get a clear shot. I made it to the trail and gave Brisco his head. Presently the shots and shouts faded.

The Butchers might come after me, but I had the utmost confidence in Brisco. He was the fastest critter on four legs, or damn near the fastest. No other horse could hold a candle to him, or hadn't yet. Besides, I had seen the horses in the Butcher corral, and they were not in his class.

I had been riding a while when I became aware something was wrong with the saddle. It felt rough and lumpy. Reaching down, I discovered I was sitting on my jacket. I had forgotten all about it. Reining up, I twisted and slid the scattergun into my bedroll, then tugged the jacket out from under me and shrugged into it. Since there was no sign of pursuit, I unstrapped my gun belt, wrapped the belt around the holster, and crammed it in a saddlebag.

I was in glum spirits when I reached Whiskey Flats. It was past midnight and the town, as usual, was still and quiet. I had told the liveryman that I would bring Brisco back in the morning, but now, after thinking it over, I rode to the end of the street. The double doors were shut and barred. I rode around to the corral, stripped off my saddle and saddle blanket and bridle, opened the gate, and shooed him in.

The boardinghouse was dark. I entered by the back door and snuck up the stairs. A few creaked but not loud enough to wake anyone.

I laid on the bed and thought about the fiasco. I had accomplished nothing. The only one I could blame was myself; I had been careless. For a professional Regulator, I would make a great dishwasher.

I wondered if maybe I had been sloppy on purpose. That sounds ridiculous, but part of me had balked at rubbing the Butchers out, and that part might have wanted things to go wrong.

Eventually I drifted into sleep. Usually I don't remember my dreams, but when I opened my eyes and sat up the next morning, images lingered. Images of a scarecrow figure in a brown hood that had chased me all over creation. In his bony hands had been a gleaming scythe that he kept trying to stick me with. "Damned silly," I said out loud.

I filled the basin with water from the pitcher and washed up. I shaved, too. Most parsons are tidy about their appearance.

The restaurant was half full. I claimed my usual seat, and right away Calista brought a cup of steaming coffee and set it in front of me with a warm smile.

"Good morning, Reverend Storm. Did you sleep well?"

"Like a baby." As lies went, it was tame compared to some I had told her.

"I expected you earlier," Calista said. "It's pushing nine."

Normally I was up at seven. I ordered eggs with sausage and toast and asked her to keep the coffee coming. No sooner had I taken a sip than a ruckus broke out in the street. Some of the customers got up to see, and a man in a bowler exclaimed, "It's the Butchers! They've brought a body in!"

I made a special effort not to seem too eager. I sat and took another sip, then slowly rose and walked to the door.

Calista was on the boardwalk, drying her hands with her apron. "I hope that's not who I think it is."

Only five of the family had come. Hannah was on a buttermilk. Ty and Clell were on either side of her, the stocks of their rifles on their thighs. Carson and Sam were as nervous as cats in a room full of rocking chairs. The body had been wrapped in a blanket and tied over a swayback sorrel. One shoe poked out of the blanket, and at sight of it, I felt sick to my stomach.

People were hurrying from every which way; the owner of the general store, the liveryman, the blacksmith, the butcher, women, children, everyone. Hannah waited until she had a crowd, then sat straighter and cleared her throat.

"You all know me. You all know my family. You know about the trouble we've been having with the Tanners. They have accused us of rustling. But we're not cow thieves and never have been. I was hoping to sit down with Gertrude Tanner and talk things out." Hannah's gaze lingered on me. "But now it doesn't matter. The time for words is past."

No one said anything. Most were staring at the body.

"A couple of nights ago four cowboys from the LT were found dead in a ravine at the bottom of the Dark Sister. The finger of blame was pointed at my family. I said it then; I will say it now. We had nothing to do with it."

"I believe you, Hannah," Calista said.

"It's good some do. But there are those who don't. Gertrude Tanner has told all who will listen that she places those deaths at my doorstep. She vowed not to rest until she's had her revenge." Now Hannah turned her sad eyes on the body. "I know Gertrude is a woman of her word, so we've been keeping watch in case her cowboys paid us a visit."

"Lord, no," someone said.

I spied a couple of LT hands at the back of the crowd. The people standing near them shied away.

"Last night someone tried to sneak up to our cabin," Hannah revealed. "Shots were swapped. Whoever it was got away, but not before the buzzard about blew one of my daughters in half with a shotgun."

Gasps and oaths greeted the news. Certain things were never, ever done, not even on the frontier. One was horse stealing. Another was cattle rustling. The third was the worst, a deed so vile, folks would not stand for it: harming a woman.

The cowboys did some shying of their own at the glares they received. "Why are all of you looking at us?" the tallest hand angrily demanded.

"Which girl is it?" Calista Modine asked. "Your oldest or your youngest?"

I held my breath.

"It's Sistine," Hannah said. "Poor, sweet Sissy." Hannah turned the buttermilk so it was alongside the sorrel. "I didn't bring her here to be buried. I have a spot near our cabin in mind for that." Hannah's lips quivered. "No, I brought her for all of you to see. Just hearing she was shot ain't enough. It doesn't make it as real as seeing with your own eyes."

Indeed, all eyes *were* on the form in the blanket. It's safe to say I was the only one who felt relief.

"Killing my daughter is the last straw," Hannah had gone on. "I won't take any more of this."

"Don't do anything rash," Calista advised. "I've sent for the Rangers. Let them handle it."

"The Rangers can't bring the dead back to life," Hannah said. "The Rangers can't arrest anyone without proof, and we can't prove the cowboys did it." She gigged the buttermilk over to the pair of cowpokes, Ty, Clell, Carson, and Sam sticking to her like pinesap. "What do you have to say for yourselves?"

"Not a damn thing, lady," the tall one snapped. "We didn't shoot your girl and we don't know who did."

"That's the gospel truth," the second cowboy said. "We're under orders not to go anywhere near your place."

"Whether you pulled the trigger or not," Hannah said, "you work for the Tanners, and that's enough blame for me." She paused. "Shoot them down like dogs, boys."

The cowboys were caught flat-footed. Much too late, they clawed for their hardware. By then Ty, Clell, and Carson had leveled their Winchesters. Sam did not level his.

The shots were a hairbreadth apart. At that range those backwoods boys could hardly miss.

The tall cowboy spun and fell, scarlet gushing from his mouth. His companion took a few steps back, gaping in astonishment at the bullet hole in his sternum; then he melted like hot wax, quivered a few seconds, and was gone.

The onlookers had been stunned into statues by the sudden violence. The whimper of a child broke the spell and the majority scattered, afraid more lead would fly.

Fortunately for the Butchers, the pair had been the only LT hands in town. Hannah climbed down, went to each body, and nudged with her toe. "Dead," she confirmed. "Sissy can rest a little easier."

"You shouldn't have," Calista said.

I felt I had to add something. Pointing at the sky, I said, "You have angered your Maker this day, sister."

Hannah tilted her head toward me. "You're a couple of days late and a couple of dollars short on common sense, Parson. This doesn't concern the Almighty. It's between me and mine and the Tanners."

"The Texas Rangers will come after you," Calista warned.

"By the time they show up I'll have settled accounts." Hannah climbed on her horse, reined around, and came over near me. "Sorry to talk to you like that, you being a man of the cloth and all, Reverend Storm. But I've lost my husband and one of my children, and I will gladly accept perdition before I will let those Tanners make wolf meat of any more of those I love." She indicated the dead cowboys. "It's war now. Out and out, guts and blood war, and the devil take the hindmost."

Chapter 10

Everything was working out just fine. The Tanners blamed the Butchers for the deaths of LT hands I had killed. The Butchers blamed the LT for Sissy, yet another name I could scrawl on the chalkboard of victims that stretched back over the years to that fateful day in the alley when I stabbed my pa.

No one suspected me. No one guessed who I was or the real reason I was there. I was free to go on killing, and the beauty of it was that if I killed with care, the blame would continue to fall on other shoulders than mine.

Thanks to Calista and her meddling, I had to do it soon. Everyone was taking it for granted that it would be a week or more before the Texas Rangers arrived, but there was no predicting. The Rangers fought hard, they rode hard—they *were* hard. It could be they would show up tomorrow. I had to be done when they got there or risk tangling with law officers as feared and as efficient as those gents in the red coats up in Canada. Like the Mounties, the Rangers possessed a fierce devotion to duty and took pride in always getting their man. Since this time I was that man, I preferred to light a shuck before they began nosing around.

I did not eat at midday. I strolled to the general store and bought coffee and jerky and a few canned goods: beans, peaches, tomatoes. I mentioned to the store owner and a few others that I needed to get out of town for a spell and commune with my Maker. I asked about the country to the south, and when I left I rode south, but as soon as I was out of sight I reined toward the Dark Sister.

I stayed well clear of the trail up to the Butcher place. Approaching from the southwest, I was soon in deep timber. I cautiously wound higher until I judged I was due south of their cabin. Then I reined north.

I had a few landmarks to go by. A ridge, for instance, I had noticed from the clearing. It was half a mile from their place. When I spotted a lightning-scarred tree, I knew I was as close as I dared go on horseback.

I did not like leaving Brisco unattended. Horse thieves were two bits a dozen in that part of the country. Stray Indians could not be discounted, either. But if I was to sneak close to their cabin undetected, I had to do it on foot.

As a precaution I led Brisco into a thicket, trampled a circle wide enough for him to lie down if he was so inclined, then shucked my rifle and was ready to commence spilling blood. I left the scattergun in my bedroll. In the daylight the Winchester afforded greater range.

I had been thinking about Sissy on the ride up. I had not known her well. She had been friendly, though, and treated me nice. And now she was worm food. It bothered me. Not that she was dead, but that I was thinking about her being dead. Normally, I never gave a thought after the fact to the wicks I snuff out. I refuse to let myself think about them. Yet here I was, thinking about her.

I spied smoke curling into the sky. Casting Sissy from my mind, I concentrated on the job. I got down on my belly and snaked through the undergrowth like an Apache, stopping often to look and listen.

I was about a hundred yards from the cabin when a cough froze me in place. As slowly as a turtle, I swiveled my head. It took fifteen to twenty seconds to spot him, he was so well hid.

It was Jordy, armed with a rifle and a brace of pistols, perched in the crook of an oak.

I was amazed he had not spotted me. Then I saw that the heat of the afternoon was getting to him. He kept yawning. His chin would droop to his chest, and when it did, he would jerk his head up and shake himself to stay awake.

I could have picked him off. One shot, and he would drop like a sitting grouse. But he was not the only fish I was there to fry and the others must not be forewarned. So I lay still and waited.

The sun was well on its downward sweep when the crackle of brush and low whistling warned me someone was coming.

Kip Butcher strolled into view, carelessly holding

his rifle by the barrel. He halted at the base of the oak and glanced up.

"You're the ugliest squirrel I've ever seen."

"Did you come to spew insults or do you have a purpose?" Jordy retorted.

"Ma says I'm to relieve you and stay out here until midnight. Then Carson will take my place."

Jordy started climbing down, saying, "Are you sure you made enough noise? The Kiowas might not have heard you."

"There ain't no Kiowas within a hundred miles."

"Maybe so. But you know better than to barge around like an elk in rut. You can bet those cowboys won't make noise when they pay us a visit."

"If they come," Kip said. "I suspect they'll think twice after what Ty and Clell and Carson did to those two in town."

Jordy did not say anything until he reached the ground. Then, "Listen to me, little brother. There's no if about it. The cowboys will come and they will come in force. We had damned well better be ready or we will damned well be dead."

"I'm as ready as you are."

"Like hell. Or you wouldn't clomp through the woods like you did." Jordy put a callused hand on his brother's shoulder. "Your problem is that you are never serious enough about things. You take life too lightly."

"I've taken Sissy's death serious enough."

Jordy gazed at the surrounding forest, his eyes passing right over me without seeing me. "Stay alert. Spot them before they spot you and get word to us pronto."

"You don't have to tell me what to do. I was there when Ma gave us our instructions, remember?"

"She's smart, our ma. Like a fox," Jordy said. "Killing those two cowpokes will make the rest come to us. We can fight them on our terms, as she puts it, and not on theirs."

Kip nodded. "There are more of them, but we'll have the edge. They don't know these woods like we do."

"It will be even better if they come at night. Most cowboys can't hit the broad side of a barn unless they're standing right next to it, and in the dark their aim will be worse."

"The one who shot Sissy had good aim," Kip remarked.

"He was using a shotgun," Jordy said, "and shotguns are like cannons. They don't need aiming. You just point and squeeze."

Kip reached up to a low limb, then paused. "Say, what if all the cowboys bring shotguns?"

"There aren't that many hand howitzers to be had in these parts," Jordy said. "Besides, we're ready for them this time."

"I sure as hell hope so." Kip went up limb by limb until he came to the fork. He hooked a leg over one limb and his other leg over another, but that did not suit him so he hooked both legs over the same limb.

Jordy was heading for the cabin and had his back to me.

I resumed crawling. I was almost to the edge of the trees when the front door opened and out ambled Daisy. I was pleased to see her and shouldn't have been. I considered raising my rifle and shooting her through the head to prove I could do it, but that was plain stupid.

Hannah emerged. They came in my direction, apparently for no other reason than to stretch their legs. They were calm and at ease, remarkable in light of the circumstances.

"—you would reconsider." Hannah's words reached me. "I've already lost one daughter. I don't care to lose you, too."

"I'm a Butcher, ain't I?" Daisy responded. "I refuse to run out on my kin when they need me most."

"It's not running, daughter. It's playing safe," Hannah said. "Calista said she would take you in. You could lie low until this is over."

"No means no," Daisy declared.

"I'd take it as a favor."

"Don't. Please, Ma. I could never live with myself if they bucked out all of you and I wasn't here to help. Why, I would march right up to the LT and call out that shrew and shoot her dead unless they shot me first."

"Consarn it, Daisy Mae. Don't be so blamed pig-headed," Hannah said, but she said it tenderly.

Daisy grinned. "I take after my ma."

"Nothing I can say or do will change your mind?"

"Not short of conking me over the noggin so you can hog-tie me and cart me off to Whiskey Flats," Daisy said.

Hannah was trying to appear madder than she was. "I should do just that to spite you. But I won't. Because you're right. You are part of this family and this family always sticks together through thick and thin."

"Now that that's settled," Daisy said, "how about you let me take a turn at keeping watch?"

"I'll think about it," Hannah said in a way that hinted she would not give it any thought at all. "In the meantime, you're not to wander off by your lonesome. You hear me?"

"Are you sure you don't want me to wear a leash?"

Her comment reminded me of their dog. I had not seen it the night I shot Sissy; I did not see it now. Yet the logical place for it to be was outside where its sense of smell and hearing could be put to good use. Where had it gotten to?

"We only have one leash and Ty and Clell took it with them," Hannah was saying. "I hope my plan works. I'm taking an awful chance."

"None of us would have thought of it," Daisy said by way of praise.

"When a pack of wolves is on your trail, you don't sit and wait for them to surround you," Hannah said. "You go after the wolves in their own den."

I was suddenly all ears.

"But what if Ty and Clell only get one or two and not all three?" Daisy asked.

"Just so long as one of those they bed down permanent is Gertrude Tanner. She's the boss of that outfit, not her weak-kneed husband. All our trouble is due to her."

"But why? What does she hope to gain?"

Hannah let out a long sigh. "I wish to heaven I knew. With all the land she has, she doesn't need our patch. Whatever she's up to, it ends as soon as Ty or Clell puts a bullet in her brain." Hannah squinted up at the sun. "They'll wait until late to move in. The Tanners won't be expecting us to take the fight to them, so your brothers should be able to slip in close."

"With Samson along it will be a cinch," Daisy said.

I realized with a start that Samson was the dog. I had to warn Gertrude. She was the one who had hired me. If anything happened to her, I wouldn't get the rest of my money. I hesitated. Here was the perfect chance to shoot Hannah and Daisy. They were so close, I could throw a stick and hit either one. But I didn't. Instead, I crawled back the way I had come until I was past the oak Kip was in. Then I stood and ran. I told myself that I had not shot them because I needed to reach the LT without delay. But I was only fooling myself.

I led Brisco from the thicket, forked leather, and applied my spurs. The Butcher homestead was a jinx, I decided. Twice now I had gone there to pick them off, and twice now fate played a wild card.

I assured myself I was doing the right thing. But I might arrive too late. It would be well after dark when I got there, and by then Ty and Clell might have struck.

Brisco raced like a Chinook. It had been a long while since I rode at a full gallop for so long and I think he enjoyed it as much as I did. Some horses were content to lounge their days away in a stall or a corral, but not Brisco. He had mustang in his blood. At heart he liked to roam wild and free, unhindered by the hand of man. In that respect we had a lot in common, him and me.

The shortest route to the LT was through Whiskey Flats. But the citizenry would wonder if they beheld the parson riding hell bent for leather through the middle of town. I had to skirt it, which added another fifteen minutes.

Chafing at a pace that would win a race, I still had miles to go when the sun sank. I was glad of that. My one worry was that some of the LT cowboys would spot me and want to know why I was in such an all-fired hurry. I had to get in, do what needed doing, and get out again with no one the wiser.

Hannah had said her sons would wait until late. Exactly *how* late was the question. Late as in sometime after supper, or late as in after everyone had gone to bed. Were it me, I would wait until the Tanners—and the cowpokes in the bunkhouse—had turned in. Never leave anything to chance was the cardinal rule I lived by. Or tried to. Life had a knack for spoiling the best-laid plans.

I had to hand it to Hannah. Striking at the Tanners was brilliant. Gertrude would never expect it, not on her very doorstep. And Hannah was right about Gertrude being the bullwhip that drove the husband and son. Remove her, and Lloyd and Phil might end the blood spilling.

Cattle appeared. Not a lot at first. The nearer I drew to the ranch buildings, the more cows there were, and where there were cows, there were bound to be cowboys. I did not come across any, however, which was puzzling.

Brisco was lathered from neck to tail when I finally reined to a halt. Swinging down, I was about to slide the scattergun from my bedroll when I changed my mind. I chose other items from my saddlebags. Better to deal with Ty and Clell quietly. And the dog. I must not forget the dog. I must not forget it could hear me and smell me from a long way off.

I had killed dogs before. I never liked to kill them because I was fond of dogs, but sometimes they had to be dealt with. I always did it quickly so they wouldn't suffer, and so they would not bark or yip and give me away.

There I was, cat footing across the prairie and thinking about dogs in general when I should have been thinking about Samson in particular, and Ty and Clell. I was forgetting the rules that had kept me alive for so long, rules I had made myself. It showed how rattled I was about Daisy.

I came on a gully I had not known was there, stumbled down the slope, and collided with someone slinking along the inky shadow at the bottom. The next instant iron fingers clamped like a vise onto my throat.

Chapter 11

In the dark above me loomed Clell Butcher. I seized his wrist and sought to wrench his hand from my throat, but he was as strong as a bull. His other hand locked on my right wrist even as his knee gouged into my gut, and he slowly bent me backward into a bow. All the while, his fingers dug deeper into my flesh.

I could not break his hold. I could not throw him off. My lungs started to ache for lack of air.

Clell grinned wolfishly. His face lowered to within an inch of mine and I could feel his hot breath on my cheek and smell the onions he had recently eaten. Suddenly he recoiled and straightened, and the next thing I knew, he had me by the shoulders and was shaking me and saying, "Parson! What in God's name are you doing here?"

I couldn't answer. I was sucking in precious breath.

"I'm sorry, Parson! Honest, I am! I had no idea it was you."

I sagged to my knees so my body hid my right hand as I slid it under my pant leg and into my boot. I suppose some folks would call my boot knife a dagger since it was double-edged and slender, but to me a blade is a blade and I always called it a knife.

A hand gently clasped my shoulder. Clell was bending over me. "I'm awful sorry, Parson. But I took you for a cowboy."

I had to swallow a couple of times before I could rasp, "I was looking for you and your brother."

"Why? And how did you know we were here?"

"Your mother told me," I managed to get out. "I know what you are up to. I came to stop you."

"This doesn't concern you, Parson. Go back to town, where you belong."

The throat or the eye? That was the question I was asking myself as he helped me to my feet. The throat did not always kill a man right off. A big bear like Clell would take a while to expire, thrashing and gurgling and maybe calling out. I had seen it before.

"Ma should know better," Clell was saying. "She's always been respectful of men of the cloth, but you could have got yourself killed."

"Where is your brother?"

Clell gestured vaguely in the direction of the buildings. "Over yonder. We drew straws. I'm watching the horses. They're up this gully."

"And the dog?"

"Samson is with Ty. Land sakes, Ma told you about him, too?"

"I can't let you murder the Tanners. We must find Ty and stop him and get out of here before the entire ranch is up in arms."

"Sorry, Parson, but no."

"Excuse me?"

"We have it to do if we're to save our family,"
Clell declared. "And neither you nor the Bible nor
God Almighty will stop us."

By then I was breathing normally and the ache
had faded and my body was my own again. "You're
mistaken." I spun and lanced the knife into his left
eye socket. The six-inch blade sliced through his
eyeball as if it were a grape. I thrust as deep as it
would go, and twisted.

Clell Butcher reacted as most men did. His whole
body stiffened and he staggered back. His mouth
opened, but the only sound that came out was a
strangled whine of disbelief and astonishment. I
tried to hold on, but warm blood was spurting from
the socket, making the hilt too slick to grip.

Clell looked at me. The white of his other eye
made it seem as big as a saucer. He tried to say
something, maybe to ask why, but all that did was
cause blood to flow from his nose and both sides
of his mouth.

Ordinarily, I let them die without saying a word.
But now I heard myself saying, "If you had agreed
to ride off with your brother and me, this might
not have happened." Who was I kidding? I could
not spare them if I wanted to.

Clell plopped to his knees. His hand rose toward
me, but he was weakening fast and his arm slumped
halfway to my neck.

"Nothing personal," I said quietly.

For a minister to take a life was unthinkable.
Clell was confused and it showed. Again he sought

to lay his big hands on me. That he had lasted this long was remarkable. Most died within five to ten seconds.

"I won't make the rest of your family suffer. You have my word."

Clell didn't hear me. He was dead. His chin had dropped to his great chest and his body slowly oozed forward until his forehead rested on the dirt. His hands were in front of him, palms up, as if he were begging a favor.

I should not have felt anything, but I did. Bending, I tugged at the knife. It was stuck. I had to work it back and forth for the longest while before it slid free. After wiping it on his shirt, I returned it to my boot.

I was up and out of the gully and hurrying toward the house when I glimpsed movement. A figure materialized next to a lit window. No, two figures, the second low and shaggy and attached to a leash.

I wanted to shout to warn the Tanners, but they wouldn't hear me. I drew the Remington, but I was not close enough.

Metal glinted at the window. The flash of the muzzle and the crack of the shot were simultaneous. Five more boomed, rolling across the grassland like peals of thunder. Then Ty whirled and bolted into the night, Samson at his side.

Soon the place would be crawling with punchers. No explanation I could offer would explain my presence. The only one who might stand up for me was Gertrude, and she was probably dead.

There is a time to fight and a time to light a shuck. A good Regulator has to know the difference. Pivoting on a boot heel, I raced toward Brisco. Once again fate had foiled me. If it wasn't for bad luck, I wouldn't have any luck at all of late.

The ride to town was a blur. I was too dazed to think. With Gertrude gone I could forget being paid the rest of the thousand dollars. I had no reason to finish the job. The Butchers were safe, a not altogether unappealing prospect.

I fell into bed fully dressed. I slept longer than I usually would and did not shuffle down to the restaurant until almost ten. No sooner did I take my seat than Calista was beside him.

"Have you heard the latest?"

"Not more bad news, I hope."

"There have been more killings," Calista related. "Last night at the LT someone shot through the parlor window at the Tanners."

"I will be happy to conduct their funeral," I offered. It would be a fitting touch. Then I could head for Denver.

"You need only conduct Lloyd's. He was shot in the head. Phil was hit in the shoulder and will live."

"And Gertrude?" I asked, thinking of Daisy.

"From what I understand, a bullet missed her by a whisker. One of the LT hands was in town a while ago. He says she is in a rage."

"At who?" As if I couldn't guess.

"You haven't heard the rest," Calista said. "After the shooting, the cowboys spread out to find the culprit and discovered the body of Clell

Butcher in a gully not far from the house. He had been stabbed."

"My word," I exclaimed. "Who did it?"

"That is what they and everyone else would like to know. It's a mystery. If Clell shot the Tanners, then who killed him?"

"What about the other Butchers? Were any of them involved?" I half hoped the cowboys had caught Ty and relieved me of the responsibility of having to take care of him myself.

"Not that anyone can prove," Calista answered. "Some of the hands thought they heard a horse gallop off." She paused. "It gets stranger. They found tracks under the window, in a flower bed. Tracks of a man, and paw prints."

I feigned surprise. "Paws?"

"That's what they say," Calista confirmed with a bob of her head. "Big paw prints, too. Some of the cowboys think they are dog prints, but others say the tracks are those of a wolf."

"Maybe they're coyote prints," I suggested.

"I'm no tracker, but supposedly there is a difference and these were definitely not made by any coyote."

"How peculiar."

Calista gazed out the window. "The whole town is buzzing like stirred-up bees. Most everyone figures the Butchers had a hand in it, but they can't figure out how Clell got himself murdered. None of the LT hands claim credit."

I saw several cowboys rein up out front. "What will the LT do?"

"Ask them," Calista said with a jerk of her thumb. "Knowing Gerty, I wouldn't want to be a Butcher. It will be all-out war now."

Sunlight spilled across the floor as the door was flung wide and in jangled two of the cowboys. One was a stocky slab of muscle who wore a Colt in cross-draw fashion. The other was a rangy bundle of sinew and bones with salt-and-pepper gristle. They ignored the other patrons and came straight toward my table.

"Reverend Storm, Miss Modine," the slab said, politely doffing his hat. "Sorry to intrude."

"That's all right, Jim," Calista said.

"Mrs. Tanner sent us, ma'am," the rangy cowboy explained. "She would be obliged if the parson, here, would plant her husband tomorrow at noon."

"I would be honored," I said.

Calista focused on the rangy one. "What is the latest, Chester? Have you found Lloyd's killer?"

"No, ma'am. Not yet." Chester realized he still had his hat on and yanked it off. "We're all for riding to the Dark Sister and wiping those varmints out, but Mrs. Tanner won't hear of it."

"That's not like her," Calista said.

Jim agreed. "It sure ain't. Especially as mad as she is. We think maybe she's leaving it for the Texas Rangers to handle."

"You shouldn't ought to have sent for them, ma'am," Chester chided. "You've gone and hobbled us, is what you've done."

"That wasn't my intention," Calista defended herself. "But you must admit this has gotten out of hand. Murders every time we turn around. Men *and* women. If it's not a job for the Rangers, I don't know what is."

"I reckon I can speak for every puncher on the LT when I say I'd rather chuck my own lead, thank you very much," Chester said testily. "It's bothersome to have lawdogs meddle."

"I'm sorry, but I would do the same had I to do it over again," Calista declared. "This isn't just about the LT. It involves the whole community."

The cowboys were disposed to debate the point, but I was hungry and nipped the argument in the bud with, "Tell Mrs. Tanner I will be out at the LT by eleven tomorrow morning."

"You can tell her yourself, if you'd like, Parson," Chester said. "She's over to the undertaker's seeing about the coffin for Mr. Tanner."

For some reason that troubled me. Why had Gertrude sent the two cowboys to ask me to conduct the service for her husband when she could just as well have asked me herself? "I believe I will go have a talk with her," I announced, rising.

"What about your breakfast?" Calista asked.

"It can wait."

Chester and Jim accompanied me to Ira Jackson's. Jackson was the best carpenter in Whiskey Flats, and as a result, whenever anyone needed a coffin, they came to him. He wasn't a real undertaker, but he was all they had.

Half a dozen cowboys lounged out front, waiting for their mistress. Gertrude emerged as I approached, saw me, and frowned. "I didn't say you were to bring him back with you," she said to Chester.

"He came on his own account, ma'am."

"I am sorry about your loss—" I began, and was peeved when she held up her hand to silence me, then motioned for me to walk with her. As soon as we were out of earshot of her hands, she stopped and faced me.

"Tell me again why I hired you?" Gertrude did not wait for me to reply but went on with, "Ah, yes. Now I remember. I hired you to dispose of the Butchers. I trust you will forgive me for my next comment, but you have done an abominably poor job."

"You can't blame your husband's death on me."

"Can't I?" Gertrude snapped. "If you were half as competent as I was led to believe, the job would be done by now." She was so mad, she practically hissed. "Not only are seven of those wretches still breathing, but the Texas Rangers will show up soon to spoil everything."

Her emotional state could be blamed on the loss of her husband, but I still did not like her attitude. "I'll finish it before the Rangers get here. I promise."

Gertrude's features pinched together like she had sucked on a lemon. "You have one day and one day only. If by this time tomorrow you have not done as I hired you to do, you may consider our arrangement no longer in force."

"I don't like being rushed."

"Frankly, Mr. Lucius Stark, I don't give a tinker's damn what you like or don't like. Your incompetence has created complications I can do without." Gertrude sniffed and started to turn. "Twenty-four hours. Not a minute more."

"You don't want to hear who killed Lloyd?"

"Tyrel, obviously."

I was impressed. "How did you know?"

"Tyrel and Clell were inseparable. They went everywhere together. What you were doing there, and why you killed one and not the other, is beyond me."

So she had figured that out, too. "I was trying to stop them."

Gertrude gave me a strange look. "You failed rather spectacularly, didn't you? Retaining your services was a mistake. You have clearly underestimated the Butchers, and you have severely underestimated me. That will cost you, Mr. Stark. That will cost you dearly." Her spine as stiff as a ramrod, she marched off.

Leaving me with the gut feeling I had just been threatened.

Chapter 12

Enough was enough. One thing after another had kept me from finishing up and getting the hell out of there. But no more. The Butchers were going to die and that was all there was to it.

Evening found me in the foothills fringing the Dark Sister. I had shut Daisy from my mind. Emotion would no longer rule me. Only cold determination. So who should I come upon unexpectedly around a turn in the trail? Who else but Daisy Mae, with her brother Sam. They had heard Brisco from a ways off and were waiting, Sam with a rifle to his shoulder.

I was in my preacher garb. The shotgun was in my bedroll, my long-barreled Remington in a saddlebag, the short-barreled Remington in my shoulder rig under my jacket, the knife in my boot. I appeared to be unarmed except for the Winchester in the saddle scabbard. Since it was only common sense to go armed in that neck of the country, it would not seem out of place for a parson to have a rifle. "Trust in the Lord, but keep your guns well oiled" was a saying that applied to everyone.

I could have kicked myself for not leaving the trail sooner. I should have cut through the woods. But I had been anxious to get it over with. Too anxious. Drawing rein, I leaned on the saddle horn and smiled. "I'd prefer if you don't shoot me, Brother Butcher," I said to the stripling.

Embarrassed, Sam jerked the rifle down. "Shucks, Parson. How was I to know it was you?"

Daisy placed her hand on my leg. "What a delight to see you again, Reverend Storm. Ma will be pleased."

"Will she?" I looked at her, horrified by the tingle that had coursed through me at her touch. Damn me to hell, but I was acting worse than a boy her brother's age. Conflicting desires tore at me: one to clasp her hand in mine, the other to draw my short-barreled Remington, touch it to her sweet face, and thumb back the hammer again and again.

"What brings you out our way?"

"I heard about Clell," I replied. "I figured your family would need some comforting."

"That's awful decent of you," Daisy said, giving my leg a squeeze.

"Everyone else treats us as if we have the plague," Sam contributed.

"Not everyone," Daisy corrected him. "Miss Modine and a few others have been nice. We do have some friends."

"Precious few compared to the Tanners," Sam said. "Most of the town is on their side."

"It's only natural. The Tanners were here long

before we were." Daisy lowered her arm. "Come along, Parson. We'll escort you the rest of the way."

Here was my chance. I could shoot them in the back. But Sam let me go by him, saying, "I'll catch up. Ma said for us to keep watch and that's what I aim to do. Give a holler when it's time for supper." He stood there watching until we came to the next bend.

Now it was just Daisy and me. I fingered the garrote in my jacket pocket, but the thought of wrapping the wire around her soft, slender throat and choking the life from her while she struggled and thrashed under me caused me to break out in a sweat.

"Are you all right, Reverend Storm? You look sickly."

"I'm fine," I said, my voice hoarse and low. To distract her I asked, "How is your family taking your latest loss?"

"About as you would expect. Ma cried for an hour last night. Thank goodness it wasn't Ty. She loves all of us as dearly as can be, but there's a special place in her heart for him, Ty being her firstborn and all."

"You are wise beyond your years."

"That's kind of you to say." Daisy smiled and touched my hand. "But then, that's why you became a preacher, I reckon. So you can go around saying kind things and being good to folks."

Why didn't I kill her then and there? What in hell was happening to me? I was so mad at myself, I shook inside.

"If you don't mind my asking, how is it a handsome cuss like you hasn't ever married? Or do you belong to a religion that won't let you?"

"I could marry if I wanted."

"That's good. I never could understand that business about how a preacher can't be close to the Almighty and a woman, both. Seems to me the Lord wouldn't begrudge a man having a companion."

"You wouldn't think so, would you?" was all I could think of to say. I wanted to rip off my collar and toss it away.

"I admire how you always think of others," Daisy flattered me. "Coming here like this. It means a lot to us."

I wished she would stop talking. I wished she would shut up and never say another word to me.

"What kind of woman would you want? To marry, I mean? Would her age matter? Or whether she was refined, like Miss Modine?"

"I've never given it much thought," I mumbled.

"You should. It's not good to go through life alone. Ma hates being alone. She misses Pa something fierce. They were special close, her and him. Always holding hands and making cow eyes, even after being married so long and having all us kids."

"She has held up well."

"She says she has to, for our sake." Daisy stared at me. "What will happen, Parson? How will this all end?"

"I can't predict the future," I responded. "But I pray it ends as it should." She could take that however she pleased.

"Ma is worried, Parson. She's heard about the Texas Rangers coming, and it can't be soon enough to suit her. She was all fired up to fight the Tanners tooth and nail after Sissy was killed, but losing Clell has changed her mind. Now all she wants is for all of us to live through this."

I was glad when the clearing and the cabin appeared. Their dog started barking, and Jordy and Carson came out of the woods. As was to be expected, they were armed with rifles and revolvers.

As I was dismounting Hannah emerged. She looked terrible, as if she had not slept in days. She had dark bags under her eyes and more lines in her face than I remembered. Deep sorrow had her in its grip, and I was partly to blame.

"Reverend." She grasped my hand in both of hers. Her eyes moistened and her lips trembled. "How good of you to pay us a visit. Come inside, won't you, and let me treat you to coffee or whatever else you would like."

Ty and Kip appeared, and Ty cleared his throat. "We would be right honored if you would say a few words over Clell. We buried him this morning next to Sissy."

"Certainly." That was when I realized I had left the Bible back in my room at Calista's.

"Would you rather do that first and then come in?" Hannah asked.

"Lead the way."

The two mounds of dirt were a dozen yards into the woods. Crude crosses had been stuck atop each. The Butchers ringed them and bowed their heads.

I racked my brain for a quote, but for the life of me I couldn't think of one.

"Whenever you are ready, Parson," Hannah politely prompted.

I stared at the mounds, wondering which was which as the crosses did not have their names carved into the wood. "Death comes to us all," I said, groping and hoping I sounded like a real preacher. "We don't want it to, but it does. Rich or poor, young or old, it comes for us when we least expect, and there is nothing any of us can do. Death is always there, always waiting." I was rambling and not sounding very biblical. "Look at the Old Testament. Moses, Joshua, Samson, they were all close to God, yet they all died. Look at the New Testament. Even Jesus was put to death. When our time comes, it comes."

Hannah and Daisy were looking at me.

"We are gathered to give our respects to two fine people, Clell and Sistine Butcher. They did not deserve to die, but they did. None of us does, but we do. Some say it's not fair and it's not right, but it's the way God arranged things, so what can we do?" I promised myself, then and there, that this was the last time I would ever pretend to be a preacher. "We ask you, Lord, to welcome Clell and Sistine into the hereafter. Look after them. May their stay in heaven be happier than their stay here. And may we one day join them in their happiness."

Some of the Butchers were fidgeting. I needed a drink. Not a glass or two but an entire bottle.

"Ashes to ashes, dust to dust. As it was in the

beginning, so shall it be in the end. The Lord is our shepherd, we shall not want. Amen."

"Amen," Hannah said, and was echoed by her brood.

I kept my head bowed until we came to the cabin. I figured they had seen right through me, but I was forgetting that most people don't expect perfection since they fall so short of it themselves.

"That was mighty fine," Jordy said.

Hannah opened the door for me. "You will have supper with us, won't you?" I opened my mouth, but she did not give me a chance to speak. "I won't take no for an answer, Parson. If I'm imposing on your good nature, so be it. I want you to stay, and that's that."

I couldn't very well tell her I had no intention of leaving until all of them were dead. "I will be happy to stay." She ushered me to the rough-hewn log table and bade me sit, then asked if I would like some coffee. When I said I would, she motioned to Daisy, who went to the stove and soon brought over two brimming cups.

"I'm so glad you're here," Hannah said as I took my first sip. "Losing Sissy and Clell has hit me hard."

"As it would any mother," I remarked.

"It was wrong to send Ty and Clell to kill the Tanners. I was better off waiting for the Rangers."

"We all make mistakes."

Hannah did not seem to hear me. "I wanted to end it, Parson. I couldn't stand the thought of losing more of those I love. I reckoned that with the Tanners dead, the killing would stop."

"I pray it does," I said.

"That's not likely. Gertrude always had a powerful hate for me and mine. Now, with her husband dead and her son laid up, she has cause to hate us that much more." Hannah bit her lower lip. "There's no telling what she'll do to get back at us. I don't mind admitting I'm worried. Mighty worried."

"The Rangers will be here soon and then you will be safe," I assured her. No one would dare tangle with the Texas Rangers. It just was not done.

"It can't be soon enough to suit me," Hannah said. "If I ask them to protect us, do you think they will see fit to guard us day and night?"

"I could not possibly predict," I answered. Unwittingly, she had given me more reason to finish the job as quickly as possible. I decided to do it right after supper. I would catch them completely unawares. Unarmed and at ease, they would be easy pickings.

To that end, I endured half an hour of small talk while Daisy made the meal. She had to do it herself. Hannah was in no mood to cook, and her brothers could not be bothered to lend a hand. When the venison was done, Daisy went to the front door and hollered, "Come and get it!" Everyone came, including Sam and the two who were hidden in the woods.

I was hungry, but I did not feel much like eating. I picked at the meat and the beans and washed what little I ate down with piping-hot black coffee.

Hannah, too, barely touched her food. Slumped in her chair, her chin in her hand, she hardly spoke the whole meal. As I pushed my plate back, she stirred. "I trust that was satisfactory?"

"As delicious as can be," I said.

"Now that you have partaken of our hospitality, what do you say to doing me a favor?"

"If it is within my power," I said gallantly.

"I don't dare show my face in town. Me nor my younguns. But I need someone to get word to me when the Rangers arrive."

"I will ride out here the moment they ride in," I pledged.

Daisy beamed at me. "Isn't he wonderful, Ma? Always ready to lend a helping hand."

"That's what men of the cloth do, daughter," Hannah said. "That, and they always turn the other cheek. It's why they're different from us ordinary folk."

"I could never imagine the parson hurting a fly," Daisy said.

How easy it is to fool people, I reflected. Most go through life with blinders on, only seeing what they want to see. There I was, a notorious Regulator, a killer many times over, and they could not see past my sheep's collar and recognize the wolf in their fold.

I was congratulating myself on my cleverness when their mongrel commenced barking his fool head off. He was tied to a stake at the corner of the cabin, giving him a good view of the trail.

"Quiet, Samson!" Ty bellowed.

"It's probably another stupid rabbit," Carson complained.

"Don't ever take anything for granted," Hannah said. "One of you go have a look-see."

Sam started to rise but froze along with the rest of his family when the dog's barking was brought to an end by the blast of a rifle. The next instant the Butchers were scrambling for their hardware. Without thinking, young Sam and Carson went to rush out the door.

"Stop right there!" Hannah commanded. "What are you trying to do? Get yourselves killed?"

Mocking laughter wafted from the woods. "Can you hear me in there? This is Gertrude Tanner!"

So much for her giving me twenty-four hours. With an effort I swallowed my fury.

"Dear God!" Hannah Butcher breathed.

Again Gertrude laughed in sheer savage delight. "Are you ready to meet your Maker? Because you are all going to die!"

Chapter 13

Tyrel sprang to the door and wrenched it open, only to slam it shut again and fling himself against the wall as rifles thundered and half a dozen slugs thudded against the door and the jamb.

"You're trapped!" Gertrude gloated. "My hands have your cabin surrounded! Try to make a break and we'll shoot you to ribbons!"

"Ma?" Sam said anxiously. He was flat on the floor, as were several of the others. Daisy had sought cover by the stove.

Hannah sidled to a window, careful not to show herself. "Hush, boy, and let me think."

I was crouched next to the table, but now I rose in a crouch and crossed to her side. She was warily peeking out. "See anything?"

"No, but I don't doubt they're out there. My worst fear has come to pass. Gertrude has us boxed in and can do as she pleases." Hannah pressed her forehead to the wall and closed her eyes. "We're goners. I should have left someone out there to stand guard."

"Never give up hope," I offered. Which was easy

for me to say since I had a way out. "Perhaps if I talk to her I can persuade her to leave you be."

Hope filled Hannah's eyes. "Would you? She might listen to you, you being the parson and all."

"It won't hurt to try." I moved past Jordy and Ty and opened the front door a crack. "Mrs. Tanner?" I bawled. "This is Reverend Storm! Tell your men not to shoot. I'm coming out."

"By all means, do. I very much want to talk to you."

As I stepped outside I heard Gertrude issue an order for the cowboys to hold their fire. She materialized out of the woods, as straight backed and haughty as ever. She was smiling a wicked sort of smile that widened when we met halfway across the clearing. I counted at least seven rifle barrels trained on me.

"Well, well, well," Gertrude said. She was dressed in black and wore an ivory-handled Colt around her waist. In her left hand was a quirt. "Paying those scum a social call, are you?"

"I'm here to get the job done." I gestured at the rifles. "You gave me twenty-four hours, remember? If I had known you were going to take matters into your own hands, I wouldn't have bothered coming out."

"I wearied of waiting for you," Gertrude said. "There's an old saying. If you want something done—"

"Do it yourself," I finished for her. "But you hired me, and I intend to wrap everything up by midnight."

"I think not," Gertrude said.

"You want to see them die with your own eyes, is that it?"

"That, and more." Gertrude grinned and tapped the riding quirt against her leg. "Oh, this is delicious. I only wish Phil was here. He would delight in the irony as much as I do."

"What irony?" I asked.

"He's laid up for a week. Doctor's orders," Gertrude said. "When I saw him lying on the floor in a pool of blood, I thought I would die. He's always meant the world to me, my boy."

"What about your husband?"

"What about him?" she retorted. "Lloyd was a fool. But then, so was I, for marrying him. I loathe weak men, and he was as weak as pond water. How curious that I chose to hitch myself to someone like him."

I had no interest in her personal life. "About the Butchers—"

"It's strange how thing works out, isn't it? Never as we expect. I had resigned myself to being shackled to Lloyd for the rest of my days, and now look. I am free to do as I want without his constant carping. You have no idea what I had to put up with."

"I don't give a damn," I said.

"Now, now. Don't be mad. I'm only doing what I intended to do all along. I never really needed you. But Lloyd insisted we hire an outsider so the finger of blame would not point at us."

"Lloyd insisted? I thought you hired me on your own?"

"Did I give that impression?"

I didn't like where this was leading. "Take your men and go."

"Haven't I made myself clear? I no longer require your services as a Regulator. I will do my own regulating from here on out."

"We have a deal," I stressed yet again.

Gertrude snickered. She was enjoying herself. "Deals, like laws, are made to be broken."

"I won't take it kindly if you back out."

"What was it you said to me a few moments ago? Oh, yes. I don't give a damn. In my estimation your reputation is greatly overblown."

I could feel myself growing mad. I never let anyone talk to me like she was doing. "Be careful."

"Or what? You'll shoot me? I wouldn't try, were I you. One wrong move, or a gesture from me, and my punchers will turn you into a sieve."

The rifle muzzles pointed at me left no doubt her threat was genuine. It only made me hotter. "I'm not leaving until I get the rest of my money."

Gertrude actually had the gall to laugh in my face. "*Your* money? In order for it to be yours, you had to earn it. Which you did not. No, the five hundred I have already paid is all I am paying, and even that was too much."

"You don't want me for an enemy."

Smirking, Gertrude put her hands on her hips. "You still don't get it, do you? Must I spell it out as I would to my late husband? How you have lasted so long is beyond me."

One more insult and I would punch her, female

or no. "Maybe it's best if I just go." I glanced at where I had left Brisco and felt my gut tighten; Brisco was gone. "What did you do with my horse?"

"We drove him off, along with their horses. After all, I wouldn't want anyone to escape, now would I?" Gertrude regarded me intently. "Tell you what. I've thought of a way for you to redeem yourself. Do as I ask and I will pay you the other five hundred. Does that sound fair?"

"I'm listening."

"Go back inside. Tell Hannah and her brats I will spare them if they throw down their guns and come out with their hands over their heads."

"They're not stupid," I said.

"Assure them I am sincere. Convince them I intend to turn them over to the Texas Rangers."

"As if you would."

"It's worth a try, isn't it?" Gertrude pressed. "And it's the only way you will get what is coming to you."

I hesitated. I might be able to talk the Butchers into agreeing. They trusted me, after all. I would assure them that as God was my witness, I would not let them come to harm.

"Well? What are you waiting for?"

"It may take me a while to convince them," I said. I glanced at the cabin. We were far enough from it, and had talked quietly enough, that there was little chance we had been overheard.

"Take as long as you need. I'm not going anywhere."

I still hesitated. Gertrude reminded me of a cat

about to eat a canary. I didn't trust her. But so what if she did not keep her word? So what if she had the Butchers gunned down? I was fixing to kill them, anyway. What difference did it make who turned them into maggot bait so long as I was paid? Shrugging, I turned. I was almost to the door when Gertrude called my name. Not Reverend Storm, but my real name.

"Oh, Mr. Stark?"

Mad as hell, I looked over my shoulder. She had drawn her Colt and was pointing it at my back. It stopped me in my tracks. "What do you think you're doing?"

"Saving myself five hundred dollars."

Gertrude shot me. There was a sharp sensation between my shoulder blades and the slug tore through my chest and burst out the front of my shirt. The impact jolted me. The world darkened and spun. Close to passing out, I lurched toward the front door and groped for the latch. I heard Gertrude laugh, and it was like having a bucket of cold water splashed in my face. My vision cleared and I stumbled to the door just as it was yanked open from within. Hannah enfolded me in her arms and pulled me in after her. None too soon. A volley from the woods blistered the door.

Jordy slammed the door after us.

Everyone else was down low. Hannah and Daisy half dragged, half carried me to a far corner and gently eased me down so I had my back to the wall. A strange weakness had come over me, and it was all I could do to hold my head up.

"She shot him!" Daisy exclaimed. "She shot the parson!"

"I wouldn't put anything past that monster," Hannah said while plucking at my shirt. "Let's see how bad off he is." She flicked my jacket aside. I tried to reach up to stop her but couldn't. Suddenly she recoiled as if I had slapped her. "What in the world is this?"

"It's a pistol!"

"I can see that, daughter." Hannah slid the short-barreled Remington from my shoulder holster. "But what in the world is the preacher doing with a hideout? I've never heard of such a thing."

"He has a rifle, too. I saw it in his saddle scabbard."

"Even preachers shoot game for the dinner table," Hannah said. "But this"—she hefted the Remington—"this is something a gambler or an assassin would carry."

I had to say something. She was close to guessing the truth. But I was so weak that all I could croak was, "Pro—tect—you."

"What did he say?" Hannah asked.

"I think he said he brought the gun to protect us," Daisy said, and tenderly clasped my hand.

Disbelief was written plain on Hannah's face.

Just then another volley peppered the cabin to the accompaniment of whoops and yips from the cowboys. The window shattered in a spray of shards. Slugs cored the door, narrowly missing Kip.

"Douse the lamp!"

Sam leaped to obey. As he rose to extinguish the

wick, a rifle cracked. He had exposed himself through the window to a shooter in the woods. The slug caught him high in the shoulder and spun him around. He braced himself against the wall to keep from falling, but would have collapsed if not for Jordy, who caught him and lowered him into a chair. It was Ty who blew out the lamp, plunging the room into darkness.

Hannah crabbed toward her youngest. "Keep low!" she cautioned. "Jordy, bolt the door. Carson and Ty, scoot over by the window."

I attempted to sit up, but my legs would not cooperate. Seldom had I felt so defenseless. Hannah had taken my Remington, leaving me with nothing but the boot knife. The shooting, though, had stopped.

The way I saw it, Gertrude had four choices. She could wait us out until we were so low on food and water, her cowboys could overrun us. But that would take days, and by then the Texas Rangers would arrive. Her second choice was to rush us, but she was bound to lose a lot of punchers. Her third option was the one I would pick: sit out there and pepper us with lead for ten to twelve hours, whittling us down so when she did give the order for her cowhands to attack, they would overwhelm us with little loss of life on their side.

As if Gertrude was able to read my mind, she shouted, and leaden hail blistered the cabin on four sides. She had not been exaggerating when she said she had it surrounded.

Laughter pealed in the silence that followed the

shots. "Are you still alive in there, Hannah? If so, you won't be for long. By daybreak all of you will be dead and your cabin burned to the ground."

Hannah was bent over Sam. Without raising her head she called out, "What did we do to you that you hate us so?"

"Wouldn't you like to know?" Gertrude rejoined. "But it will stay my little secret this side of the grave."

"Please, for the sake of my children, don't take the law into your own hands. Turn us over to the Texas Rangers."

"Beg all you want, but my mind is made up. None of you are getting out of there alive. That includes your parson friend, in case he's still breathing."

God, how I hankered to blow out her wick. In my fury I clenched my fists and realized my strength was returning. Pain was setting in, as well. My temples pounded and my mouth became as dry as Death Valley. I did not have the warm, wet feeling deep inside, that warned of internal bleeding, which was a good sign. Nor was blood leaking out of my mouth and nose.

Daisy had slid over by her mother, but now she returned and wanted to know, "How are you holding up?"

I had to lick my lips and swallow a few times before saying, "It's no worse than being stomped by a bull. How is your brother?"

Bending so close her warm breath fluttered my cheek, Daisy said, "The bullet nicked his shoulder bone, but Ma thinks Sam will live."

"We can't stay cooped up in here," I said.

"What else can we do? Ma says it would be suicide to make a break for the woods. They would drop us one by one as we go out the door."

That they would. "Give me a revolver or a rifle and I will cover you," I offered. My thinking was that the cowboys would chase after them, giving me the chance to crawl into the woods and hide.

Daisy misunderstood. "You are the noblest man I've ever met. But we're not about to run off and leave you."

At that juncture something struck the front of the cabin with a loud *thump*, and seconds later a flickering glow lit the window.

"Dear Lord!" Hannah cried. "They're trying to set the cabin on fire!"

That was the fourth choice.

Chapter 14

A bucket of water was on the counter. Jordy grabbed it and ran to the window, where fingers of flame were licking at the sill. To douse them, he had to lean out and upend the bucket. The moment he did, a rifle cracked off in the trees. Jordy dropped the bucket and tottered back, his right arm suddenly limp.

Hannah and Daisy rushed to render aid. They brought Jordy over near me and had him sit. Kip joined them and handed his mother his belt knife, which Hannah used to cut open Jordy's sleeve. She gingerly examined the wound. The slug had drilled Jordy above the elbow, shattering the bone and leaving an exit hole the size of a walnut. Blood pumped in a torrent.

"We have to stop the bleeding," Hannah said. "Daughter, rip a sheet into strips. Kip, find me something to use as a splint."

I was feeling weak again. I stared at my own wound, wondering if I would live. Internal bleeding was not always apparent. If I was bleeding inside, there was nothing Hannah could do for me. I thought of Gertrude's treachery and yearned to slip a garrote around her throat or, better yet, strangle her with my hands.

I had only myself to blame for being shot. When I started in the regulating business, I would never turn my back on someone like Gertrude. I had become too sure of myself, too careless. I had taken to assuming my reputation would protect me.

As I watched the glow at the front of the cabin grow, I did something I had not done since I was knee high to a foal. I prayed. I asked God Almighty to let me live so I could have my revenge on the woman who had done this to me. With every iota of my being, I prayed. When it hit me what I was doing, I grinned at my silliness.

Long ago I learned that God never answered my prayers. As a boy, night after night, I prayed that my father would stop beating my mother. Night after night, I prayed he would stop drowning himself in drink and treat us as a father was supposed to treat us. But my prayers did no good. My father did not stop drinking. He did not stop beating her. He did not treat us as a caring father should.

I had heard that God answered the prayers of others: Folks have told me that the Almighty answered theirs. Why God never answered mine, I couldn't rightly say. Maybe I made God mad at me somehow. Maybe I prayed wrong. Whatever it was, as I sat there with that bullet hole in me and realized I was praying, I not only grinned, I had a lump in my throat.

Then the moment passed, and the cowboys were

whooping and hollering and peppering the cabin with lead. The flames outside were now visibly licking at the sill, and spreading rapidly.

The Butchers were huddled together and Hannah was talking in urgent but hushed tones. I could not hear what she was saying. Jordy had been bandaged, but he was as pale as paper. Sam looked even worse.

I tried to crawl to them, but my arms would not support me. I was able to sit back, but the effort left me exhausted. I must have passed out because the next thing I knew, hands had hold of me and I was being dragged across the floor. I sucked in a deep breath and the pain made me cough and sputter.

Hannah's kindly features floated above me. "Be still, Parson, and listen. We don't have much time. Our cabin is filling with smoke. We can't stay or we'll be burned alive. We have to try for the woods. But we can't take you with us."

"What—?" I began, but she hushed me with a finger to my mouth.

"I'm sorry, but we can't. Jordy and Carson are too weak to help carry you, and it will be all the rest of us can do not to get ourselves shot."

I felt a hand in mine, squeezing gently. A small, slender hand. Daisy's hand. I heard a scraping sound and saw Ty sliding the table aside.

"We're going to put you in the root cellar," Hannah went on. "It's the best we can do. If we live, we will come back and fetch you as soon as we can." Hannah held the short-barreled Remington where I could see it, then slid it into my shoulder holster. "Here. The Lord only knows what you are doing with this, but it might come in handy." She regarded me intently. "I wish we had time to talk. I have a feeling things aren't as I thought they were, but that's neither here nor there now. We're all in the same boat, and it's sinking."

"They'll be expecting you to make a break for it," I was able to wheeze.

Hannah's features became etched with sadness. "I know. We all know. But we have to do it. There are enough of us that maybe we can shoot our way out." She smiled and said in earnest, "Good luck to you."

Partial darkness enfolded me. I was being lowered into their root cellar. I smelled dank earth. Near me hung a slab of jerked venison. To my left lay a sack of potatoes. A blanket was placed under me.

Hannah and Tyrel and Carson and Kip filed up the steps, but not Daisy. She sank down beside me and tenderly touched my cheek. "I don't want to leave you, but Ma says it's best. At least this way you have a slim chance of living."

"Don't go." I was sincere, much to my amazement.

"I have to. They're my family." Daisy's eyes were the loveliest eyes I ever gazed into. "Before I do, I'd like an answer out of you. An honest answer."

"About what?"

"Are you a preacher or aren't you?"

I didn't hesitate. "Of course I am."

A smile lit Daisy's face. "I knew it. I knew you wouldn't lie to us. And your hideout gun?"

"I told you. I brought it to help protect you if I had to. It belonged to my pa."

Daisy kissed my cheek. Not a peck, but a lingering kiss that was the best kiss of my life. Then she straightened and said hoarsely, "This ain't fair. But don't you worry. I'll be back for you. No matter what. You believe me, don't you?"

"Sure," I said.

Hannah appeared in the opening. "Daisy! Come on! There's so much smoke we can barely see. We have to leave. We have to do it now."

"Coming, Ma." Daisy smiled and caressed my chin. Turning, she bounded up the steps.

I opened my mouth to call out to her to be careful, but the trap door closed. Now all I could do was lie there as helpless as a newborn while the cabin burned down around me.

Presently I noticed gray wisps worming between the boards above me. The floor had enough chinks and cracks that a lot more smoke was bound to get in. Thin slivers of light penetrated too. I looked about but could not see much.

I was straining my ears, and I heard it. I heard the front door slam open and the shooting began. In my mind's eye I saw the Butchers race out into the night, firing as they went. How many made it to the trees depended on whether Gerty had thought to bring cowboys from the sides and rear of the cabin to support those in front. Judging by the din, she had.

The shooting went on and on.

I drew my Remington. I wanted to rush out and help the Butchers. I rose on my elbows, but that was as far as I got. The root cellar turned topsy-turvy and I passed out again.

When I came to the shooting was over. Smoke half filled the root cellar. I heard loud crackling and hissing and snapping. After a bit I thought I heard something else—laughter. Female laughter.

The cabin was in flames. Soon the floor would burn, right down on top of me. Hannah had meant well, but I would be roasted alive.

To my left, past the sack of potatoes, was an earth wall. Girding myself, I rolled onto my side. My head swam and I thought I would pass out again, but I didn't. Levering my forearms, I inched toward the sack. A simple potato sack, yet crawling over it was like crawling over a mountain. It hurt. It hurt like nothing ever hurt my whole life long. I broke out in a sweat. My chest felt as if iron bands were wrapped tight, squeezing the life from me. But I made it. I crawled over the potatoes and lay spent and limp between the sack and the wall.

The crackling and hissing grew louder. A tremendous crash signaled the roof was collapsing.

Marshaling my energy, I gouged at the dirt with both hands. It was not as hard-packed as I feared. I dug as fast as I could, aware that the root cellar was now nearly full of smoke. I clawed and scooped and scooped and clawed and made steady headway.

Another crash spurred me to greater speed. Smoke seeped into my nose and mouth. I started to cough, but quickly smothered my mouth with my sleeve. If Gertrude and her cowboys were still out there, they might hear me

Taking short, shallow breaths, I continued to dig. My fingers ached and my chest was a welter of agony, but I did not stop. I could not stop. I scraped and gouged, scraped and gouged. Soon I had a niche almost as long as my body and a foot wide. It was not much, but it had to do.

Wedging myself in, I reached behind me, cupped the dirt I had dug, and covered my head and back as best I could until exhaustion caused me to collapse. I lay completely spent, scarcely able to breathe, as the crackling and hissing swelled to the roar of an inferno.

The heat was unbearable. I felt like I was being fried alive. Sweat poured from me in great drops, soaking me, drenching my clothes. I swore I was giving off steam. Just when I could not take it anymore and was about to scream in torment, the roar began to fade. I was hot, ungodly hot, but I did not grow any hotter.

I lapsed in and out of consciousness until after a while I opened my eyes and the roar was gone. But not the hissing. And not the acrid odor of burned wood and burned other things.

I stayed where I was. It would take hours for the wreckage to cool enough for me to make my way out of the root cellar. As weak as I was, I was content to stay put, and to marvel at my deliverance.

But I was putting the cart before the horse. Suddenly I heard the clomp of feet, and the person I hated most in this world barked orders.

"Look everywhere! He has to be here. There won't be much left, but I want to see what there is with my own eyes."

"Why go to all this bother over a Bible thumper?" a cowboy responded. "We know he didn't get out."

"It's too hot," another said. "We'll burn ourselves."

"Do as I tell you!" Gertrude commanded. "It's important I find him. Chester, you poke around in that corner. Brewer, over by the stove. Sutton, you take the root cellar."

Boots clomped closer. "What a mess," the man who had to be Sutton said. "My pants will be so black they'll need washing."

Farther off a puncher remarked, "Folks won't take kindly to a man of the cloth being killed."

"They'll string us up for sure if they find out," said another.

Gertrude did not appreciate their comments. "Hush up, both of you. There's not a shred of evidence to link us to this. Quite the contrary. The arrow we'll leave will point the blame at hostiles."

"Isn't that a Kiowa arrow, ma'am?" Chester asked.

"Yes, it is," Gertrude confirmed.

"Where did you get it, if you don't mind my askin'?"

"We can thank my late departed husband. His cousin gave it to him. We'll leave it where it's bound to be found. Seton will add the icing to the cake, as the saying goes."

Laughs and snickers greeted that tidbit. I wondered why. And why the name Seton was vaguely familiar.

"I've got to hand it to you, ma'am. You've thought of everything."

"I always do," Gertrude stated matter-of-factly. "I've had a lot of practice. My husband was next to worthless when it came to making decisions. I made the LT what it is today, not him."

The cowboys did not say anything.

"Lloyd was lily-livered. Remember those nesters we drove off back in seventy-seven? I gave the order, not him. And those rustlers we hung? Lloyd would have turned them over to the law. But not me. I believe in handling my own problems. Like these wretches we've just exterminated."

"Their rustling days are over," a cowboy remarked, and again all of them laughed.

"Yes. The cows," Gertrude said.

I was so intent on what they were saying that I had forgotten about Sutton, but I was reminded of him when I heard him cough. He was close, very close, and I tensed, thinking he would find me and call out to the others. But much to my amazement, he didn't. Instead, Gertrude called down to him.

"Anything down there?"

"No, ma'am. A lot of burned boards and burned food, but that's all."

"Come on up, then. Powell, give him a hand." Gertrude paused. "I don't understand it. Where can the body be?"

"Maybe the reason we can't find it is because there's nothing left of him," someone suggested.

"No, there is always something," Gertrude informed them. "Bones. Teeth. Remains of some kind."

She was right. I once had occasion to burn out a squatter, and when I sifted through the ruin, I found a thigh bone and the brittle bones of one hand and his teeth. Oh. And his glass eye.

"We can search all night if you want, Mrs. Tanner," a cowpoke said. "But that fire could be seen from a long ways off. We might have visitors."

"Unfortunately, we just might," Gertrude conceded. "To our horses, then, gentlemen. We will avoid Whiskey Flats and return to the LT with no one the wiser. Tomorrow afternoon I'll ride into town and be suitably shocked when I hear about the massacre."

Approximately ten minutes later the thud of hooves filled me with relief. It was short-lived. I started to twist but couldn't move. Not through any fault of mine. I was pinned.

Now I understood why Sutton had not found me. The floor had caved in, and I was buried under it.

Chapter 15

I twisted my neck around to take stock and nearly gouged an eye out on a thin spine of charred wood that had once been a floorboard. I discovered I had been wrong. Only part of the floor had caved in, a wedge-shaped section that had collapsed within an inch of my cranny and within an inch of crushing my skull like an eggshell.

Gathering my strength, I rolled over on my other side. It was a tight squeeze, but by worming my body a bit deeper into the niche, I succeeded. I placed both hands against the still very warm boards, and pushed. They would not budge. Panic gripped me at the thought I might be trapped. To die of hunger and thirst had always struck me as a horrible way to cash in one's chips. I would much rather go quick, with a bullet or a blade to a vital organ.

A crossbeam held the section of floor together, but the crossbeam was loose; I could see it jounce and shake when I pushed.

I tried a different board. It and two others next to it were the most badly burned. Sheer joy coursed through me as, creaking loudly, it gave way. Not a lot, maybe a foot or so, but it was enough that when I pushed the other two boards, I created a gap wide enough for me to wriggle through.

The effort cost me, though. I lay still and spent, caked with sweat. My chest did not hurt, which surprised me. I wanted to examine the wound, but it would have to wait. Presently I felt strong enough to sit up. I gazed at where the steps had been only to find them gone. They had been burned to ashes. Again panic stabbed through me. I could not possibly jump high enough to hook my elbows over the edge and pull myself out. Then I noticed a smoldering mound that had once been stockpiled provisions.

Bracing myself against the fallen wedge of floor, I slowly stood. It took everything I had. I leaned against the blackened boards until I could shuffle to the mound and gingerly lift my foot. It was spongy but solid enough to support me. With my hands on the dirt wall, I rose high enough to poke my head and shoulders out of the root cellar.

A cool breeze fanned my face, a breeze so wonderfully welcome and refreshing that I was content to stand there and do nothing but breathe deeply for a while. Stars speckled the firmament, and by the position of the Big Dipper I figured it had to be close to two in the morning. Were it not for the east wall of the cabin, which was still burning, I would be in total darkness.

It was strange. Fires are fickle beasts. The roof was gone, the west and north walls had been burned to the ground, yet most of the east wall and part of the south wall were largely intact. Parts of the floor had been burned through; other parts were barely scorched.

I had to get out of that hole. I extended my arms over the edge as far as they would go and attempted to lever myself out, but the instant I put my weight on my chest, agony racked me. I nearly blacked out.

It was some time before I could focus my thoughts. Obviously, I wasn't going to climb out. I needed something to hold on to. The stove was still standing, but it was out of my reach. The only piece of furniture left, oddly enough, was a chair, but it, too, was too far away.

I noticed that I was close to a corner of the root cellar. Carefully raising my right leg, I found that I could brace my boot against the other wall. Moving slowly so as not to tire myself, I poked and jabbed at the earth. My intent was to make a foothold I could wedge my boot in, but the fire had somehow hardened the dirt and jabbing at it was like jabbing at rock. Brittle rock. I persisted, sweating torrents. Twice I had to stop to catch my breath and wait for my head to stop spinning. But at last I had a roughly round hole I could stick part of my boot into.

Pressing my forearms flat, I thrust upward with my leg. Again my chest protested and my head swam, but I slid up and over the rim and crabbed forward until I lay spent and hurting on the floor.

More minutes went by. I might have lain there longer, but the odor of charred flesh roused me. In the center of the east wall the badly burned door hung open on one hinge. Just inside, consumed by the flames where he had fallen, was the body of Sam Butcher. I could tell it was him because he had been the shortest and slimmest of the men.

I forgot my own condition in my concern for the Butchers. Or, rather, one of the Butchers. I stood up. My legs were like mush and I swayed as I walked, but I made it out the door, wary of the flames that continued to lick the wall.

I nearly tripped over another body sprawled just outside. It was Hannah. The fire had blistered her feet, but the rest of her was untouched. She was riddled with bullets and must have been dead when she fell. Powder marks on what was left of her brow suggested that after she was down, someone had walked up to her, put the muzzle of a gun to her forehead, and blown the top of her head off.

Only one person despised the Butchers that much.

The next body was a few yards farther. Kip had been shot in the chest, stomach, and thigh. Spent shells showed that he had fought on after he was down.

The rest made it across the clearing. Carson had dropped a few steps into the trees. A hole the size of an apple in his right temple had proved to be the fatal wound. He had been scalped.

I turned to look for more bodies. Belatedly, it dawned on me that I had not drawn my Remington. Granted, Gertrude and her cowboys were long gone, but for me not to have a gun in my hand told me I wasn't thinking straight. I remedied my oversight and lurched deeper into the woods.

When I spotted Ty I thought he might be alive. He was sitting with his back to an oak, his rifle across his lap. His eyes were fixed right on me. "Tyrel?" I said, but not too loudly. He did not answer.

It took ridiculously long to reach him. I had to move at a turtle's pace. Only when I was up close did I see the hole where his left eye had been.

I did not want to go on. I knew what I would find and I did not want to find her. I knew what it would do to me, and what I would do. Apparently there was no end to my foolishness.

But I did go on. I searched and searched and was about ready to give up when a whisper stopped me in my tracks.

"Parson?"

I had almost stepped on Jordy. He was on his back, his torso leaking crimson like a sieve. He, too, had been scalped. I eased onto a knee and propped an arm under me so I would not pitch onto my face as I bent over him. "Is there anything I can do?" Not that I cared, but a real parson would.

Jordy had to try twice before he gasped, "The others? My ma? My brothers?"

I could lie to him. But I responded, "Dead, I am afraid."

"Ma too? I lost track of her when we ran from the cabin."

I nodded.

"That bitch. That wretched, vile bitch. Sic the

Texas Rangers on her, Parson. Tell them what she's done. Make her pay."

"Gertrude Tanner will get what is coming to her," I vowed. Then: "You haven't asked about your sister. Did Daisy get away?"

Jordy's features clouded. "I don't think so. I heard her scream. Heard them laugh. She can't be far."

"Lie still. I will be back to see what I can do for you." I went past a thicket and a pine and there she was. A flattened ring of vegetation testified to the fact she had fought fiercely. I stared and stared, numb outside and in. To do what they had done to her was unthinkable. Abusing women was not done. It was worse than murder, worse than rustling, worse than stealing a horse.

I admit that, when judged by the standards most people live by, I had done some terrible things in my life. A lot of terrible things, actually. Murder, many times over. I have stolen on occasion; I helped myself to the money and sometimes the personal effects of those I killed. I was coldhearted. I was ruthless. I could be vicious when crossed. I was all of that, and more. But I had never violated a female. I never stooped to one of the foulest atrocities a man can commit. Lucius Stark, the Regulator, considered by many to be as wretched a human being as ever drew breath, never did *that*.

I staggered over and dropped to my knees. I wanted to touch her, but she was covered with blood from her neck to her knees. They had slit her throat after they were done.

I never hankered to kill anyone as much as I did

those LT hands. They weren't cowboys. They were vermin. I vowed to make their extermination my main goal in life. Theirs, and one other.

I clasped Daisy's hand. In life she had been so beautiful, so warm, so full of vitality. Now she was pale and still and cool to the touch, her once lovely eyes blank slates. I let go of her hand and it fell limply to the ground. Soon that would change. Soon she would stiffen and her complexion would become waxen and her eyes would glaze and she would begin to give off the special smell of death.

"I can't have that," I said aloud. "I will bury you." The others needed to be buried, too, but someone else could take care of them. I was only interested in Daisy.

Then Jordy called my name. Reluctantly, I stood. The dead could be ignored. The living were another matter. I returned and squatted at his side. "I found her," I announced.

"Tell me."

"You do not want to know." I examined him more closely and confirmed the testimony of my eyes. I sat back, tired from the exertion.

Jordy's eyes fluttered. He was having difficulty breathing. "Damn him!" he spat. "Damn him to hell for what he did to her!"

"Don't you mean 'them'?" I said.

"No." Jordy licked his lips. "The others were laughing, but it was just the one. I heard him after he was done."

"What did he say?"

"How she fought like a wildcat."

From somewhere deep inside me boiled a surge of red-hot lava.

"How she was the best he ever had."

The night spun but not from my wound.

"How she was better than a whore he had down in Texas." Jordy uttered a low moan. "Oh, God. Not to her. She was the sweetest gal ever."

I had to force my vocal cords to work. "His name? Did you happen to catch his name?"

"No. I wish I did."

"Anything that would help me. Anything at all." The LT hands did not know it yet, but they were all on my list. Gertrude and Phil were near the top, one rung below whoever was to blame for Daisy.

"I'm sorry."

Jordy was quiet so long, I figured he had died. But then he spoke again.

"One thing might help you. He called her 'little sugar.'"

"Little what?"

"His exact words. The 'little sugar' fought like a wildcat. The 'little sugar' was better than a whore he had once. He kept a keepsake from the 'little sugar.' He never called Daisy by name. Maybe he didn't know it."

"Or didn't care." But before I was through, he would. Something else Jordy said caught my interest. "What was that about a keepsake?"

"I don't know. It's what I heard him say."

Again he was still for a considerable spell. When he broke his silence, I could barely hear him.

"Will you really see that they pay, Parson?"

"Of course." He had no idea.

"You won't turn the other cheek? You being a man of the cloth, and all, you won't forgive and forget, will you?"

I looked at him. He was dead anyway, so what difference did it make? "Ever heard of Lucius Stark?"

"Stark?" Jordy repeated, puzzled. "Where have I heard that name before?"

I did not give him any clues. He had to earn it.

"Wait. Now I remember. Isn't he an assassin? Goes around the country killing folks for money?"

"I'm Lucius Stark."

"Beg pardon?"

"You heard me."

"But—" Jordy said, and did not say anything more for a good long while. Finally he exhaled and croaked, "I'll be damned. Was it us you were after?"

"Yes."

"You son of a bitch. Who hired you?"

"Gertrude Tanner."

"But she's the one who shot you!" Jordy chuckled, then snorted, then burst into merry laughter broken by gasps and groans. He laughed and laughed and went on laughing even as blood trickled from the corners of his mouth. I guess he couldn't stop. He was the only man I ever saw who laughed himself to death.

I rose and would have kicked him except my legs were not steady enough. So I settled for saying, "It wasn't that funny."

Until that moment I never felt true hatred. The kind that causes the pulse to quicken and the head to hammer and every nerve to tingle with the throbbing urge to take life.

I fought down my rage and cast about for something to dig with. A broken tree limb was handy. It nearly killed me, and the grave was much too shallow, but I gave her a decent burial.

The coyotes and buzzards could have the rest of the Butchers.

I had work to do.

Chapter 16

Three weeks. That's how long it took for me to mend. Three weeks, with me chafing at every minute that went by.

All I thought about was Gertrude and the LT. I lived, breathed, and ate revenge. I considered various ways to go about it. The quickest was to rig kegs of black powder under the ranch house and the cookhouse and blow the Tanners and their hired hands to hell and back when they sat down to supper. But that would be *too* quick. Too merciful. I did not want them to die in an instant's time, feeling little pain. I wanted them to die slowly. I wanted them to suffer. I wanted them to know why they were dying, and feel the fear the Butchers had felt, trapped in the cabin with no way out.

That was fitting for the cowboys. For Gertrude and her son and the son of a bitch who murdered Daisy, I had something special in mind.

So for three weeks I hid on the Dark Sister and plotted. I did not have a horse. Brisco had disappeared the night of the attack. Either he ran off or they stole him. I did not have provisions, but I got by. Game was everywhere, and I camped in the hollow close to the stream, so I never lacked for water.

I had plenty of guns. I took every weapon the Butchers had, and their gun belts, besides. I ended up with six rifles and seven revolvers. Four of the rifles were Winchesters, the rest were older single-shot models. I chose the newest of the Winchesters and a bandolier Jordy had been wearing. Most of the revolvers were Colts. I'm partial to Remingtons, but I settled on a pair of Samuel Colt's brain-children. They were near identical army .45s with seven-and-a-half-inch barrels. Basic wood grips, not fancy pearl or ivory. The front sights had not been filed off, as I had done with my Remingtons, and the ejector rods were still attached.

Every day I practiced handling them. Drawing, cocking, twirling, spinning until they became as much a part of me as my hands. It was important. Don't ever let anyone tell you all pistols are the same. They are not. Each kind has its own special feel. The trick is to become so slick with whichever model you choose that you can draw and shoot straight without thinking about it. Just up and squeeze and bang!

There was another reason I took the guns and the gun belts. It was the same reason I made it a point to find and take the arrow Gertrude left.

When I wasn't practicing or hunting, I spent a lot of time in a thicket close to the east wall of the cabin. No one showed up until the evening of the second day after the slaughter, and then it was Calista. I heard her galloping up the trail long before I saw her. I almost rose out of hiding to greet her. Almost. She reined to a stop and sprang from the saddle, horror etched in her face. She went from body to body, saying, "Oh, my God!" over and over. She cried over Hannah. Fifteen minutes she was there; then she swung on her sorrel and raced for Whiskey Flats.

I figured it would be morning before more came, and I was right. Half the town turned out. They came on horseback. They came in wagons. Some brought the kids. They gawked at the bodies, they remarked on the wounds, they allowed as how it was an outright massacre. A few commented on the absence of firearms. Several others speculated that Indians were to blame since two of the Butchers had been scalped.

Calista had already seen it all, so she stood to one side. I overheard when the owner of the general store came over to her.

"You were right. There's no sign of the parson anywhere. Are you sure he came out to visit them?"

"I'm positive, Tom," Calista said. "He told me he was going to pay his respects, and I saw him ride out of town."

"Strange. Unless the Indians took him."

"If it was Indians," Calista said.

"Jordy and Carson were scalped."

"Anyone can lift hair."

"They've been stripped clean of weapons and ammo. Indians do that, too," Tom mentioned.

"Anyone can steal weapons, too."

"Why do you refuse to believe it was Indians?"

"Because we haven't had Indian trouble in years. The Comanches no longer roam at will, and the Kiowas know better."

"If not them, then who?" Tom asked.

"You know the answer to that as well as I do," Calista said. "She vowed to wipe them out and they've been wiped out."

"That's a strong accusation to make without proof."

"You agree. You just don't want to say so."

"What I think isn't important. Without evidence, it counts for nothing." Tom regarded the charred debris. "Gertrude is the wealthiest woman in west Texas. She has a shark for a lawyer and cowboys who would die for her."

"Are you saying you're scared of her, Tom?"

"You're damn right I am, pardon my language. She would make a formidable enemy. I, for one, do not intend to antagonize her unless I have good cause."

Calista gestured. "You wouldn't call this good cause?"

"Don't take that tone with me. I liked the Butchers, Hannah especially. I liked them as much as you did. But now they're dead and I'm alive and I aim to stay that way." Tom studied her. "What do you plan to do?"

"Don't worry. I'm not about to ride out to the LT and accuse Gerty to her face, if that's what you're thinking."

"Then what?"

"I'll have a private talk with the Rangers when they get there. Which I hope to God is soon."

"Tomorrow."

"What?"

"A drummer told me. He ran into Texas Rangers a few days ago. They said they had to wrap something up, then they were headed for Whiskey Flats. Expected to arrive on Wednesday. That would be tomorrow."

"You should have told me sooner."

"What difference does it make? We'll let them hash it out. If they go after Gerty, so be it. But I wouldn't count on it."

"We can't let her get away with this. Not this, we can't."

The store owner shrugged. "What will be, will be. I'm not a lawman. I'm not related to the Butchers. I have no stake."

"Other than common human decency."

"That's not fair, Calista. No one is more fair than I am. I don't charge outrageous prices like some do."

"I'm talking about human lives and you're talking about canned goods."

Tom sighed and shook his head. "There is no talking to you when you get like this. Look yonder. They're about ready. I'll go lend a hand. But you be careful, hear? Don't go tangling with Gertrude Tanner unless you have more to back you up than suspicions."

"I'll do what I have to."

Some of the men had brought shovels. They formed a burial detail, and the Butchers were planted in a row to the north of the cabin.

No one found Daisy's grave. I had seen to that by covering it with leaves and pine needles and brush.

Everyone gathered to pay their respects. They formed a half circle and bowed their heads, and there was a lot of coughing and fidgeting.

Calista began. "I guess it's up to me. I knew them as well as anyone and probably better than most. They were decent folk. They never imposed. They were always friendly. Hannah Butcher was as kindhearted a woman as ever lived."

"She sure was," someone agreed.

Calista acknowledged the comment with a smile. "For some time now the family has been under a cloud of suspicion. They were accused of being rustlers. We all know by whom. But Hannah denied it, and I believed her. I visited them many times and never saw any cows or fresh beef or hides."

Muttering broke out, and a portly man said, "It's a good thing Gertrude Tanner isn't here to hear you say that. She doesn't take kindly to being called a liar."

"It's the Butchers we should be concerned about," Calista responded. "Specifically, who killed them. It seems to me that the person who pointed the finger of blame is at the top of the list."

"Is this a funeral or isn't it?" a disgruntled listener complained.

"Sorry," Calista said, but she did not sound

sorry. She gazed skyward. "Lord, we commit the souls of these good people unto your care. Watch over them and preserve them. We ask this in your son's name. Amen."

A chorus of amen's were added. They started to drift toward their horses and wagons.

Calista was last. She gazed at what was left of the cabin, then at the woods. I thought for a second she spotted me, but she showed no sign of it and walked to her horse.

I watched her ride off with mixed feelings. Part of me had wanted to reveal myself. The other part, the part that hired out his gun for money, held me in check. No one must know I was alive.

That night I slept fitfully. I tossed and turned, racked by a nightmare. In it, I was trapped in the burning cabin. I was pinned and helpless, the flames licking nearer and nearer. Just as I caught on fire, I woke up. I was caked with sweat, yet my mouth and throat were as dry as a desert. Weakly, I made it to my feet, and the stream. After slaking my thirst, I kindled a small fire. I had some rabbit left over from supper, and I was famished. Dawn was not far off, so it would suffice as breakfast, too. While the meat roasted on a spit, I examined my wound. I was worried about infection, but there was no sign of any.

The sunrise was spectacular. I sat munching on the juicy meat as pink, orange, and yellow splashed the eastern sky. It occurred to me that I had never really admired a sunrise before. I was always so caught up in myself and what I was doing.

The thought troubled me. I was becoming soft. What did I care about sunrises and sunsets and such?

Still, it *was* a sight to see, the sun seeming to float up out of the earth, a great blazing golden globe that shone like fiery burnished gold. It brought the birds to life and warmth to the new day.

I spent most of the morning in the thicket by the cabin. Noon came and went and still no sign of anyone. I was about to return to the hollow when hooves drummed, and shortly thereafter in they rode.

There were two of them. Both were middling sized. Both sported woolly mustaches. Both wore two revolvers. The badges pinned to their shirts gleamed as they reined to a stop. One dismounted while the other shucked a Winchester from his saddle scabbard and levered a round into the chamber.

You hear so much about the Texas Rangers that when you see them, you half expect them to be as big as giants. But these were as ordinary as pie, or almost. It's hard to describe, but one look and you knew these two were two of the toughest hombres to ever draw breath. It wasn't that they strutted around like roosters. Not at all. It was in how they held themselves and in how they moved.

The one who had climbed down was crisscrossing the clearing, reading the sign. He was good, too. He pointed at where Hannah had fallen and said, "This here was the mother."

How he could tell was beyond me. A puddle of dry blood marked the spot, but it could be anyone's blood. Then he hunkered and indicated footprints in the dirt near the cabin door.

"Heavyset woman. Small feet. Quite a jumble here. But I'd guess she came out last."

"Do we dig up the graves, Dee?" the Ranger on the bay asked.

"A few we might have to. Given my druthers I wouldn't, but some of the townsfolk swear it was Injuns."

"And my ma is the Queen of England."

Dee snickered. "If she were, Les, you wouldn't be dodging lead for a living. You'd be off in some castle somewhere, diddling the maid."

"Why, pard, I'm affronted. It would be the maid and the cook and their cousins, if they had any."

I smiled along with them. So the Texas Rangers liked their women as much as the next man. It was a revelation.

Then more hooves pounded up the trail, and into the clearing trotted Calista Modine, Tom from the general store, and Webber, the butcher. Tom and Webber were what you could describe as two of Whiskey Flats's leading citizens.

"Are we late?" Calista asked. "I thought you said to meet you here at one."

"You're not late, ma'am, we're early," Dee said.

"We came on ahead to scout the country," Les elaborated, "and to read the sign." He swung down. "It's too bad the townspeople came up here yesterday. They made a mess of any tracks that might have helped us."

Dee nodded. "The bodies should have been left as they were."

"Now hold on," Webber said. He was a big, beefy man with a gut that bulged over his belt. "It wouldn't be Christian to let the scavengers gnaw on them."

"And we weren't entirely sure you would show up when that drummer claimed you would," Tom said, defending the burials.

Dee and Les ambled toward the mounds, Dee saying to Calista, "Show us which was which, if you would be so kind, ma'am." After she went down the row, attaching a name to each mound, he stepped to the third one and tapped it with his boot. "So this here is Jordy Butcher's? And you say he was one of those who was scalped?"

"Yes." Calista was wringing her hands as if she were nervous.

Les handed his Winchester to Tom and dropped to his knees. "I reckon our hands will have to do."

"You're not doing what I think you're doing?" Webber asked, aghast.

"Unless you would rather do it," Les said.

The Rangers went at it like badgers and had Jordy unearthed in no time. Each body had been wrapped in a blanket and the ends tied. Dee took one end and Les the other.

"This is most unseemly," Webber groused as the blanket parted.

"We do what we have to," Dee said.

The proceedings were interrupted by yet more hoofbeats, heralding the unexpected arrival of none other than Gertrude Tanner.

I wedged the Winchester to my shoulder.

Chapter 17

Gertrude was not alone. Four cowboys were along. Or maybe it was only three. The fourth wore a black Stetson, a Carlsbad hat, and a black leather vest. On his right hip, butt forward, was an ivory-handled Smith & Wesson. It was rare for a cowboy to indulge in a revolver that cost more than most punchers earned in three or four months. He had curly blond hair and a wispy blond mustache, and from the way he sat the saddle, it gave the impression he was fond of his reflection.

Gertrude rode straight to the graves and wasted no time in pleasantries. "What in heaven's name do you two think you are doing?"

"We're on a maggot hunt," Les said.

Dee paused in the act of unwrapping the body. "Pay him no mind, ma'am. I take it you are Mrs. Tanner? We've heard about you."

"Then you know I do not suffer fools gladly," Gertrude declared. "Even those who pride themselves on being lawmen." She placed both hands on her saddle horn. "I will ask you one more time. What in heaven's name are you doing?"

"Making sure these folks were buried right-side up," Les replied. "It's against the law to bury someone facedown. They could smother."

"Is he insane?" Gertrude snapped at Dee.

"Only every other Sunday," Dee said. "The rest of the time he's only half loco."

The cowboy in the black Carlsbad gigged his roan closer. "Enough silliness. Those tin stars don't give you the right to treat a lady with disrespect."

"You're right as rain, puncher," Dee said.

"I'm not no damn cowpoke," the man in the black hat said.

Les was studying him. "Not that what we do is any of your damn business. But if it will smooth your hackles, I'll apologize to your boss if she'll tell us what in heaven's name she's doing here."

"Someone should shoot him," Gertrude said.

Dee smiled a crooked smile. "That would be murder, ma'am, and it appears there has been enough of that already."

"What are you implying?"

Flipping the blanket, Dee uncovered Jordy Butcher from the shoulders up and pointed at Jordy's head. "This man has been scalped."

"Yes. So? Indians scalp whites all the time."

Les made a clucking sound. "Not true, ma'am. Some Injuns do, yes, but only some of the time. Fact is, more whites have scalped Injuns than Injuns have scalped whites, if you count the giants the Injuns say lived here before the Injuns came, since the giants were white."

"Give me a pistol and I will shoot him myself," Gertrude said.

Dee ran a finger across Jordy's head. "Do you see how deep the cut is, ma'am? And how much hair was lifted?"

"So?"

"So Injuns don't cut down to the bone. They stick the tip of their knife under the hair and peel it like an apple."

"Maybe this one had never done it before," Gertrude suggested.

"That could be, ma'am." Dee continued to be as polite as a politician on the stump. "But Injuns generally don't raise all the hair. They always leave some. Which proves to me that this here fella was scalped by a white man. And if he was scalped by a white, then it was whites that did the killing, and if whites did the killing, then my partner and me aim to find out who and put them behind bars or plant them, their choice."

Gertrude was boiling mad and trying not to show it. "I see. And you would be willing to swear in a court of law that whites were to blame?"

"Any day of the week."

"And twice on Sunday," Les chimed in. "Although the courts are usually closed on Sundays on account of it being the Lord's day and all."

A peculiar thing happened. Gertrude smiled. "You two are not the simpletons you present yourselves as. That was neatly done, gentlemen."

"Thank you, ma'am," Dee said.

"My ma raised me to always be neat," Lee added.

Gertrude lifted her reins. "Well, I only came to meet you and I've done that, so I'll be on my way."

"Be looking for us to visit the LT, ma'am," Dee informed her. "We have a few questions to ask."

"Maybe more than a few," Les said.

The rider in the black hat was squirming in his saddle like a sidewinder on a hot rock. "These lawdogs rile me, Mrs. Tanner. They surely do."

"Now, now, Mr. Seton. The Rangers deserve our highest respect. When they come out to the ranch, they must not find our hospitality wanting."

I stirred in my hiding place. There was that name again, and again it stirred a faint recollection. Then I remembered. Saloon gossip had it that a gent named Seton had made a name for himself down along the border. Not as much of a name as Hardin or Thompson or Fisher but enough that most hard cases fought shy of him.

I was not the only one who had recognized the handle. Dee and Les swapped glances, and Dee said, "Did we hear right? You wouldn't happen to be Bart Seton, would you? The same Bart Seton who took part in the Duxton-Rodriguez scrap?"

"I might be."

"Why, son, you're plumb famous," Les said. "They say four Mexicans drew on you in a cantina and when the smoke cleared you were the last man standing."

"There were five Mexicans," Seton amended. "But killing greasers doesn't hardly count for much. They never amount to spit with a six-gun."

"You're welcome to your opinion," Dee said, "but I've met a few who could put a hole in the center of a playing card at twenty-five paces."

"You've strayed a far piece from the Rio Grande," Les commented.

Gertrude spoke before Seton could. "That's my doing, gentlemen. We've had a problem with LT cattle being rustled. I sent for him when it first started."

"You weren't fixing to take the law into your own hands, were you, ma'am?" Dee brought up.

"Perish forbid, Ranger. I always abide by the law. Ask anyone. I only wanted to protect what is mine." Gertrude reined around and gave a little wave. "It was instructive making your acquaintance. Until we meet again." She smiled and lashed her reins.

The dust had not yet settled when Calista declared, "She was lying. I never set eyes on Seton before today and I've been out to the LT more times than I can count."

"I never saw him, either," Tom said, "and most everyone hereabouts stops at my store at least once a month."

Dee shrugged. "It's not important. He's not wanted, as near I can recollect."

It was important to me. I needed to learn exactly when Gertrude had sent for him. Was it before she sent for me? Or after? If before, then why had she bothered to send for me when she had him on her payroll? If after, was Seton supposed to finish the job if I couldn't? Or was there more involved? Either way, I didn't like it. I didn't like it one little bit.

The Texas Rangers were giving Jordy Butcher a second burial. My ears pricked when Dee said,

"Tell us more about the preacher who disappeared. We'll want to question Mrs. Tanner about him, too."

Calista described me in remarkable detail, down to the small scar on my chin. I never imagined she noticed so much. She ended with, "He was just about the sweetest man I've ever known."

Les had glanced up sharply at the mention of the scar, and Dee and him swapped looks again.

That was a bad sign. I was wanted in Texas. My regulating had taken me to Dallas, El Paso, and San Antonio. Combined, that tallied to eleven less people in the world. After each job I skipped Texas a jump ahead of the Rangers. To say they hankered after my neck in a noose was putting it mildly.

Dee was speaking. "Well, Leslie, I reckon we're about done here for now. Let's go nose around elsewhere."

"I'm always ready for a good nose, Deeter," Les said.

Webber the butcher was surprised. "What about the rest of the bodies? Aren't you going to dig them up, too?"

The two Rangers were lowering Jordy into his grave. "You can if you want," Les answered. "But one a day is my limit."

"We've proven it wasn't Injuns," Dee said, "and that was the whole point."

"But the others were shot to pieces," Webber said. "If you dig out the bullets, can't you tell what kind of guns were used?"

Les laughed. "Dig lead out of days-old corpses?

That woman was right. Someone here is loco, but it's not me."

Dee was also amused, but for a different reason. "The slugs wouldn't tell us all that much, anyhow. Who ever heard of such a thing?"

"I just thought—" Webber said, but did not finish.

"You will be careful, won't you?" Calista said to Texas's finest. "Gerty won't let you put her behind bars."

"I doubt she'll try to bushwhack us, ma'am," Dee responded. "It would only bring more Rangers down on her head."

"She's clever, this one," Les said. "She'll try smoke and smiles to keep us off her scent."

"Then you believe she is behind it?"

Dee and Les began pushing dirt back over the body, and Dee answered, "Let's just say she's at the top of our list at the moment. But suspecting someone and proving they are guilty can be a mighty wide river to ford."

"I hate to admit it," Les said, "but we don't always get our man. Or our woman. I hear tell there's an outfit up in Canada that says it does, but Canadians just like to hear themselves brag."

"So don't get your hopes up," Dee cautioned.

Still, Calista was encouraged. I was not. I did not want the Rangers poking about in what I considered a personal matter. If they arrested Gertrude before I was ready to deal with her, I didn't know what I would do.

Who was I kidding? Of course I knew. I would

not rest until everyone involved suffered the same fate, or worse, as Daisy and her family. I owed it to myself. I had been shot and nearly burned to death. If that didn't give me the right to bring the LT to its knees, nothing did.

The Texas Rangers and the townsfolk were walking to their mounts. Calista invited the lawdogs to stop by her place later for a meal. "It's on me. My way of saying thanks for helping us."

"We're just doing our jobs, ma'am," Dee said.

"But I'm never one to pass up free grub," Lee assured her.

My own meal that evening was roast venison. I shot a doe. I couldn't carry or drag it to the hollow, so I cut off a haunch and dragged that. Meat, lots of meat, would restore me to my old self, and over the next several weeks I did more to reduce the Dark Sister's wildlife population than all the predators in Texas.

Three weeks, it took. Three weeks, wishing every second that I was restored to my usual vigor and vim.

Then one morning I woke up, stood, and stretched, and didn't feel an ache or pain anywhere. To test myself, I decided to climb up the Dark Sister higher than I had ever gone before. I was at it for hours, until I came, quite unexpectedly and much to my amazement, out of the forest into a green meadow.

It was not the meadow that amazed me. It was the ornery four-legged cuss and the Butcher mare he had taken up with. The whole time I was down by the cabin suffering and barely able to move, my not-so-trusty steed was dallying with a filly in their own little high country paradise.

"So this is where you've been?" I said as Brisco came up to me. The mare hung back because she did not know me, which was just as well for her. The tart.

I patted Brisco and scratched around his ears and marveled that my saddle was still on. The cinch was loose and the saddle was smeared with dust and dirt and grass, but it was in one piece and none of my effects were missing. "Looks like my luck has turned," I remarked.

The mare did not want to leave. The hussy shied when I rigged a hackamore, but I threw a loop around her neck and brought her along anyway. It pleased Brisco, but I was thinking that the Apaches claimed horseflesh was downright tasty.

God had been good to me. I was fit again. I had my own revolvers and my rifle and plenty of ammo. I had two horses and my saddlebags with the tools of my profession. Some might take it as a sign the Almighty was on their side, but I was more practical. If there was one thing I had learned from reading Scripture, it was that the Lord was powerful fond of blood. He loved spilling it and loved watching it spilled, and I was about to treat him to a spilling the Angel of Death would envy.

My last day on the mountain started early. I was up at first light. Breakfast waited while I went upstream to a pool. Stripping, I jumped in and swam about for all of a minute. The water was too cold.

Teeth chattering, I climbed out and hopped up and down until I felt halfway alive again. I quickly dressed. Once back at the hollow, I rekindled the fire. I was not in the mood for squirrel meat, but it was all I had.

In my saddlebags I kept a small mirror. The man who stared back was not me. It was a ragged hermit with an unkempt beard and a tangled mop. I shaved and trimmed my hair.

After removing my parson's garb—gladly, I might add—I donned my spare shirt and pants, and polished my boots. When I was done I looked like a whole new man, and felt like one, too.

I placed my shoulder holster and the hideout in my saddlebags and strapped on my long-barreled Remington. I had lost my hat on that night I would never forget. My coat had been so badly singed and so caked with soot, dirt, and grime that I had discarded it long ago.

I was as ready as I would be.

I walked over to Brisco, unwrapped the mare's lead rope, and forked leather. I headed east. As I passed the charred timbers that had been the Butcher cabin, I touched a finger to the middle of my chest and felt the new scar under my shirt.

Those responsible were going to answer for it.

I couldn't wait to start.

Chapter 18

I did not use the trail. I could not risk being spotted. Then there were the two Texas Rangers to keep in mind. They complicated things. They could be anywhere, at any time. Rangers were notorious for popping up when you least expected and least wanted them to.

I swung to the south and was winding down a canyon toward the foothills when a strange sound reached my ears. I drew rein and listened. It sounded like two rocks were being smacked together, and it went on and on until I gigged Brisco and warily led the mare lower.

The canyon widened. Boulders and brush choked the bottom, but there were few trees since there was no water. I veered to where the shadow from the canyon wall was deepest.

The sound grew louder. Much louder than the *chink* of Brisco's and the mare's hooves. Soon I heard voices, although I could not tell what they were saying. I came to a bend and stopped. After swinging down, I looped Brisco's reins around a bush. He was well trained and would not go anywhere. I was not sure of the mare, so I secured the lead rope to a boulder.

Sliding the scattergun from my bedroll, I loaded both barrels and stuck extra shells in my pocket. On cat's feet I glided along the wall. At the bend I peeked past the edge.

Three horses stood in a row, their reins dangling. A fourth, a pack animal, was nearby.

Two of the three riders were attacking the base of the canyon wall with picks. The third watched, a shovel in his left hand, the long handle across his shoulder.

I could scarcely credit my good fortune. The three weren't prospectors. They weren't townsmen. They were cowboys. Specifically, LT cowboys. I remembered them from when I was out to the ranch. Whether they took part in the slaughter of the Butchers was unimportant. They rode for my enemy, and anyone who worked for my enemy became an enemy whether they wanted to be an enemy or not.

One of the punchers stopped swinging his pick, stepped back, and wiped a sleeve across his sweaty face. "I hate this. I just hate this."

"Don't start, Jack," said the cowboy with the shovel.

"Hell, Brennan, you hate it as much as I do," Jack snapped. "We're punchers, not desert rats. We signed on with the LT to herd cattle, not play at being pocket hunters. I'd rather swing a rope than this damn heavy pick."

The third cowboy lowered his pick. "Complain, complain. That's all you ever do, Jack."

"Tell me you like doing this, Porter," Jack challenged. "Tell me it as if you really mean it."

"We get paid extra," Porter said. A red bandanna rode high on his neck. His clothes were caked with dust.

Jack would not relent. "I don't care how much extra she pays us. She should hire someone else to do her damn collecting."

Brennan snorted like a bull. He had the shoulders of one, too. "Will you listen to yourself? Name me one other outfit where the punchers make as much as we do? Ninety dollars a month. That's twice what most hands earn."

"Admit it," Porter said to Jack. "You like the extra money as much as we do. So quit your bellyaching and get back to work."

"What if those two Texas Rangers find us?"

"They're in town, Jack," Porter said. "We saw them in front of the livery, remember?"

"They could have followed us," Jack sulked.

Brennan leaned on the shovel. "But they didn't. We kept a sharp watch. No one knows we're here except Mrs. Tanner and her son."

"And Seton," Porter said. "Don't forget Bart Seton."

"Why she hired him on, I'll never know," Jack groused. "He hardly does a lick of work. Spends most of his time up at the house. And don't tell me she's giving him quilting lessons, neither."

Porter glanced down the canyon. "One of these days that mouth of yours is going to get you shot. If Seton heard you say that, he would bed you down, permanent."

"Bart Seton doesn't scare me," Jack declared.

"Then you are a natural-born fool," Porter said. "Bart Seton would scare anyone with a lick of common sense."

"Enough jawing," Brennan said. "The sooner we fill those packs, the sooner we can head back to the ranch."

Filled the packs with *what*? was the question on my mind. They had chipped quite a pile from the rock wall. Ore of some kind. Glittering streaks gave me a clue. Not yellow streaks, but grayish streaks.

Jack and Porter stepped to the wall and resumed chipping away. They were intent on what they were doing. Brennan had his back to me.

Straightening, I went around the bend. I made no attempt to hide. I strolled toward them as casually as you please. When I was an arm's length from Brennan, I halted, leveled the scattergun, thumbed back both hammers, and smiled. "Howdy, boys."

Brennan whirled so fast he almost dropped the shovel. Porter and Jack stopped swinging their picks and their jaws dropped down to their belts.

"Don't let me interrupt," I said. That close, the vein gleamed brightly. Not solid silver, but a rich vein nonetheless. It ran along the bottom of the wall from where Porter and Jack were standing for another twenty yards. Seven sizable pockets had previously been dug out.

"It can't be!" Brennan blurted. "You're dead."

"No, you are." I let him have a barrel full in the face. His head exploded like a melon. The stump of a neck and the body swayed, then pitched backward, the shovel clattering noisily. I swung the scattergun at the other two. "Who's next?"

Jack and Porter threw their picks down and their arms into the air. "Don't shoot, Parson!" Jack bleated. "Please don't shoot!"

I circled so I was in front of them and far enough back that they couldn't jump me. "I'm no Bible-thumper. My name is Lucius Stark."

Porter's eyes about bugged out. "Who did you say?"

"Are you hard of hearing?"

"Lucius Stark the Regulator?" Porter was horror-struck. He took a step back. "What do you want with us?"

"I need answers. Which one of you wants to go on living?" I did not say how long.

"I do!" Jack cried.

I emptied the second barrel into Porter. At that range the buckshot did not spread much. The blast lifted him off his feet and smashed him against the wall. As limp as an overcooked noodle, he oozed to the ground. His chest reminded me of chopped beef.

Jack had shrunk into a crouch with his arms over his head. "Don't kill me! Don't kill me!" he wailed.

"Stand up."

Quaking like an aspen leaf, Jack obeyed. He mewed like a kitten when he saw me reloading.

"How long have the Tanners known about this silver vein?"

He glanced at Porter, his Adam's apple bobbing. "I can't rightly say. Months, I reckon."

"How many months?" I prodded. "Think real hard."

"The first I heard about it was four or five months ago. But others knew before me. The one you should ask is Ben Winslow, the LT foreman."

"Could it have been eight months?" I recalled Hannah saying that her husband vanished about that time.

"I reckon it could."

That tallied with the number of pockets if you counted the one they were digging. "The Tanners send some of you out here once a month for silver, is that how it goes?"

Jack had to think about it. "Now that you mention it, yes. But you keep saying the Tanners. It's always Gerty who does it, as far as I know."

"Lloyd didn't know about the vein? Her son doesn't, either?"

"I can't speak for them. I'm only telling you what I know, and what I know is that Gerty always sends us."

"Why was Everett Butcher murdered?"

"Was he?"

I took a half step and pointed the twin muzzles at his face. "You can join your friends right this instant if you want."

"Honest, mister!" Jack squawked. "I heard

about him going missing, sure. But no one ever said he was murdered."

"Were you in on killing the rest of the Butchers?"

He tried. He looked right at me and spoke much as Moses must have when he came down from Mt. Sinai with those tablets. "As God is my witness, I had nothing to do with it."

"How many hands were with her?"

"Only a few."

Two lies. I was sure then. But I had a few more questions. "Why doesn't Gertrude file a claim on this silver? Why keep it secret?"

"You would have to ask her."

Although I pretty much had the next answer figured out, I asked anyway. "What does the ore have to do with accusing the Butchers of being cow thieves?"

"Again, you would have to ask Gerty."

"I will," I informed him. When the time came. Right now I lowered the scattergun as if I had changed my mind, but I did not lower it all the way.

Jack's relief was amusing. He sought to gild the cage by saying, "Listen. I won't say a word about you shooting Brennan and Porter. I'll get on my horse and ride out of the valley and never come back. I swear on my ma's grave."

He should not have mentioned graves. I blew off his right foot. He screamed as he fell and flopped about like a fish out of water, only a lot worse, caterwauling like a gutted wildcat all the while. I put up with as much as I could, then walked up to him and rapped him on the noggin. He was only out for a few minutes. In that time I went through the pockets of his friends. It proved profitable. Porter had sixty-five dollars on him; Brennan had over a hundred.

Two of their horses had run off. I didn't mind. It fit with my plan. The remaining horse and the mule I added to the string behind the mare.

Jack stirred and opened his eyes. He looked about him, his eyes glazed, uncomprehending until he saw the blood. "Oh God!" he wailed, and blubbered like an infant.

My shadow fell across him and he jerked back in terror.

"Who did the girl?"

"What?" He was shaking so bad, his teeth were chattering.

"Calm down and concentrate. Which one of you raped and killed Daisy Butcher?"

"I told you, I wasn't there."

I blew off his left foot. This time I let him thrash and convulse until he lay spent and whimpering. Then I stomped on his left arm to get his attention. "Once more. Who raped Daisy Butcher?"

Tears flowed down his cheeks. He broke into great, racking, pathetic sobs. "Why won't you believe me?"

"Because you're a lying son of a bitch."

He had a shred of spunk left. "You have no right!" he shrieked.

"I do it because I can, boy, and that's all the right I need."

Jack's brow puckered and he blinked tears away. "I don't understand."

"We're born with the right to do as we please. But those who run things don't want that because if we do as we please, we upset their apple cart. So they make laws that say we can't do as we please, and if we break those laws, they send tin stars after us to blow out our wicks."

The loss of blood had turned him pale and weak. "I never thought of it like that." He gave his head a vigorous shake. "I feel sleepy."

"That's normal."

"Finish me," he pleaded.

"There's no rush." I stepped back and hunkered. The key now was to keep him aware. New pain would serve, and he had a lot of body left.

His eyes swiveled toward me. "Right or not right, how can you do this to someone?"

"I told you. I don't live by the same rules as everyone else. But then, you don't entirely live by them yourself, or you wouldn't have helped Gertrude Tanner wipe out an innocent family."

"They were rustlers!"

"No, boy, they weren't. She lied to you just as you've lied to me. And lies always come back to bite us in the ass."

"Please end it. I can't take any more."

"Sure you can. I've whittled on some for hours. You, I figure it will be thirty minutes yet before the loss of blood sends you to hell, where you belong. Between now and then I can do a lot of whittling."

"What do I have to do? Beg?"

"It would go in one ear and out the other." I hefted my knife.

He grasped at a straw and it was a good one. "What if I told you where Gerty keeps the silver she hasn't shipped off on the stage yet? Would you give your word to get it over with quick?"

I kept my word.

Chapter 19

I had more to do before I rode off.

I dragged the three bodies about thirty yards closer to the mouth of the canyon and propped them against boulders. Anyone who came to investigate why they failed to return to the LT would spot them right off. I was in need of a hat, so I helped myself to Jack's. It was brown instead of my favorite color, black, and it had a narrow brim instead of a wide brim, as I liked, and a high crown instead of a low crown, which I preferred, but it fit. I also shrugged into his vest and tied his bandanna around my neck so that from a distance I might pass for a cowpoke.

Snagging the lead rope, I climbed on Brisco and rode out of the canyon. I did not head east toward the Tanner spread. Instead, I reined left, seeking a way to get above the canyon. A game trail pockmarked with deer tracks was a likely prospect.

It took forever. The trail had more twists and switchbacks than I cared to count. Eventually, though, I stood on the lip of the canyon wall directly above the silver vein. Behind me, a boulder-strewn slope rose to thick timber.

"They'll do nicely," I said to Brisco. Swinging back on, I climbed higher, avoiding a patch of talus. Above it, clustered like eggs in a hen's nest, were a score of boulders of various sizes. I went past them and drew rein.

It might work. I put my shoulder to one of the smaller boulders, dug in my heels, and pushed. The boulder gave a little, but only a little. I braced my shoulders and tried again. Again it moved a few inches. This would not do.

I climbed back on Brisco. Leaving the other horses for the moment, I unwound my rope, tossed the loop over the boulder, and dallied the other end around the saddle horn. I gigged Brisco to one side, and down, and when the rope became taut, jabbed my spurs. For a few moments Brisco strained. Then the boulder began to slide, gaining speed as it went. I unwound my rope from the saddle horn. The boulder careened off another, smaller boulder, dislodging it, and this second boulder tumbled after the first. A third boulder bounced down the slope. And a fourth.

The boulders struck the talus. Loose dirt and rocks cascaded down, the rope whipping like an angry snake behind the first boulder. More and more talus was dislodged as the avalanche I had created hurtled toward the rim.

The roar it made reverberated the length of the canyon. Tons of earth and rocks poured down, raising a thick column of dust that billowed into a spreading cloud. It gave the illusion that the whole mountain was breaking apart.

Eventually the clamor ended. Dismounting, I carefully walked to the lip and peered over. The entire vein was buried by a mound that rose halfway up the wall. It would take weeks to dig through.

Gertrude would throw a fit. Chuckling, I reclaimed the mare and the other horses and made my way down the mountain to the grassland. To avoid running into any townsfolk I looped wide to the south.

I was in no hurry. It would take half the night to reach the LT, which suited my purpose just fine. Outnumbered as I was, I had to rely on my wits to whittle the odds. Darkness was an ally that I aimed to use to full advantage.

About two hours had gone by when I spied a couple of riders to the north. They were heading west but reined toward me to cut me off. I didn't like that. I liked it even less when the sun flashed off metal on their shirts.

This was the last thing I needed. I quickly bunched the bandanna around my chin so it would appear I had just pulled it down—and to hide my scar. When they were fifty yards out I drew rein and raised a hand in friendly greeting.

"You must ride for the LT," Dee said as he came to a stop.

"Yes, sir." When dealing with the law it always paid to be polite. "Are you those Rangers I've heard about?" It also paid to pretend to be as dumb as a tree stump.

Les smothered a chuckle and nodded. "That we are, mister. I reckon our badges gave us away. What might your handle be?"

"Jack, sir."

"Jack what?"

"Jack Walker, sir."

"You don't say? One of the most famous Rangers of all time was named Walker. Maybe you've heard of him. Captain Sam Walker came up with the idea for one of the very first Colts."

Now, everyone west of the Mississippi knew about the Walker Colt and the part it played in Texas history. But I said, "You don't say?" When I played a stump, I played a stump.

"You wouldn't happen to be related, would you?"

"Not unless my ma was keeping secrets from me."

Les laughed and smacked his thigh. "That was a good one. But tell me. You haven't seen hide or hair of the missing parson, have you?"

I admired how he slipped that in as slick as you please. "No, sir, I sure haven't."

Dee was regarding my string with an interest that troubled me. "We were out to see the Tanners this morning. Nice people, Gertrude and her son."

The world was going to end. A Texas Ranger had told a lie. For me, it was another in an endless pack. "The nicest."

"How long have you worked for them?" Dee asked.

"Oh, about four years, I reckon." I needed to be shed of them, but I could not think of a good enough excuse to ride on.

"What did you think of the Butchers?"

"Sir?"

"Did they strike you as the kind to rustle cattle? We've been told they were as honest as the year is long, and that the mother, Hannah, kept a tight rein on her whole litter."

"What are you saying, sir? That you don't think they stole our cattle? Mrs. Tanner says they did and I believe her."

"Of course you do," Dee said. "You're loyal to the brand." He was as clever as his partner. "But did you or anyone you know ever actually *see* the Butchers steal cows?"

"I never did, no." I lifted my reins as a hint I was ready to move on. I might as well not have bothered.

"Nor did any other puncher we asked," Dee revealed. "Yet you would think someone had."

"Not if the Butchers did the stealing at night."

Les lost his smile. "I didn't just fall off the turnip wagon, Mr. Walker. Your outfit has hands ride night herd."

He had me there. I recovered with, "But we can't be everywhere at once. It's mighty easy to slip in and help yourself to some cows and slip out again."

"How many head were taken, altogether?"

"I can't rightly recollect."

"Where did the tracks lead?"

"You would have to ask Mrs. Tanner."

"Is there anything you *do* know?" Dee asked.

"Only that I need to get these strays back to the ranch and I'd be obliged if I could be on my way."

"Strays?" Les repeated. "Even the claybank with the saddle?"

"Yes, sir. That there is one rambunctious critter. Threw its rider and lit out to see the world."

"It doesn't look very rambunctious to me," Les said.

Dee inadvertently saved me by waving me on. "We've detained you long enough, Mr. Walker. Give our regards to your employer and her son."

"Will do." I touched my hat brim and smiled and rode at a walk in order not to arouse suspicion. But I couldn't shake the feeling I already had. I was tempted to look back but didn't until I had gone half a mile. They were riding west.

Lesson learned. I swung farther south to lessen the chance of running into someone else. The change of clothes would not fool someone who had seen me up close. Or had seen me on Brisco.

The day waned and a few stars blossomed. My stomach growled, but it could growl all it wanted.

Along about midnight I encountered a herd of LT cattle. They had bedded down over a wide area, and from a distance reminded me of nothing so much as squat tombstones. I immediately drew rein and listened.

On trail drives cowboys riding night herd often sang to the cows to keep them calm. These cows were on their home range, and there should not be any such need. But there still might be a night guard.

And there was.

I heard him humming, not singing. He was north of the herd and coming around it in my general direction. Quickly dismounting, I opened a saddlebag and took out the item I needed. Silence was called for. Holding it in my right hand and Brisco's reins and the lead rope in my left, I walked toward the rider.

I saw the night herder before he saw me. He had stopped humming. I waited until he was quite close and saw that his chin had drooped to his chest. I greeted him with "Are you awake or asleep?"

The cowboy gave a start and reined up. His hand swooped to a revolver, but he did not draw it. "Who's there?" he blurted.

"Jack," I said, doing my best to imitate Jack's voice. I started toward him, wishing the hat's brim was wider.

"Jack Walker?" the cowpoke said, taking his hand off his hardware. "Where in hell have you been? Mrs. Tanner came out to the cookhouse at supper and she was mighty upset that you boys weren't back yet. She sent Bart Seton and some others to the canyon to find you."

"Long story," I said.

"She was worried you might have met up with those Texas Rangers. I never met a nosier pair of gents in all my born days."

"It's their job to be nosy." I was not quite near enough. Another five or six steps should do it.

"Do you have a cold? You don't sound quite right."

"Same as always." I let go of the reins.

"Barker is riding herd with me. I can have him rustle up some coffee."

"No need," I said. By then I was next to his horse. I grabbed his leg, yanked it free of the stirrup, and heaved. He squawked as he went over, scrabbled madly for the saddle horn, and missed. He landed on his back and promptly rolled up onto the balls of his feet and clawed for his revolver, but by then I was around the horse and behind him, and had a short wooden handle in each hand. His hat had fallen off and I slipped the wire over his head and around his neck in one quick flick. He reached for the wire. They always reach for the wire instead of reaching for me, giving me the second I needed to plant both feet and pull on the handles with all my might.

The cowboy tried to stand up, but I kneed him in the spine. Gurgling and spitting, he continued to claw at the wire, which had dug a quarter inch into his flesh and was digging deeper. He would do better to grab for my wrists, which he presently did, but I was braced, my wrists and elbows locked, and all he could do was pluck frantically at my sleeves. It had no effect. Bit by bit I garroted the life from his body. When he was finally still, I slowly straightened. I was caked with sweat and breathing hard.

There was no sign of the other night herder. Usually they circled on opposite sides of the herd. I had a few minutes before he came around to this side.

Squatting, I went through the cowpoke's pockets. He had close to two hundred dollars on him. No wonder the LT hands were so devoted to Gertrude Tanner. She was paying them better than any other outfit in Texas.

I tried on his hat, which had a nice, wide brim, but it was too small. Throwing it aside, I lifted the body and draped it over his saddle. I used his own rope to tie him on, and gave the horse a swat on the rump. Off it went, bearing its grisly burden.

I put the garrote back in my saddle and palmed my boot knife. I climbed on Brisco and circled the herd, holding the knife next to my leg.

The other cowboy, Barker, was singing "Rock of Ages," of all things. He was more alert and jerked his pistol the moment he saw me.

"Who's that?"

I resorted to the same trick. "Jack."

He lowered the revolver but not all the way. "Where in hell have you been? Mrs. Tanner was fit to have kittens."

"So I've heard." I did not look at him but at the ground. Since there was no moon, the ruse should have worked. But suddenly he pointed his revolver at me again and I heard the click of the hammer.

"Hold it! You're not Jack!"

I smiled, and did not stop. "No, I'm the parson. Couldn't you tell? Peace be unto you, brother. Didn't I see you at Lloyd Tanner's funeral?"

Confusion rooted him for the few moments it took me to bring Brisco alongside his horse.

"Reverend Storm? I don't understand. Why did you just call yourself Jack and why are you wearing his hat and vest?"

"So I could do this," I said. Lunging, I thrust the knife into his belly, burying the blade to the hilt, while at the same instant I seized hold of his wrist and pushed the muzzle of his revolver into his belly. I didn't expect him to squeeze the trigger. It must have been a reflex. The revolver went off, the shot muffled some but not enough.

Barker stiffened. He stared at me in puzzlement, then slumped from the saddle, dead as dead could be. The knife slid free and warm blood splashed my hand.

Some of the cows had stood up but none ran off. They were fat and lazy, these LT cattle.

I gazed in the direction of the ranch buildings. They were miles away yet. I deemed it doubtful the sound would carry that far, but taking things for granted in my profession was an invite to an early grave.

I dismounted, wiped the knife clean on his pants, and slid it back into my boot. I tried on his hat. It fit, but it, too, had a short brim. I kept the one I had.

Sixty more dollars went into my saddlebags. I tied Barker onto his horse, swung the horse toward the ranch, and gave it a slap.

Two more accounted for, and a lot more to go.

Chapter 20

Most jobs I get in and get out fast. I have to, because once I start to earn my pay, tin stars butt in and do their best to stop me.

This job was different. I was not being paid. What I had in mind, I was doing on my own. It was strictly personal, and as such, I was free to take liberties I would not ordinarily take.

Killing the cowboys was not enough. I wanted Gertrude to know I was on the loose. I wanted her to know I was coming for her. She was formidable, but she was human and it was bound to affect her nerves.

With that in mind, I rode past the bunkhouse, past the cookhouse, and on past the stable. Several horses in the corral perked up, but none whinnied. I did not stop until I came to the main house.

All the lights were out, as well they would be at that hour. Sliding down, I tied the packhorse and the claybank to the rail. When Gerty saw them she would know I knew about the silver vein. She would send riders to the canyon. They would return with the news that her precious silver vein was buried under tons of rock and dirt. It should make her mad as hell.

I admit I was breaking every rule I live by. I had lasted as long as I had in my business because I never took needless risks. I always did my work in secret except for the ears I took as proof I had done the work. This time I would not bother with ears. I had no need to prove anything to anyone.

This was for me, and me alone.

I had saved my parson collar, and as a crowning touch, you might say, I took it from my saddlebags and wrapped it around the saddle horn of the horse I had just tied to the rail. The collar was in bad shape from my ordeal in the cabin, but there was no mistaking what it was—or who had worn it.

Stepping back, I smiled. That should do nicely. I regretted I would not be on hand to see Gertrude's reaction.

I forked leather. Not a lot of night was left and I had to find someplace to hole up before daylight. It did not take a lot of savvy to figure out that when Gertrude realized I was alive, she would have her cowboys scour the countryside.

I reined Brisco toward the Fair Sister. Unlike its sibling, the mountain was largely bare of vegetation. But it had foothills, and beyond, a similar maze of canyons, ravines, and gullies. Plenty of spots for a man to hide.

Dawn was breaking when I came to the far side of the mountain. A narrow canyon looked promising. The ground was solid rock, so my horses left few tracks. The walls were high and would shield me from the sun. The only drawback was that it was a box canyon. If I was discovered, the only way out was to shoot my way out. But I wouldn't mind that. I wouldn't mind that at all.

I hobbled Brisco and the mare, spread out my bedroll, and was asleep within minutes of my head touching my saddle. I slept wonderfully. I dreamed that I dropped Gertrude Tanner into a huge cauldron of bubbling water and watched as she was boiled alive. It was rare for me to dream so vividly. When I woke up, I lay there a while, remembering and relishing.

Twilight had fallen when I emerged from the canyon with the mare in tow. She was used to me by now and did not balk or otherwise give me trouble.

I roved north in search of another herd and found one within tobacco spitting distance. I reckoned on finding a cowboy or two, as well, but the cows were unattended.

I made for the ranch. I expected it to be a beehive. From a quarter of a mile out I watched and watched and saw no one. I moved closer and watched some more. Again, except for a few lit windows, nary a sign of life anywhere.

I took a gamble. As brazen as brass, I rode in. No one challenged me. There were no shouts or shots. I waltzed into the stable as if I owned the spread. Most of the stalls were empty. Evidently the hands were all off somewhere.

The tack room had what I needed: a saddle, saddle blanket, and bridle for the mare. I had just tugged on the cinch one last time and was turning to lead the two horses back out when hooves clattered. I hurriedly led Brisco and his sweetheart into adjoining stalls, then hid in another and drew my Remington.

The hoofbeats slowed. Spurs jingled, and into the stable strode a cowboy leading a lathered dun. He and his mount were caked with dust. They had come a far piece, and I had a hunch where from.

I did not show myself until he had stripped the dun and placed it in a stall. As he turned toward the double doors I came up behind him and jammed the Remington's barrel into his spine.

The cowboy froze. It was Chester, the rangy cowboy from the restaurant. "What's the meaning of this?" he asked without turning his head.

"Get rid of your iron."

He did.

"Where is everybody?"

"Most everyone is off with Mrs. Tanner. They rode out about ten this morning."

I believed him. I sidled around so he could see me. "Let me guess. She went to the Dark Sister to check on her silver."

"I'll be damned," the cowboy said. "You. Here of all places. Mister, you've got more sand than most ten hombres."

"When do you expect her back?"

He gave himself away by hesitating. "Anytime now."

I kicked him in the left knee and he crumpled in agony. He was smart enough not to cry out. "When did you say?"

"Sometime tomorrow," he hissed between clenched teeth. "She's staying the night in the canyon. Has the whole outfit digging like gophers to get to the vein."

"Why aren't you with them?"

"She sent me back to tell her son what you did."

"Phil is here?"

He stopped puffing and glared at me. "Tell me why, mister. Why did you kill Brennan and those others? And Barker and Steve? What did they ever do to you?"

"Were you at the Butcher cabin, Chester?"

"No."

I pistol-whipped him across the temples, not once but twice, and he slumped over, unconscious. Twirling the Remington into my holster, I took the rope from the saddle he had thrown over the stall. I fashioned a noose and threw it over a beam, then slipped the noose around his neck. Leading Brisco into the aisle, I looped the other end of the rope around the saddle horn, and waited.

Chester was not out long. Groaning, he blinked and slowly sat up, feeling groggily about his throat. "What the—?" he croaked.

"Don't try to take it off," I warned.

Fear restored his senses. He swallowed and looked at me. "This ain't right. Turn me over to the law and have me put on trial."

"It's no less right than slaughtering the Butchers," I remarked. "As for a trial, I'm your judge, jury, and executioner. The least you can do is take your medicine like a man." I smacked Brisco. For a few moments Brisco strained into the rope. Suddenly the cowboy was yanked off the ground and clean into the air.

Kicking wildly, Chester pried at the noose, then at the knot. But only for a few seconds. His left hand dropped to a belt knife I had overlooked. Unsheathing it, he slashed at the rope but missed.

I was growing careless. I ran to a nearby mound of straw and seized the long handle sticking up out of it.

Chester cut the rope. He was not that high, but he sprawled to his hands and knees. He had not noticed me. Rising on his knees, he frantically tugged at the noose. He never loosened it. I saw to that by spearing him in the chest with the pitchfork. He arched his back, grabbed the handle, and tried to wrench the tines out.

"That's for Daisy," I said.

Chester locked eyes with me, eyes wide with shock. I saw the spark of life fade, just as you see the light of a lamp fade as you turn it down. He only convulsed once, and that was that.

I left him there. I brought the mare from the stall, and as I passed the body, I noticed his hat. Black, with a wide brim and a low crown creased on the sides. I preferred a round crown, but I tried it on anyway. It was tight, but it fit. "Thanks," I said, and kicked its former owner in the teeth.

I walked the horses up to the main house rather than ride. No one was peering out. I went up the steps to the porch as quietly as a church mouse, and peeked in. The parlor was well lit, but I saw no one.

With my back to the door, I reached behind me and knocked. I had to do it three times before footfalls sounded in the hall.

"Who is it?"

I was in luck. It wasn't one of the servants. Slumping to disguise my height, I answered, "It's Chester, Mr. Tanner. I have a message for you from your mother."

Phil opened the door, grumbling, "It's about damn time. I can't stand sitting here twiddling my thumbs. What is the news?"

I drew the Remington as I faced him. "It's not good, I'm afraid. But you and your bitch of a mother have only yourselves to blame for double-crossing me."

"Stark!"

"One and the same. Are you going to stand there catching moths in your mouth or invite me in?"

Slowly backing up, Phil raised both hands. "I'm unarmed. You wouldn't shoot a defenseless man, would you?"

The stupid questions I get asked. I followed and closed the front door behind me. "Where are the servants?"

"Gone. They usually leave an hour before sunset."

"So it's just you and me?" I can't say how happy that made me. It must have shown.

"Now hold on. I don't like that look. It wasn't me who double-crossed you, it was Mom. Hell, man, I didn't know she had hired you."

Could it be? I wondered. I wagged the Remington. "Into the parlor." He obeyed, moving to the settee to sit. I leaned against the jamb. "Do you honestly expect me to believe your mother kept it a secret?"

"You've seen how she is. She's the one who runs things, not me. She even bossed Pa around."

He was good. This would take a little doing. "Why did she want the Butchers out of the way?"

"The silver, why else?"

"All she had to do was file a claim and it was hers. The Butchers didn't own the Dark Sister." All they had a legal right to was their homestead. Which made their slaughter that much more meaningless.

"There was a hitch," Phil said. "My mother didn't discover the vein. Someone else did."

"Who? One of your hands? Did some of your cows stray up into the canyon and a puncher spotted the silver?"

"No, it was Everett Butcher."

A hole in the quilt had been filled. I confess I was somewhat taken aback. "Did he file?"

"He was going to. He came into Whiskey Flats, into the saloon, smiling and treating everyone to drinks. He had a good deal to drink himself. Then he headed east and ran into my mother on her way into town." Phil paused. "Mother and him never did get along. He always thought we looked down our noses at his family, but that's not entirely true."

"Save your lies for someone who will be taken in by them."

"All right. Maybe Mother despised them. But I never had anything against the Butchers and neither did my father until the rustling started."

"Which your mother conveniently blamed on the Butchers," I observed. "But tell me more about your ma and Everett."

"Everett was drunk. He told her about the silver. Gloated how his family would soon have as much money as ours, and how they would build a fancy house and wear fancy clothes and show everyone the Tanners no longer ruled the roost."

"Your mother must have liked that."

"She was furious. She struck him with her whip. It made Everett mad, and he grabbed it. She ordered him to let go, but he laughed at her. So she did the only thing, in her estimation, she could. She pulled the derringer she keeps in a special pocket in her dress, and shot him."

I had no trouble imagining Gertrude Tanner doing it. Nor would anyone who knew her. "What did she do then?"

"Somehow she got him into the buggy and brought the body back to the ranch," Phil related. "She had Brennan and Wilson take Everett and bury him. Then she sat down with my father and me to decide what to do about the silver."

"Go on," I said when he stopped.

"Mother wanted it for herself, but she was afraid Everett might have told Hannah and the rest of his family about the vein. If he went missing, and Mother filed a claim, the Butchers would put two and two together."

"And figure out your mother had a part in his disappearance."

Phil nodded. "Exactly. So she came up with the idea of getting all the Butchers out of the way by accusing them of being rustlers."

"Only they never stole a single head."

Again he nodded. "But it gave Mother the perfect excuse to wipe them out. Then she could file safely. She never counted on Calista sending for the Texas Rangers."

There it was. The whole mess in a walnut shell. "How are you in the kitchen?" I asked.

"I beg your pardon?"

"I'm hungry enough to eat a buffalo. Lead the way."

Uncertainty lining his features, Phil Tanner rose and practically tiptoed past me into the hall. As I fell into step, he glanced over his shoulder. "Be honest. What do you intend to do with me?"

"It depends on how well you cook."

Chapter 21

Phil Tanner kindled the stove at my request. I was being polite as could be, and it puzzled him. But there was no need to rush. Thanks to his mother's greed, we had the place to ourselves.

While he got the stove going, I made a circuit of the kitchen. I took a butcher knife off a counter and placed it in a drawer. I also peered into the pantry. Then I sat in a chair with my back to a wall and my boots propped on the table. My spurs scraped the wood, but I didn't care. I had the Remington in my lap.

"There," Phil said, rising. He was nervous. He kept glancing at me as if he expected me to riddle him with lead. "What would you have me do now?"

"Bacon and eggs strike my fancy." I had seen both in the pantry. "Reckon you can handle that?"

"I don't do much of my own cooking, but yes, I think I can manage." He stepped to the pantry door.

"No tricks," I warned.

"No tricks," Phil repeated. He was not in there

long. When he came out, he had the bacon and a bowl of eggs. He walked stiffly to the counter and set them down. "How do you want your eggs?"

"I've always been partial to scrambled."

"How many?"

"Eight should do me. With six strips of bacon. Toast. And coffee."

He resented having to do it, but he set about preparing my meal with studied care. I sensed he was afraid to make a mistake. I did not tell him that killing, or the prospect of killing, sometimes made me hungry.

"I've heard of you, you know," he said as he laid the bacon strips in a pan. "You're downright famous."

I allowed as how there was some gossip about me in saloons and such, but I wouldn't go that far. "Wild Bill was famous. Billy the Kid was famous. Jesse James was famous. Compared to them I'm nobody."

"They say you've killed upwards of fifty people. Is that true?"

"Folks exaggerate." I set the Remington on the table with a loud *thunk* and he jumped and glanced around. "I'd like some soup, too. How about if you put on a big pot of water to boil."

"Soup with bacon and eggs?"

"I like to eat soup with every meal," I said, ladling it on.

The pot he selected was not nearly large enough.

"Bigger than that," I said. "The biggest damn pot in this whole damn kitchen."

After some clanging and clinking, he brought over the largest pot I had ever seen. "Will this do?"

"Nicely," I said.

When people are nervous, they talk a lot. He was no exception. "Don't take this wrong, but I'm surprised the law hasn't caught up with you yet."

"I'll share a secret," I responded. "The law in one state can't do much if you make it across the border into another state before they can catch you."

"But how about when you return to states where warrants have been issued for your arrest?"

"You sneak in and sneak out." I made a show of stretching. "So long as you're not wanted where you live, you're safe enough."

"But what if the other states find out where that is?" Phil brought up. "Can't they have you arrested and brought back?"

"Sometimes. It helps if you have a judge or two in your pocket." I considered it a necessary expense.

Phil had avoided the subject he really wanted to bring up for as long as he could. Now he coughed and said, "It was my mother who shot you, not me."

"I was there, remember?"

"All I'm saying is that she hired you and she shot you, so if you should be mad at anyone, it should be her."

Disgust welled up in me, but I tempered it with, "You love your mother that much, do you?"

"Tolerate her, is more like it." Phil began cracking eggs. "You've seen how she is. Could you love a woman like that?"

"She gave birth to you."

"So? From as far back as I can remember, she's treated me as if I can't pull up my britches without her help. She treated my father the same way. Now he's dead, thanks to her." Phil was building a head of steam. "She's never satisfied, that woman. We have a prosperous ranch, or it would be if she didn't spend money faster than we make it. Until the silver came along, we were lucky to break even most years."

"You don't live in a sod house," I reminded him.

"Sure, we live high on the hog, mainly because of her. She always has to have the best. The best clothes. The best furniture. The best buggy. None of that comes cheap. I haven't even mentioned her jewelry."

I had noticed that Gertrude was partial to necklaces and bracelets, some studded with diamonds.

"You make it sound as if I should love her just because she's my mother. But a parent has to earn love, just like everyone else, and my mother hasn't earned mine. To be perfectly frank, Mr. Stark, I loathe her. I loathe her with every fiber of my being."

Inwardly, I smiled. He had a flair, I'll grant him that. I was curious how far he would take it.

"She is to blame for you sitting there holding that revolver on me," Phil said while fluffing the yolks and whites. "If anyone deserves to die, it's her, not me."

"You think so, do you?"

Phil turned, his face alight with hope. "I *know* so. Which is why I want to make you an offer."

"How do you mean?" As if I could not guess.

"How would you like ten thousand dollars?"

"My fee is a thousand."

"But surely you wouldn't mind making ten times that amount? No one in their right mind would. All you have to do to earn it is kill my mother."

There. He had gotten it out. I pretended to ponder.

"No one need ever know. It would just be between you and me." Phil's enthusiasm was a wonder to behold. "I'll pay you half in advance and half when she is six feet under."

"I can't."

"Why not? What do you have to lose? You're planning to kill her anyway, aren't you? For what she did to the Butchers? Then why not get paid for doing it? It makes sense to me."

"You have that much money handy?"

Phil thought he had me. He showed more teeth than a politician giving a speech. "No, but I can get it in, say, a week to ten days. What do you say?"

"Ten thousand dollars is a lot of money," I admitted. "But with your mother dead, you'll have the ranch and the silver all to yourself."

That gave him pause. "So?"

"So you stand to be able to pay me a great deal more than ten thousand." I let him consider that a few moments. "Killing her would be the greatest favor anyone ever did for you. It should be worth a lot."

"How much?" Phil bleakly asked.

I pulled an amount out of thin air. "Fifty thousand would suit me. I could retire on that much." Which was true.

Phil appeared to have swallowed a cactus. He blinked and sputtered, "Fifty thousand it is, then. Under the same terms. Half in advance and the rest when my mother is in her coffin."

"Be sure you don't burn my meal," I said.

"What?" Phil turned back to the stove, and swore. He darted to a cupboard for a plate and filled it to overflowing with the eggs and sizzling strips of bacon. He brought them over, then scurried to fill a cup to the brim with hot coffee.

"Don't forget my toast."

"What about the soup?" Phil asked, nodding at the large pot. The water wasn't boiling yet.

"Let it heat up more," I said. I slid the Remington into my holster and motioned for him to sit across from me. He was being so reasonable, I couldn't see him trying to jump me.

As carefully as if he were sitting on broken glass, Phil eased down in the chair. "I must say, you are not at all how I expected."

"Is that so?" I said with my mouth crammed with eggs.

"My mother made it sound as if you were a coldhearted cutthroat who could never be trusted. But she was willing to spend money anyway to hire you. She would do anything to get her hands on that silver."

He had blundered and did not realize it. I swallowed and remarked, "So she talked it over with you before she hired me?"

Phil sat back. "Why, yes, I suppose she did, at that. Although she did not give me a say in whether we did. It was her decision and hers alone. Just as it was her decision and hers alone to shoot you in the back, giving you no chance to defend yourself. Despicable. Truly despicable."

"That she shot me in the back or that she didn't kill me?"

His laugh was more akin to a bark. "I'm glad she failed. Her mistake is my gain. If she had shot you in the head, we wouldn't be having this discussion."

I forked a piece of bacon into my mouth. It was thick with fat and dripping with juice, exactly how I liked it.

"May I ask you a question?" Phil ventured.

Absorbed in the bacon, I grunted.

"How will you do it? Kill her, I mean? Will it be quick and painless or will she suffer? Were it me, I would stake her out like the Comanches do and skin her alive."

"Your own mother?" I said. And to think, he had the gall to call *me* coldhearted! Talk about a kettle calling a pot black.

"What difference does that make? You've killed women, haven't you? Mother said you had. That's why she sought you out in particular. She said that only someone as ruthless as you were reputed to be could kill someone as nice as Hannah Butcher, or as sweet as her daughters, Sissy and Daisy."

Suddenly I lost my appetite. I considered jamming the fork into one of his eyes but stuck with my original notion.

"I could never murder anyone but my mother," Phil blathered on. "I hate her that much."

"I try to keep my personal feelings out of my work," I said. Although, since the attack on the cabin, that wasn't true.

"How much longer will you keep at it? Your work, I mean?"

"None of your business," I growled. I was tired of playacting, tired of toying with him like a cat toyed with a mouse.

Alarm furrowed Phil's features. "Why are you mad? Is it something I said? If so, I apologize."

"I don't know what gave you that idea." I stood and walked to the stove. The water in the pot was beginning to bubble. Another minute or two and it would be hot enough.

"Good. We should be friends, the two of us. We are partners, after all, in the sense that we are plotting a crime together."

I touched the pot handles. They were wood, not metal, and posed no problem.

Phil did not know when to shut up. "I wish I could see her face when you do it. Would you let me? I would be willing to pay extra for the privilege. A hundred dollars, just to see her face. No! Make it a thousand!" He laughed viciously. "Won't she be surprised? I daresay it will be the shock of her life."

"Death usually is," I said. The water was boiling nicely.

"What an exciting life you must live. Vastly more exciting than being a nursemaid to a bunch of cows."

"It has been kind of exciting around here of late," I mentioned as I lifted the pot a few inches.

"Hasn't it, though? It will almost be a shame to have everything back to normal. Maybe then those Texas Rangers will stop snooping around. They worry me. Do they worry you?"

I walked toward the table holding the pot in front of me. Some sloshed over the rim and nearly splashed my hand.

"What are you doing? I thought you wanted soup."

"I've changed my mind." I set the pot on the floor near his chair. Placing my hands on my hips, I bent down to give the impression I was peering into the water.

"What in the world are you doing?" Phil leaned toward the pot. "What do you see in there?"

"Boiled Tanner," I said. In a twinkling I had the Remington out and struck him over the head. He crumpled, but I caught him before he fell flat. He was dazed but not out. Sliding a leg under his chest to hold him steady, I shoved the Remington into my holster to free both hands. Then I moved behind him, let him slump to his knees, gripped both his wrists, and bent his arms as far back as they would go.

The pain revived him. "That hurts!" he shrieked. "What are you doing? We had an arrangement."

I started to force his face toward the pot.

"Wait! No! You can't!" Phil struggled, but I had a knee between his shoulder blades, and the leverage. "What about the money? Kill me and you won't get it!"

"You offered me a thousand to watch your mother die," I said. "I'm giving up a lot of money to see you do the same."

Phil bucked and twisted but could not break my grip. *"Why?"* he wailed. "In God's name, tell me why!"

I told the truth for once. "This is for Daisy."

His screams filled the kitchen. They filled the house. They went on for a long, long time.

Chapter 22

At three in the morning Whiskey Flats was a cemetery. Only a few windows glowed and they were in houses at the outskirts. The saloon, the stores, the livery, the restaurant had all long since closed.

I came in from the north, riding the mare and leading Brisco. I had switched back and forth to keep them fresh.

The hunted had become the hunter. I was searching for the Texas Rangers. They were a thorn that needed clipping. Worse, they were bound to try harder to find me once news of Phil Tanner's fate reached town.

I reached the main street through a narrow gap between the general store and the butcher's. The hitch rails were empty. Across the street was the restaurant. I could not go in the front. I crossed to an alley that brought me to the rear. Dismounting, I removed my spurs and crept to the back door. Calista did not keep it locked. I gingerly tried the latch, and pushed. The top hinge squeaked but not loud enough to wake anybody.

Her room was on the second floor, at the front.

I slunk up the stairs and down the hall. A few of the boards creaked, but again, not loud enough that it would startle her boarders into wakefulness.

Her door was bound to be bolted. I crouched and scratched at it with my fingernails. She had a cat named Butch who spent as many nights out romancing the town's female cats as he did snuggled in Calista's bed. I was hoping he was off with a feline lady friend.

Calista took forever to wake up. I heard rustling, and a yawn, and the scrape of her feet. "Butch?" she said softly.

The instant the bolt rasped, I straightened and put my shoulder to the door. I caught her off guard. She stumbled back and had to grab hold of the bedpost to stay on her feet.

"What in—" Calista blurted, and put a hand to her cheek in amazement. "You! Alive!"

"Pleased to see you again, too," I said, quietly closing the door, then throwing the bolt. I leaned back, my thumbs hooked in my gun belt. "Did you miss me?"

Calista was wearing a chemise as a nightshirt. A thin white chemise that was molded to the shape of her body and left nothing to be guessed at. I must have been staring because she wheeled and clutched a robe that had been thrown over a chair and hastily donned it. When she turned she had composed herself. "To say I'm surprised would not be entirely honest."

"Oh?"

"A lot of LT cowboys have died in the past few days. The Texas Rangers are of the opinion you are to blame."

"Parsons don't generally go around bucking folks out in gore."

"But you're not a preacher, are you? You never were. The Rangers think you might be a notorious assassin by the name of Lucius Stark."

"When did they come to that conclusion?" I was interested to know.

"Yesterday. They've had their suspicions. Something to do with a scar. They're mad as can be about the trick you played on them."

"What trick would that be?"

"You know very well. You pretended to be an LT puncher by the name of Jack Walker. Les was sure he should know you from somewhere, but he didn't catch on until later." Calista paused. "It's true, isn't it? You really hire yourself out to kill people?"

"I didn't come here to talk about me."

"Oh, God." Calista sat on the edge of the bed and bowed her head. "And to think I was fond of you."

"Was?" I said.

"You can't expect us to continue being friends." She made it sound like the most insane thing in all creation.

"I don't see why not," I responded. "I'm still the same man I was when I dressed as a parson."

"But you're *not* a parson, which is the whole point." In her exasperation, Calista balled her fists. "How could I have been so dumb?" She gestured sharply. "I want you to leave and never return."

I didn't move. "I'd be obliged if you would hear me out first."

"Nothing you say could possibly be of interest to me."

"Not even the fact that Gertrude Tanner hired me to exterminate the Butchers? Or that she was the one who murdered Everett?"

That pricked her. She was intrigued despite herself. "How do I know you're not making that up?"

"Someone had to hire me or I wouldn't be here. Someone who could afford my thousand-dollar fee."

"My word. You rate yourself highly, don't you?"

Her sarcasm stung. "I rate my skills highly. But I don't walk around with a mirror strapped to my chin, if that's what you're implying."

"Skills?" Calista repeated, and laughed me to scorn.

"Not everyone can core an apple at two hundred yards with a rifle, or twenty-five yards with a revolver. Not everyone can stick a knife in a bull's-eye nine times out of ten. Not everyone has the patience to lie as still as a log a whole night or day, waiting for a perfect shot." I confess I was stretching things. With a rifle I was good out to a hundred yards, with a revolver, maybe ten. I much preferred to use the scattergun or the garrote or the knife. "And not everyone can squeeze the trigger when a person is in their sights."

"My, my," Calista sniffed. "You recite all those accomplishments as if they are traits to be proud of."

"Do you want to hear about Gertrude or not?"

"If you insist. But your skills, as you call them,

do not inspire much confidence that you will tell the truth."

I was about to say I would never lie to her, but that would make me the world's biggest hypocrite.

"I'm waiting."

I gave her all of it, or nearly all, from the moment I arrived in Whiskey Flats until right then. I left out the part about my feelings for Daisy. I left out that it was me who shot Sissy. I also glossed over the gore. And I sure as hell left out how I had boiled Phil Tanner alive.

Calista did not say anything for a spell. When she finally did it was not to accuse me of lying, but rather, "You think you know someone, but you never do. Gerty has always been headstrong. Arrogant, even. But I never suspected she could stoop so low."

"Now you know."

Calista gave me a peculiar look. "Why did you come here tonight? Why put yourself in danger to see me?"

"Everyone in town is asleep. I'm not in that much danger."

"More than you realize. Those two Texas Rangers are in the room at the far end of the hall."

My skin crawled at the blunder I had made. Word was, Rangers slept with one eye open. Sure, it was an exaggeration, but no one ever took them by surprise. It was always the other way around. I put my ear to the door but did not hear anything.

"So why did you?" Calista was focused on me as if the answer meant a great deal to her.

"To ask for your help."

"You can't be serious."

"You're the only real friend I have here," I said. The only one left, anyway. "I was hoping I could rely on you."

Calista smiled a strange little smile. "I thank you for the compliment, but I do not, as a general rule, make it a habit to associate with hired killers."

"That was uncalled for." I was beginning to regret my decision.

"Fair enough." Calista leaned back. "Simply because you have me curious, what exactly is it you want me to do?"

"Help me take care of those two Texas Rangers." I realized I had worded it wrong when her eyes widened and she went as rigid as a board and came up off the bed as if I had pricked her backside with a needle.

"How dare you! What manner of man are you that you can possibly think I would help you kill someone?"

"Slow down," I said.

She stormed over to me and poked me in the chest. "Don't tell me what to do, Mr. Lucius Stark! I am not like you. I can never do what you do. For you to imagine I can is an insult!"

Her voice was rising. I had to say something quick or she would wake everyone. "I'm not asking you to help me kill them. I'm asking you to help me not kill them."

That stopped her. "I'm confused."

"If you will sit back down and listen instead of

chewing my head off, I'll explain." I gently took her by the shoulders and guided her to the bed. She did not resist although I swore she shuddered at my touch. Amazing how when you dress like a parson everyone adores you, but when you kill folks for a living, suddenly you're about as adorable as the plague.

"I'm listening. This should be interesting."

More sarcasm. I ignored it and pressed on. "I don't want to have to kill the two Rangers if I can help it. The Texas Rangers are a close-knit outfit. Harm one and the others won't rest until they hang you or treat you to lead."

"That's true," she conceded.

"Believe what you want of me," I said, and then mimicked her, "but I do not, as a general rule, make it a habit to kill lawmen. It brings more trouble down on my head than it's worth. I avoid tin stars as much as possible. I'd like to avoid these two Rangers, too, but now they'll be trying harder than ever to find me—" I had erred, and she caught on immediately.

"Wait a second. Why would that be?"

I wanted to kick myself.

"What have you done? Who have you murdered now?" Her hand rose to her throat. "Not Gertrude!"

"Not her," I responded, thinking to myself, *Not yet, anyway*. "Will you let me finish, or not?"

"Continue."

I sat on the edge of the bed. The smart thing to do was to stay by the door, but in my eagerness to convince her, I did not do the smart thing. "I need to take the two Rangers by surprise so I can disarm them."

"What then? Do you shoot them when they are defenseless?" Calista stopped and frowned, then said softly, "I'm sorry. That was uncalled for."

"I figure if I can disarm them, I'll take them to the south ten miles or so and leave them afoot, then come back, finish what I have to do, and be gone before they return." My original notion was to have her send word to them, inviting them to her restaurant.

Calista gazed deep into my eyes. I had the impression she was trying to peer into my soul. As if anyone ever could.

"Well? Will you help or not?"

"I need time to think about it."

"You have five minutes." I could have given her until daylight, but her insults had rankled me.

"I need more than that. You're asking me to break the law. I could be thrown behind bars."

"I would never put you at risk." I placed my hand on hers, but she would not permit the contact and slid hers onto her lap.

"Please don't. It's bad enough you betrayed my trust. Don't pretend you care when you don't."

I thought of Daisy. "You would be surprised how much I can care. Killers have feelings like everyone else."

Calista touched her fingertips to her forehead and said, "You say the darnedest things. I don't know what to make of you. I honestly and truly don't."

"I'm just a man, like any other."

"No, you are not. Most men would never do what you do. But let's not go into that again." Calista ran her hand through her hair. "What would you have me do?"

"It's simple. Go to their room. Knock, and when they answer, tell them that you heard a noise outside and looked out your window and saw me riding down the street."

"That's all?" she said when I did not go on.

I nodded. "They'll come rushing downstairs, half asleep and strapping on their revolvers. It will be easy for me to get the drop on them. I'll make them chuck their hardware and the three of us will ride out of town with no one the wiser."

"You won't shoot them?"

I stood up. "What must I do to convince you? Swear on a stack of Bibles?" As if that made any difference.

"I would rather you didn't. You have insulted the Lord enough for one life." Calista offered a tiny smile to show she meant no slight.

"I suppose I have, at that." I grinned.

Calista gnawed on her lower lip a bit. "You honestly and truly won't harm them in any way?"

"I told you. I don't want every Ranger in Texas after me."

"But if you strand them, how will they fend for themselves without horses?"

"They're Texas Rangers," I reminded her. "They're tough as rawhide. They can live off the land like Comanches. They'll be fine." She was on the verge of agreeing. I could see it in her face.

Suddenly there came a loud thump on the door.

"Lucius Stark! We know you are in there."

Calista gasped.

"This is Deeter Smith of the Texas Rangers. You are under arrest! Come out with your hands in the air, or by God, we will break in and shoot you to pieces."

"Damn!" I said.

No one had ever accused the Texas Rangers of making idle threats.

Chapter 23

I was trapped with no way out except the window and it was a two-story drop to the street. If I didn't sprain an ankle I could run down the alley to Brisco and the mare, but the Rangers were bound to give chase and catch me before I lit a shuck. I needed a brainstorm and I needed it quick.

It was the other Ranger who gave it to me. "Miss Modine? This is Leslie Adams. Are you all right? Has he harmed you?"

I drew my Remington. "I haven't yet, but if you break down that door, she's as good as dead." I winked at Calista, but she was not amused.

"What are you doing in there with her?"

I heard muffled sounds and a few cries from other rooms. The other boarders were waking up.

"Answer me!" Les commanded.

"I needed a place to lie low for a few days," I replied. "I figured I could scare her into letting me have a room. I didn't know you two were here."

"You are a mangy polecat," Les declared, "and I can't wait to attend your hanging."

Dee stuck to the business at hand. "Open the door and toss out your weapons or there will be hell to pay."

"Back off or I'll shoot the woman!" I grabbed Calista by the arm and hauled her over to the door. "Tell them I mean it," I said, placing the muzzle against her temple.

Calista glared, but she called out, "Ranger Smith? He has a gun to my head. He might mean what he says."

"Of course he means it, ma'am," Dee responded. "He's killed women and children at one time or another."

Recoiling, Calista whispered to me, *"Children?"*

I shook my head.

Les shouted, "Don't you worry, Miss Modine! We won't do anything that will cause you hurt."

"That's nice to hear!" I yelled. I had to keep them busy so they would not have time to think. "Have the other boarders stay in their rooms and keep quiet! Then you go into yours, close the door, and give a holler!"

"What then?"

"I walk out as sassy as you please," I answered, "with my pistol to the lovely lady's head and my finger on the trigger."

"You miserable bastard," Les said.

"I won't wait all night!" I told them. Enough commotion, and other townsfolk would wake up.

The Rangers did not respond. I heard them ordering boarders to go back to their rooms, and saying how everyone should calm down.

"Sorry about the ruckus," I said to Calista.

Our shoulders were brushing, and when she leaned toward me, her breath fanned my neck. "I'm sorry you're not who you presented yourself as. I liked you. Liked you a lot."

"Nothing has changed."

"That is the most ridiculous statement I have ever heard. Everything has changed, and you know it as well as I."

"I'm not the ogre people claim." Not in my own eyes, and those were the ones that counted.

"How can you be so blind? Don't you have any scruples? Any morals? Have you lived by the gun for so long that to you it seems normal?"

"Those Texas Rangers live by the gun and I don't hear you speaking ill of them," I remarked.

"You're comparing yourself to them? Lucius, you *break* the law, they *uphold* it. Surely even you can see the difference."

"They shoot people for a living. Oh, they wear badges so it's nice and legal, but they pull the trigger for money, the same as me. The only real difference is that they do it for the government and I do it for ordinary folks." If you could call Gertrude Tanner ordinary.

Calista gave me the saddest look. "You poor, deluded soul. You are worse off than I thought." She raised her hand to my cheek. "What would it take to have you come to your senses?"

"My senses are just fine," I snapped. And they

told me that the hall was silent now, save for the fading jingle of spurs.

"Stark!" Dee Smith yelled. "We're going into our room, as you wanted, and we'll keep the door closed!"

"Not so fast! Unbuckle your gun belts and leave them in the hallway." I would collect them on the way out.

"We can't do that," Les shouted.

"Quit stalling or I shoot the woman!" I wasn't fooled. They were bound to have spare revolvers in their saddlebags. But not spare gun belts, and I would take delight in dropping theirs into a horse trough on my way out of town.

A door slammed.

I released Calista, threw the bolt, and slowly opened her door a crack. At the other end of the hall were the two gun belts. "Stay close," I whispered. I eased the door open the rest of the way and stepped out. Hopefully, none of her boarders would try to be a hero.

I started toward the stairs, then realized she wasn't following me. I looked back. She was framed in the doorway, the portrait of sorrow.

I beckoned, but Calista didn't move. Instead, she said quite plainly and loudly, "I'm sorry, Lucius. I won't be a party to your dastardly deeds. I won't help you trick the Rangers. You are on your own, and may God help restore you to some semblance of a decent human being."

I should have seen it coming. I should have known she would do what she did next, namely, cup a hand to her mouth and bawl at the top of her lungs: "Rangers! I'm safe! Do with him as you please!"

Maybe I was stupid to trust Calista. Maybe it was silly of me to think she was different, to expect her to overlook my past deeds because she felt a spark of friendship. To some folks, and she was one, the straight and narrow might as well be the Eleventh Commandment.

At her yell, the door at the other end of the hall opened and Leslie Adams banged off two swift shots. The only thing that saved me was that just as he fired, I lunged toward the stairs. The slugs missed me by a whisker—and cored Calista in the act of swinging her door shut. The familiar *thwack thwack* of lead ripping through flesh jolted me as much as it jarred her. She looked down at herself in disbelief.

"What have I done?"

Calista folded at the knees. I ran to her and scooped her into my arms and kicked her door closed after us. Carefully setting her on the bed, I examined her, and felt sick inside.

"Lucius?" Tiny dark specks had appeared at the corners of her mouth. She clutched at thin air. "Lucius?"

I clasped her hand. "I'm here." Boots clomped in the hall, and more commotion erupted.

Calista swallowed, then said softly, "I'm sorry. That was wrong of me."

What the hell could I say?

"Please forgive me. I don't hate you. Truly, I

don't. I just don't understand you, is all—" Calista coughed, and the tiny specks became large drops.

"You shouldn't talk," I said. I almost added, *You damned stupid fool.*

"I'm dying, aren't I? Oh, God. I don't want to, Lucius. I want to live. How could this happen?"

She had brought it on herself, but again I held my tongue. A fist struck the door so hard, the entire door shook.

"Stark? Miss Modine? What's going on in there?" It was Leslie Adams, the man who had killed her.

Fury roiled up in me like lava in a volcano. Whirling, I fanned the Remington, smack at the center of the door. Part of me shrieked not to, that if I killed a Texas Ranger, I was as good as dead myself. But I didn't care. I banged off three shots and was rewarded with a thud and a groan.

"Les!" Deeter Smith cried.

"Haul him down the hall!" I shouted. "And stay away from this door or you'll get the same!" I began reloading.

Calista was unnaturally white and breathing shallow. "Lucius? What have you done now?"

"I killed the son of a bitch who shot you."

"Oh, Lucius. He didn't mean to."

I thrust the Remington into my holster, sat beside her, and held her hand in both of mine. "Is there anything I can do? Would you like some water?" A pitcher and a glass were on her nightstand.

"You'll have every Ranger in Texas after you. You know that, don't you?"

Here she was, her life fading, and she was more concerned about me. "All you had to do was help me disarm them."

"My principles wouldn't let me."

"Your principles have gotten you killed," I said more savagely than I intended, and instantly regretted it. I squeezed her hand. "Sorry. You did what you thought was right."

Footsteps drummed on the stairs. The boarders were fleeing. Someone commenced shouting out in the street, spreading the news of the shoot-out. Soon the whole town would be up in arms.

Calista heard them. "You should go."

"I'm in no hurry."

"They have you cornered. They will surround the building. You won't stand a chance."

"I like to pull the trigger, remember?"

A sigh escaped her. "Why must you be so cruel? You misunderstood. Those are my friends out there. People I have known for years. I don't want them harmed." Calista blinked, and a tear trickled down her cheek. "Promise me, Lucius. Promise me you won't lift a finger against them."

"I give you my word."

"Thank you." Calista smiled. She tried to lift her other hand but lacked the strength. "You see? There is hope for you. Change your life around before it's too late. Will you do that for me?"

"You ask an awful lot," I said.

"You're not bad clear through, Lucius. There is

a spark of good in you. You have proven that by staying with me."

I had another reason, but I kept it to myself. "Are you sure you don't want some water?"

"No, Lucius. But you are a dear." Calista closed her eyes. "I feel so tired. There's no pain, though. None whatsoever. Isn't that odd?"

"I'm glad there isn't." I tried to see out the window, but the angle was wrong. Someone was hollering for rifles to be passed out. Another man was arguing that they should rush me.

I barely heard Calista when she whispered, "I always figured to die in bed of old age. I never reckoned on anything like this."

"It's not always up to us." No one appreciated that fact more than me. "But I imagine that I won't die in bed, either."

Calista opened her eyes. "Will you do me another favor, Lucius? I hate to ask, but no one else is handy."

Now someone was shouting for a ladder to be brought so they could climb to the second-floor window.

"What sort of favor?"

"I have a sister in St. Louis. Get word to her for me. You'll find her address in the bundle of letters in the top drawer of my dresser. I never made out a will. I didn't see the need. But I want everything I own to go to her. My parents are dead and I don't have anyone else."

"I'll get word to her," I lied.

"You're sweet, Lucius Stark. You behave all

mean and gruff, but deep down you are a lamb. That is why I am confident you can change. Give up killing and find something worthwhile to do with your life."

The window suddenly shattered in a shower of glass. A rock had been thrown through it.

"Mr. Stark? Can you hear me in there? This is Tom Fielding. I own the general store. Miss Modine is a friend of mine. Is she all right? Is she alive?"

Before I could answer, the door shook to another blow. "Stark! My pard just died! You have one last chance to send Miss Modine out and give yourself up."

There I was, caught between the townsmen in the street and Texas Ranger Deeter Smith in the hall. I had been in some tight situations before but never one where the cards were so stacked against me.

"Lucius?" Calista breathed.

"I'm still here."

"I can't see you. Everything has gone black." The tip of her tongue traced her lips. "I'm scared, Lucius. Hold me, will you? Please."

Heedless of the blood on her robe, I hugged her. She was as cold as ice. It would not be long.

Something thumped against the front of the house below her window. I did not need to look out to know what it was.

Again the door shook, and Deeter Smith growled, "You have one minute. Then I'm coming in whether you send her out or not!"

Calista trembled, and uttered a tiny, "Oh!" She arched her body, let out a long breath, and was gone.

I rose and drew the Remington. The good citizens of Whiskey Flats thought they had a curly wolf trapped. They were about to learn that cornering a lobo did not come without a cost.

Chapter 24

I looped my left arm around Calista's waist and hoisted her body off the bed. She flopped like a limp sack and I steadied her as I moved to the door. "I'm coming out," I shouted to the Ranger. "I have the woman with me. If you or anyone else tries to stop me, she dies."

Silently counting to ten, I jerked the door open. I was careful to stand to one side, but no shots boomed.

Deeter Smith was halfway down the hall, backing away, his empty hands out from his sides. "I don't want the lady hurt. Don't start throwing lead."

I moved toward the stairs without waiting for him to reach the other end. It proved a mistake. I had taken only a couple of steps when Calista slumped forward and sagged like a puppet with its strings cut.

The Texas Ranger abruptly stopped. "What's wrong with her?"

"I had to slug her." I hoped he would accept the lie. Otherwise, things were bound to become mighty violent mighty quick.

Dee's eyes narrowed. "What's that on her robe and on your clothes?" He raised his voice. "Miss Modine? Can you hear me?"

"Can't you see she's out cold?" I said. The stairs were only twenty feet away. I walked faster.

"Unconscious, or dead." Smith had made up his mind which. "You miserable scum!" he barked, and stabbed for his Colt.

It was brave, but it was reckless. I already had the Remington in my hand. I fired before he cleared leather, not once but twice. He staggered against the wall and collapsed.

I was a fine one to brand him reckless. I had just added another Texas Ranger to my tally. From now on, the Rangers wouldn't rest until they stood over my grave and clapped one another on the back.

But that was a worry for another time. Right now I had to make it to the ground floor and out the back to the horses. I took another step, when up the stairs charged half a dozen townsmen, all armed. The foremost spotted me and let out an excited bellow.

"There he is!"

"Don't shoot! He has Calista with him!"

I pointed the Remington at them. "Back down the stairs! Pronto! Or you'll be burying your friend here before the day is out!" They started down and I took another step—and stumbled. I had tripped over the hem of Calista's robe. I caught myself and stayed on my feet, but Calista nearly slipped out of my grasp and her hair fell from her face.

"Look!" the townsman exclaimed. "There's blood on her clothes!"

"I don't think she's alive!" cried another.

"Kill him! Shoot the vermin!" urged a third.

Howling with outrage, they barreled up the stairs, firing as they came. I hurled Calista at them and snapped off two shots, then spun and ran to her room, slamming the door behind me. Slugs ripped into the wood as I angled toward the window.

They would take a few minutes to regroup. I swiftly reloaded, and as I was inserting the last cartridge, a face appeared at the pane. It was Tom Fielding, the owner of the general store. He opened his mouth to shout something, and I sent a slug through the center of it.

Seizing the chair, I whipped around and threw it. The glass exploded outward. The chair must have struck someone lower on the ladder because there was a shrill squawk.

I ran to the window. No one was on the ladder, but there had to be twenty or more incensed citizens clustered about Fielding and another man at the bottom. In the few seconds their attention was diverted, I reached down, wrapped my left hand around the top rung, and shoved.

The ladder crashed to earth among them, knocking several over. The confusion and panic that resulted gained me the moments I needed to hook my right leg over the sill, then my left, and lean out. I was two stories up, but there were plenty of cushions below. I pushed off and dropped.

"Look out!" a woman screeched.

I slammed into the back of a portly man in a nightshirt. It was like falling into a vat of dough.

My left knee hit bone and my leg spiked with pain, but otherwise I was unhurt and on my feet before those around me realized what had happened. I shot one man in the chest, another in the head, snatching the second man's revolver as he fell. Screams and shouts added to the bedlam as I plowed through them, scattering those not quick enough to move aside.

Packed so close together as they were, no one dared fire for fear of hitting someone else.

Then I was in the street and sprinting for my life, zigzagging as I ran. I had always been fleet of foot. Now it would be put to the test.

"There he goes!"

"Shoot him!"

Several tried. Slugs sizzled the air uncomfortably near and there was a tug at my sleeve. I made it to the boardwalk, and the saloon. The door was shut and no doubt locked, so I used the big window. Throwing my arms over my face, I crashed into it shoulder first.

My luck held. I wasn't cut. I raced for the rear, hoping there was a back way out. I had never been in the saloon before. It would not have been fitting when I was pretending to be a parson.

The howls of my pursuers spurred me into flying down a short hall. I came to a door. A flick of a bolt and the wrench of a latch and I was in the cool night air, just as the mob crashed in through the front.

I turned east and sped to the gap between the general store and the butcher's. Some of my pursuers burst out of the saloon and spotted me as I darted into it, but I doubted they guessed my intent.

I sped to the main street and was elated to find it temporarily empty.

The townspeople had fallen for my ruse. I had led them away from Calista's—and my horses. Most of them, anyway.

A figure filled the window of her bedroom, and a finger pointed. "There he is! He's right there! Get him, somebody!"

I shot the town crier in the throat and he staggered out of view. Somewhere, a rifle blasted, kicking up dust inches from my boot. But I made it to the alley. It was nearly pitch-black. Which explains why I collided with someone coming the other way. We were both running flat out, and the impact slammed both of us to the ground. I landed on my back, the breath knocked out of me, the few stars visible overhead swirling and dancing.

"You damned idiot!" the townsman bellowed.

I forced myself to sit up. The man was doing the same.

"Fowler, is that you? Why in hell don't you watch where you're going? I about busted a rib."

"I'm not Fowler," I said, and shot him. Heaving erect, I jumped over the deceased.

Two men were standing guard over Brisco and the mare. They had heard the shot and were almost to the alley when I hurtled into the open. Both had rifles, but neither had his leveled.

Stupidity always costs us. In their case it was

lead to the head, and then I was in the saddle and galloping south with the mare in tow.

Bedlam ruled Whiskey Flats. Lanterns and lamps were blazing all over the place, and despite the shots and screams, most of the women and a few kids had ventured outdoors and were milling about.

I was in for it now. I had shot the living hell out of that town. They would send for more Rangers. A lot more Rangers. Or they might even contact the governor and ask for the army to be sent. Either way, I was running short on time. I had to finish up and get out of there. Once I was across the state line I would be safe.

Or would I? The Rangers might not let a little thing like a boundary keep them from coming after me. Or someone in government might think to hire the Pinkertons and sic them on me. The last thing I wanted was those bloodhounds on my trail.

It could be that in shooting two Texas Rangers, I had shot myself in the foot. The state of Texas might go so far as to post a bounty on my head, and if the bounty was large enough, I'd have every peckerwood bounty seeker from here to Hades and back again after my hide.

Evidently the townsfolk had had their fill of me. No one gave chase. I rode for a while, then reined east toward the distant Fair Sister and the LT.

I tried not to think of Calista, but she crept into my thoughts anyway. I never meant to get her killed. Using her to snare the Rangers had seemed like a good idea. How was I to know it would flare up in my face? I consoled myself that her highfalutin airs were more to blame than I was. Her and her morals! I was good enough for her to associate with when she thought I was a parson. I never had understood an attitude like that. But then, I didn't judge people.

Some would say that it was wrong for me not to share their scruples. In their eyes I *must* be evil. But who gave them the right to decide what a person could and couldn't do? What made them good and me bad other than their belief I had to be wrong because I did not think like them?

Folks claimed I did not have a conscience, but that was not true. The guilt of killing my father always bore down on me like the weight of the world on that Atlas gent I heard about when I was small. It was one killing I truly regretted, along with that of my wife. The rest were just business. Some men farmed for a living, some were lawyers, some owned stores and saloons or whatnot. Me, I killed people. It was my profession, to get fancy about it.

I was good at killing and I liked doing it, and I would as soon go on doing it until I was too old and puny to shoot straight. But the rest of the world would have it otherwise. They would not let me be. To them I was a rabid dog that must be destroyed at any and all costs.

It was hardly fair.

I sighed in frustration. You would think that after twelve years I would be used to the finger-pointing and the name-calling, but it never did sit well with me that I was considered a lowly coyote because I sheared sheep.

A sound intruded on my thoughts, and I glanced

over my shoulder. Whiskey Flats was a nest of fireflies in the distance. I discovered I had drifted toward the road to the LT and was paralleling it. The sound I'd heard had been hoofbeats.

A pair of cowboys were heading for the ranch.

A slap of my legs, and I moved to cut them off. I reached the road and drew rein in the middle. I did not palm my Remington or shuck my Winchester. Another minute and they came to a stop.

"You're blocking the road, friend," a young puncher said, pointing out the obvious. He had a moon face and looked to be all of eighteen.

"Do we know you?" asked his companion, the slab of muscle who had been at the restaurant with Chester. Jim, his name was.

In the dark they did not recognize me. I smiled and said, "Where's the fire, boys?"

"Back in town," the young one said excitedly. "Lucius Stark gunned down a couple of Texas Rangers and a woman."

"And seven others, besides," Jim said.

"Did you see it?" I asked.

"I wish," the young one declared. "We were with Matty Blaylock, the dove from the saloon. She let us have pokes for five dollars."

"We heard the ruckus," Jim related, "but by the time we got our clothes on and down the steps, Stark had lit a shuck."

"It sure was a sight to behold!" the young one marveled. "Bodies and puddles of blood everywhere. People crying and cursing."

"We saw them carry the dead Rangers from the

boardinghouse," Jim said. "Can you imagine? Stark killed two at the same time. That's hardly ever done."

"I wouldn't want to be in his boots when the rest of the Rangers find out," the younger puncher commented.

"We're on our way to tell our boss," Jim said. "She'll be mighty interested in the news."

I shifted so my right hand was on my hip. "Would you give her a message for me?"

"For you?" the young one repeated.

"If it's not too much of a bother," I said. "You're going that way anyway."

They glanced at each other and Jim said, "What are you talking about, mister? Who the blazes are—" He stopped and flung an arm out. "Damn me for a fool! Ike! It's him!"

"Him who?"

"Lucius Stark!"

Ike gulped and straightened. "What do we do?"

Jim had his hand poised above his Colt. "If we draw at the same time, he can't get us both."

"All I want is for you to deliver a message. But if you're that anxious to die, then slap leather and to hell with you."

"What's this message you keep talking about?" Jim asked suspiciously.

"Tell your boss I am coming for her. No more hide-and-seek. I am going to ride right up to her front door and blow her brains out." The truth was, I had something a lot slower and a lot more painful in mind.

"You have your nerve!" Ike spat. "Let's gun him, Jim. Here and now."

Jim was studying me as if I had dropped from the sky. "No, Ike. We'll do as he wants. Let him come. Because you and me and the rest of the boys will be there to welcome him with more lead than he can chew on in a month of Sundays." He used his spurs.

His young pard reluctantly followed suit, glaring at me as they went past.

I had thrown down the gauntlet. It would end, one way or another, before dawn. The odds were not favorable, but I had been bucking the tiger for longer than I cared to recollect. The only difference was that this time I was sticking my head in the tiger's mouth for me.

Chapter 25

Given a choice between her cows and herself, I was confident Gertrude Tanner would choose her own hide over her cattle. So I was not the least surprised to find another herd unattended by cowboys. She had called all her hands in to deal with me.

Given a choice between riding in alone or having help, I chose the help. So what if they had four legs and were some of the dumbest brutes in creation. That might seem harsh, but cows spend their days chomping grass into their bodies at one end and oozing it out the other end. It didn't call for a lot of brains.

I approached the herd, circling so I was behind them, then let out with a whoop and a holler and waved my arms. My best guess was that there were about five hundred head, a lot of cows for one man to handle if I was on a cow trail headed for Dodge or Abilene. But all I needed to do was point them in the right direction and give them cause to panic, which cows were fond of doing anyway.

It helped that the cattle were accustomed to being herded. A few strayed off, but for the most part they stayed close together as I drifted them eastward. A pink flush blazed the sky with the promise of a new day. Another fifty or sixty head appeared and I reined over and gathered them up.

I would never make a good cowboy. Spending my days watching a bunch of cows graze and rest is not my notion of excitement. A cow chewing its cud is about as boring as any animal can get.

I didn't like how cows smelled, either. They made it worse by constantly doing their business, one or the other, and the stink was enough to make you gag.

Come to think of it, cows were a lot like people, only they did not put on airs. More important, many had horns and weighed as much as horses and, when spooked, could be fearsome.

I had seen the aftermath of a stampede once. It was up in Montana. I came on an outfit out on the range the morning after a thunderstorm agitated their cattle to a feverish pitch of raw fear, and a bolt of lightning unleashed that fear in a flood of hooves, horns, and destruction. The cattle crashed right through the camp, smashing the chuck wagon to kindling, scattering the cavvy and trampling the cavvy man and five others into the ground. I saw the cavvy man, or what was left of him, a pulpy scarlet lump with shattered bones jutting like white spines. His head was so much goo with an eyeball in the middle. Only one. The other was missing.

Yes, sir. When it came to a stampede, the best a man could do was hunt cover and pray.

A mile from the ranch I had several hundred head. A tingle ran through me at what I was about to do. I could be as devious as Gertrude Tanner any day.

The sun was above the horizon when I drew the Remington. I aimed at the sky and triggered three shots while screeching like a berserk Comanche.

I once heard from an old buffalo hunter that buffalo can go from standing still to a dead run in the blink of an eye. Now I got to see cows do the same. The ones at the rear bolted, pushing against those in front of them, and they, in turn, pushed against the cows in front of them. It was like dominoes. Three shots, and my improvised army swept toward the buildings like Lee charging the north at Gettysburg.

It was a glorious feeling. I laughed and fired another shot. The pounding of thousands of hooves, the rumble of the ground, the lowing of the cattle, created a thunderous din. A cloud of thick dust rose in their wake, screening me as I reloaded.

Presently shouts broke out, and sporadic shots. Gertrude's hands were trying to turn the herd. I imagined them stumbling from the bunkhouse, not quite awake and tugging into their clothes, to behold the horde bearing down on them.

I hoped Gerty was watching, maybe from an upstairs window, her heart in her throat. If she had a heart, that was. More than likely she had a block of ice. Ice certainly flowed through her veins. She was, without a doubt, the most ruthless person I had ever met, male or female, and that was saying a lot.

I looked up, and drew rein. The cows had slowed and were breaking to the right and left. I glimpsed the stable and the corral. A puncher was on the top rail, whooping and waving his hat. Cows passed under his boots, so close he could touch them with his toe if he wanted. Suddenly there was a loud crack and the fence began to sway. The press of cattle proved to be more than the rails could bear. With a splintering crash, the corral fell apart and the cowpoke on the top rail was pitched into their midst.

His screams were horrible.

I looped wide to reach the main house. The cattle should keep the cowboys busy long enough for me to pay my respects to Gertrude. I had never wanted to kill anyone as much as I hankered to kill her. It was all I could think of: her cowering before me, me shooting her in the knee, then the elbow, then the shoulder. That was for starters. Before I was through she would suffer as few ever suffered since the days of Noah and his ark.

The cloud of dust that hid me from the cowboys also hid the cowboys and the buildings from me. I thought I spied the cookhouse. I did see a shed splinter and split apart. Then the dust ahead partially cleared, and the main house loomed before me.

The cattle were being funneled between the house and corral. The north side was clear. As I brought Brisco to a halt, a revolver cracked. My hand leaped up of its own accord, my Remington replied, and a cowhand slumped over the sill of a window, his smoking revolver falling from fingers gone limp.

Springing down, I ran to the window, shoved him to the floor, and hooked a leg over and in. My spurs were still on, but no one would hear them jangle over the clamor outside.

The inner door was ajar. A glance showed the hallway was empty. I was debating which way to go when a yell from upstairs decided for me. My back to the wall, I sidled to the stairs.

The whole house seemed to be shaking. Beams creaked overhead. A door slammed, but where, I couldn't say. I went up two steps at a stride and stopped short of the landing. More shouts drew me to a front bedroom. It had two windows. They were open, and crouched next to each was a cowboy. Not just any cowboys but my acquaintances from the ride out, Jim and Ike.

The racket made by the cattle was fading. From over by the bunkhouse came a holler. "Any sign of him?"

Jim cupped a hand to his mouth. "No! Not yet!" He leaned out the window and looked to the right and left. "Where in hell can he be?"

"I wouldn't do that, were I you," Ike said. "You're a mighty tempting target."

Jim drew back in and swore. "Why doesn't he show himself?"

Ike endeared himself to me by saying, "Stark's not dumb. What did you expect? That he'd waltz right into our gun sights?"

By then I was only a few feet behind them. I cleared my throat and said, "Only a greenhorn would do that."

They spun, or began to, turning to stone when they saw the Remington. Ike looked as if he were about to lay an egg. Jim had more savvy and was not flustered, which made him the more dangerous of the pair.

"Set your revolvers down and slide them toward me," I directed. Ike obeyed, but Jim balked. I trained the Remington on him. "If you want to die I'll oblige you." He didn't. He placed his Colt on the floor and pushed.

"When Bart Seton and you meet up, you're dead."

I paid his bluster no heed. "Pay attention. I'll only ask this once. Where is Gertrude?"

"We don't know," Jim sneered.

I shot him. Not in the head or the chest but in the calf. Blood spurted, and he howled and clasped the wound and rolled about while gritting his teeth and puffing like a steam engine.

"I'll ask once more. Where is your boss?"

"Go to hell!"

I thumbed back at the hammer and said, "The

next one is through the ear. One last time. Where is she?"

Jim had grit, I'll give him that. "I'll never betray her, you murdering bastard!" he snarled.

"Suit yourself."

Ike chose that moment to spring. I have only myself to blame for being caught off-guard. I did not keep one eye on him as I should have, and I did not see the knife until he lanced it at me. I skipped backward, but he nicked me, damn him, in the right wrist. Not deep and not painfully, but a warm sensation told me he had drawn blood. I twisted and squeezed the trigger, but he twisted, too, at the exact instant I fired. The slug seared his side but did not drop him. Suddenly he was on me, swinging wildly, and I found myself battling for my life.

I backpedaled and pointed the Remington. Steel rang on steel as the knife blade deflected the barrel. My shot went into the ceiling instead of into him. Then he had my wrist in a grip of iron and I had his in the same. Locked together, we strained like two bucks with their antlers locked. I was bigger, but he was solid sinew and was desperate to hold on to me.

Out of the corner of my eye I glimpsed Jim gamely crawling toward his revolver and leaving a crimson smear on the floor.

Other cowboys might show up at any moment. I hooked a boot at Ike's knee, but he sidestepped. I pivoted and tried to toss him over my hip, but he dug in his boot heels and would not be thrown. He was tougher than he looked. But he was a man, a young man, at that, and he lacked my experience. I feinted to the right and swung left, but I could not unbalance him. I feinted to the left and swung right, but again he defied me. Then I feinted right, and went right, jerking him completely off his feet. The next moment he was on his back and I was on top of him with my knee on his chest, slowly forcing the knife toward his throat.

Ike cried out and was able to stop the knife from descending.

Meanwhile, Jim had dragged himself almost to the Colt. He extended his arm but he was a hand's width short. Levering an elbow, he inched forward. He smiled grimly as he wrapped his fingers around the grips and swung toward me. He had a clear shot and he did not hesitate.

I was counting on that. His finger tightened on the trigger, and I threw myself onto my side, hauling Ike up after me so that he was on top just as the Colt went off. They were astounded, the both of them. Jim, that he had shot Ike. Ike, that he had been shot. The slug caught him in the jaw and blew off a portion of his face.

Warm blood spattered my neck as I heaved and kicked with both legs. My boots slammed into Ike's chest and catapulted him toward the window. Rolling, I aimed at Jim as he aimed at me. I fired first. This time I shot him smack between the eyes. I swiveled. Ike was rising, his shirt drenched wetly scarlet, fire in his eyes, as with a desperate leap he sought to bury his blade in my body. My slug smashed into him in midair. He was dead when he hit the ground.

Winded, I rose and replaced the spent cartridges. I was surprised no one had come to help them. The house should be crawling with cowboys.

I heard voices outside and sprang to the window, careful not to show myself. The stampede had made a shambles of the sheds and the outhouse.

I did not know how many were left. Out there somewhere was Bart Seton, and it was him I wanted the most. I had a hunch about him, and if it bore out, he deserved to suffer as much if not more than Gertrude.

Unexpectedly, a cowboy broke from the stable, running toward the house. He did not notice me. I doubt he heard the shot that spun him around and pitched him into eternity.

I waited but no more appeared.

Something wasn't right. I had a vague sense of unease. It spurred me into heading for the stairs. Extreme caution was called for, and I made no more sound than a mouse. A quick glance at my wrist showed that Ike's knife had barely broken the skin and the bleeding had stopped.

The house was ominously still. I was on the third step when I realized what was bothering me. Not once had I heard Gertrude, or Bart Seton, bark commands, or say anything else. They were conspicuous by their silence.

I had a hunch why. I bounded down the stairs and down the hall to the front door. Throwing it wide, I darted onto the porch. No shots greeted me. No shouts, either. I crouched behind a post and waited, but nothing happened.

"Damn her," I said aloud.

I sprinted around the house to Brisco and the mare. Since I had not run into anyone coming from the ranch on my way there, I had three directions to choose from. I figured Gertrude and her companions went east, past the Fair Sister. A week's ride or so would bring them to Clementsville. It had a town marshal, and she could ask for his protection. She could also send for the Texas Rangers or even a federal marshal. One mention of my name and they would come running.

I gigged Brisco to the rear of the house. Much to my delight I found fresh tracks. I could not tell exactly how many were with Gertrude, but it was plain she was not alone. No doubt Bart Seton was always at her side. Plus however many cowhands were left. The sign showed they had ridden out at a gallop. Which suited me fine. Their horses would soon tire. By switching from Brisco to the mare and back again, I was confident I could overtake them well before nightfall.

I couldn't wait. Gertrude and Seton had a lot to answer for, and I was just the hombre to see that they did. No one had ever gotten the better of me, and I would be boiled in tar if they would be the first.

I reminded myself not to be cocky and was about to spur Brisco when I realized I was forgetting something. I dismounted and left the horses there and walked back to the front of the house.

A haze of dust hung in the morning air, the tiny motes sparkling like pinpoints of gold.

I could spare half an hour. For Daisy's sake, as well as the rest of her family's, I should do this right. Word would spread and be a powerful lesson to anyone who hired me in the future.

Never rile a Regulator.

Chapter 26

Three lanterns in the bunkhouse were more than I needed. I splashed the kerosene from all three over the bunks and the walls, then scooped hot coals from the stove and dropped them onto a bunk I had liberally sprinkled. Smoke immediately curled toward the rafters.

The cookhouse was my next stop. I soaked an apron with kerosene and placed it on one of the long tables. I added the curtains and a wooden spoon and pieces of a chair I smashed against a wall. As the flames grew I backed out, then headed for the stable. There I found only one lantern hanging on a peg. I upended it over the hay in the hayloft and soon had flames licking at the rafters.

I walked to the main house and stood on the porch and admired my handiwork. The bunkhouse was fully ablaze, the cookhouse was cooking nicely, and thick gray coils rose from the stable.

One more, and I would be done. I turned to go inside and happened to glance in the direction of Whiskey Flats. "What the hell?" I blurted.

A quarter of a mile away were five riders approaching at a gallop. Unless I was badly mistaken, they couldn't be cowboys. The punchers were either dead or with Gertrude. Then who? I wondered as I moved to the side of the house and drew the Remington. Hopefully, they had not spotted me.

They came straight to the house and reined up in a flurry of dust. As I had guessed, they were townsmen, and they were armed.

A stocky man in a bowler dismounted and stared aghast at the burning buildings. "My God! Will you look at that! We're too late."

"Check in the house, Howard," an older man with stooped shoulders urged. "See if she's in there."

Howard complied. I heard him clomp about, upstairs and down, and in a few minutes he reappeared, breathing heavily. "I found two men, both dead. Jim Unger and Ike Fraykes."

"Damn. But no sign of Gertrude?"

Howard shook his head. "We might as well head back to town, Bill. We can't be of any help here."

I was glad I had left Brisco and the mare behind the house rather than in front. In a few minutes the townsmen would be gone and I could get on with destroying the ranch.

"Where is everyone else?" a third townsman wondered.

"Surely he can't have killed them all," said a fourth.

Howard had lifted a foot to a stirrup, but paused. "Maybe we should look around for more bodies.

We came all this way. We might as well do something."

The older man, Bill, was staring at the house with his brow knit. Suddenly he exclaimed, "Son of a bitch!" and drew a Merwin & Bray pocket pistol from under his jacket.

Alarmed, the others produced revolvers. Howard lowered his foot and clumsily unlimbered what looked to be a Smith & Wesson. "What's wrong? What did you see?"

"The house isn't burning."

"No, it's sure not." Howard glanced at the house and then at Bill. "What difference does that make?"

Bill glanced toward the corner and I ducked back. I heard him say, "Don't you get it? Any of you? He wouldn't burn the other buildings and not burn the house, too. Do you know what this means?"

Howard was not the sharp razor of the bunch. "No, I can't say as I do. Suppose you tell us."

"It means he's still here."

I was fit to be tied. Why did they have to butt their noses in when I was almost done? The easy thing to do was get on Brisco and light out after Gertrude, but the man called Bill was right; I couldn't burn down the rest and not burn down the house, too. The house contained everything Gertrude held dear.

There were five of them, but they were townsmen, so I should have an edge. I stepped into the open with my Remington leveled.

"There he is!" Howard squawked.

I fired and had the satisfaction of seeing my target deflate like a punctured water skin and fall from his saddle. I would have shot the man next to him, but Bill cut loose with that Merwin & Bray, three swift shots that struck the corner near my head and seared my cheek with flying slivers. For a townsman, old Bill was uncommonly slick.

I ducked back again. I was angry at them for sticking their noses in and I was angry at me because I refused to leave. I had done more than enough killing the past few days, and honestly and truly had no hankering to add these Good Samaritans. They should have stayed in town where they belonged.

A horse whinnied. Shoes scraped the porch.

I risked a glance and saw the man I had shot sprawled on his belly, dead. There was no sign of the other four. I took it that they had sought cover in the house, but then Howard showed himself at the far end of the porch and snapped a shot. I jerked back and it missed.

From inside the house came Bill's voice. "Mr. Stark? Can you hear me out there?"

There was no sense in not answering. They knew where I was. "No, I can't hear you," I hollered, and chuckled at my little joke.

"Give yourself up, Mr. Stark, and I give my word that we will take you back to town unharmed."

"That's awful kind of you," I said in disgust.

"It's in your own best interests. We've sent for the Texas Rangers and they're likely to shoot you down on sight. At least if you go with us, you get to live until the trial is over."

"It will be a week or more before the Rangers can get here," I said. By then I would be well shed of Texas, and good riddance.

"You're mistaken, Mr. Stark. Those two you killed, Deeter Smith and Leslie Adams, were part of a company scouring the mountains north of here for renegades. The rest of the company will be here by tomorrow afternoon at the latest."

Unwelcome news. A company of Rangers once held off hundreds of Comanches. If they caught up to me, I didn't stand a chance in hell.

"We came to tell Gertrude," Bill had gone on. "We never expected to find you here. But since you are, you might as well be smart and give up. We'll treat you decent. I give you my word."

"You have it backwards," I said. "You're the one who should be smart and take your friends and go. I won't shoot. I promise."

"Even if we trusted you, which we don't, we can't just up and ride off. I would never be able to live with myself."

"Be sensible," I said, knowing full well that sensible people were as rare as hen's teeth.

"That's strange, coming from you. How sensible was it for you to shoot up our town and kill all those poor souls? How sensible is it for you to do what you do for a living? You can no more claim to be sensible than you can claim to be kind."

He had a point. One person's sensible is another's folly. But I was not there to bandy words. I raised my voice. "Listen! All of you! Think of your loved ones. Your families and friends. Your wives and kids. Think of the tears they will shed if you don't come home."

"You are a mangy cur," Bill declared.

I tried a different tactic. "The chore of tracking me down and ending my days belongs to the Rangers, not to you."

"I beg to differ, Mr. Stark. Those were our friends you murdered. Calista Modine was as decent a woman as ever drew breath. You have too much to answer for, for us to turn our backs."

"I did not kill Calista," I said quietly to myself. They would not believe me if I told them the truth.

"Mr. Stark?" Bill said. "No man is invincible. Eventually we all meet our Maker. You might think we will be easy to take, but we won't. I was a lawman once, years ago, in Ellsworth."

That explained his ability with a six-shooter.

"What will it be, Mr. Stark?"

I was becoming angry. While we stood there sparring, the wicked witch of west Texas was making good her escape. I had to get this over with quickly.

"I've met men like you before, Mr. Stark," Bill said. "Men who felt they were above the law. Or, rather, a law unto themselves. But none of us have the right to decide who lives and who dies. We're none of us God, Mr. Stark, although, Lord knows, a lot of us behave like we are. In the end we always

have to answer for our deeds. You have the choice
of how you answer for yours. You can either go
out in a blaze of smoke and blood, or you can
submit to a trial and take what comes."

It occurred to me that he was talking too much.
Almost as if he was doing it on purpose to distract
me. I glanced over my shoulder, but no one was at
the far corner of the house. I glanced up at the
windows above me—and my gut churned like a
pond in a tempest. One of the townsmen was lean-
ing out a second floor window, taking deliberate
aim. I threw myself to the ground at the selfsame
instant that his revolver boomed. Pain exploded in
my left shoulder. I landed on my side and snapped
an answering shot that added a hole where his eyebrows met his nose.

Curse me for my stupidity! I had fallen for one
of the simplest ruses of the law trade. I was hit and
I was bleeding. I had to find out how bad, but I
could not do it there. Rising, I watched the windows as I ran toward the back of the house. No
one else appeared. They were playing it cagey.
Bill's doing, I bet.

I had made enough blunders for one day. I
stopped and peered past the corner before ventur-
ing around it. Cold rage seized me. Brisco and the
mare were gone. While Bill had blathered, Howard
or the other townsman had snuck around and led
my animals off.

This could not be happening. I was being out-
thought and outfought by a pack of amateurs. Until
that moment I had not taken them seriously. I did

now. *What would they expect me to do?* I asked myself. Either charge after my horses or barge into the house through the back door.

I did neither.

Never taking my eyes off the windows, I ran twenty-five yards to the outhouse. It had been destroyed in the stampede and lay in scattered sections. The door was largely intact, lying flat in the grass. I hopped over it, turned, lifted it with my good arm, and stretched out underneath on my left side. My shoulder throbbed, but I grit my teeth and bore it. The pain reminded me not to make another mistake.

Near the top of the door was a small opening in the shape of a crescent moon. I peeked through. No sign of any of them yet. Grunting, I shifted and pried at my shirt. The slug had drilled me under my collarbone, sparing the bone and going clean through. I had been lucky. But it was bleeding and would weaken me if the bleeding did not stop.

The pain I could take. I had always prided myself on being able to handle pain that would have other men weep and whine.

Suddenly I felt dizzy and sick. I closed my eyes and waited for the spell to pass. I hoped to God I wouldn't pass out. It would be just my luck for them to find me when I was as helpless as a baby. It would embarrass me to be taken like that. I always imagined that when my time came I would go down in a hail of lead. To be taken unconscious and under an outhouse door—no, that would not do at all.

I opened my eyes and looked through the crescent moon.

Howard and another townsman were slinking along the rear wall. They came to the back door and Howard warily opened it. The other townsman watched the corner and the windows. They thought I had gone inside. Neither had bothered to glance toward the outhouse.

Ordinarily, this would be like snatching a pie from a four-year-old, but my clipped wing was stiffening. In a little while it might be next to useless. Torment washed over me as I pressed my left hand to the door to brace it, and slid partway out from under.

Howard entered the house. I centered the Remington on the other man's back, between his shoulder blades. At my shot he stumbled, his arms flung out to keep from falling. He started to turn and I shot him again, in the back of the head.

Howard reappeared. He stared at his friend, then gazed wildly about, swinging his revolver from side to side.

I watched him through the crescent moon. He did not stay there long, but spun and ran inside. I slid out from under the door, made it to my feet, and jogged to the far corner. I was hurting bad when I got there. It was all I could do to focus.

Howard must have heard me. He poked his head out the back door. I shot him through the ear. He tottered a step and collapsed, one leg against the door, keeping it from closing.

Now it was Bill and me. I was in no condition

to have our battle of wits drag out. But how to end it quickly without getting myself killed?

Another bout of dizziness brought bitter bile to my throat. I swallowed it and started toward the front of the house, only to have the world spin like a child's top. I sank down with my back to the wall and sat catching my breath. The nausea was awful. I considered crawling away and hiding, but I was too weak. I managed to draw my boot knife and switch it to my left hand, holding it so it was concealed under my wrist. Thinking of the wicked witch, I bowed my head.

The ratchet of a hammer being thumbed back jarred me. I looked up into the muzzle of the Merwin & Bray. A boot pinned my Remington to the ground.

"You should have surrendered to me," Bill said. Bending, he snatched the Remington. I did not resist. "How bad is it?"

"Bad," I croaked.

"Can you stand?"

"Not on my own."

Bill hunkered. He trained the Merwin & Bray on my face while parting my shirt to examine the wound for himself.

I had one chance and one chance only. I thrust my knife into the base of his throat and sheared the blade upward. The last sound I heard was the Merwin & Bray going off.

Chapter 27

I slowly came to. I was cold and stiff, but I was alive. Above me stars sparkled. I went to sit up and felt a weight on my legs. It was Bill, lifeless, his eyes wide and his mouth agape. My blade was still embedded in his throat. I rolled him off and painfully pushed to my knees.

I had lost most of the day. By now Gertrude Tanner was miles away. Disgusted with myself, I slid my knife out of Bill's throat, wiped the blade on Bill's shirt, and replaced it in my boot. Reclaiming the Remington, I walked unsteadily to the front of the house. I half feared the townsmen had given Brisco and the mare slaps on their rumps and sent them galloping off, but thankfully, both horses were tied to the hitch rail.

As much as I hankered to go after Gertrude, I had my shoulder to think of. I heated water on the stove, cut a sheet into strips, and did the best I could bandaging myself. The bleeding had stopped, and I could move my left arm a little without causing too much pain.

I needed food and rest. I toyed with the notion of staying the night, but the company of Texas Rangers were due the next day. I put a pot of coffee on and helped myself to eight eggs and six strips of bacon from the pantry.

The meal invigorated me. I had energy to spare as I busied myself filling a sack with food and tying the sack to my saddle, then splashing kerosene in every room of the house and setting the house on fire.

By the grandfather clock in the parlor it was pushing ten o'clock when I strode outside and swung onto the mare. Leading Brisco, I at long last headed east. Once beyond the Dark Sister I threaded through darkling hills and on across a broad windswept plain.

I was bound for Clementsville. Closer by three days was a small settlement called Three Legs, named after an old-timer who had lost a knee to a Comanche arrow and had to use a cane ever after. Three Legs amounted to no more than a gob of spit, but it had a saloon, and Gertrude was bound to stop there if she continued east as I believed she would. There was always the possibility she would turn to the southeast instead. Eventually, that would take her to places like San Antonio or Austin, or maybe even all the way to the Gulf, and Corpus Christi or Galveston. Due south about a hundred and sixty miles was the border with Mexico. But to reach it, she'd have to pass through some of the most inhospitable country anywhere, filled with hostiles and outlaws. Due north lay the border with New Mexico. It was a lot closer, but the mountains there were infested by Apaches, and only a fool baited Apaches in their lair.

Gertrude, for all her faults, was no fool.

So east it had to be, and east I traveled, switching horses every two hours. Now and again I would rise in the stirrups and hope to spot a distant campfire, but morning came and I had not caught up. I was tired, but I pressed on.

Hate will do that. I had never really hated anyone before, not like I hated Gerty. My hate was a red-hot flame burning deep inside of me, and the only thing that could quench the flame was her lifeblood.

At noon I happened on the charred embers of a fire made the night before. I found where five mounts had been picketed, and footprints. I had figured there were more left than that, but maybe some had had enough and lit a shuck.

Evening came, and my eyelids were leaden. I turned in early to get an early start and slept the sleep of the exhausted. A couple of cups of coffee, a few pieces of jerky, and I was ready to resume the hunt.

The plain was not completely flat. Here and there were grassy knolls. I had passed a score without incident when a bright gleam atop a knoll up ahead galvanized me into action. I was riding Brisco. With a jab of my spurs I broke into gallop. Simultaneously came the crack of a rifle. Forgetting about my shoulder, I swung onto the off side, hanging by one leg and the crook of my elbow. My wound shrieked with pain and I nearly lost my hold, but somehow I clung on and made for the shooter.

A cowboy rose in plain sight, a Winchester wedged to his shoulder. He tried to fix a bead, but there was not enough of me showing. He shifted, and I would swear he was aiming at Brisco's head. In the hope he would not shoot my horse if I was not on it, I let go and tumbled. My bad shoulder bore the brunt. Agony spiked through me. My temples pounding, I rolled onto my belly and drew the Remington.

The cowboy had seen me drop and gone to ground. I began to crawl in a half circle toward the knoll. I figured he would stay put since he commanded the high ground, but in a short while I saw the grass sway off to my left. The blades parted, framing the pockmarked, weather-beaten face of my would-be killer. He was staring toward where I had dropped from Brisco, not where I was. I took aim but let him crawl a few yards closer before I squeezed the trigger.

The cowboy was still alive but would not be for long. He glared up at me and groped for his rifle. I kicked it out of his reach.

"Where are the others?"

"Go to hell." Blood dribbled over his lower lip and down his chin. His hand was pressed to the neck wound, but it would only buy him a few extra minutes of life.

I had no sympathy for him. "You should have stuck to punching cows."

"Wanted the money," he gurgled. "Extra thousand dollars."

Gertrude was getting desperate, I reflected. "I'm surprised she didn't have Bart Seton wait for me instead of you. He's her hired killer."

The cowboy snorted, and scarlet drops sprayed from his nose. "He's more than that, mister. A lot more."

Gertrude and Seton? Why not? So what if her husband had been dead only a month or so.

He coughed and was racked by a spasm that ended with him as white as snow and dripping sweat. "Finish me," he said. "As a courtesy."

"You don't deserve it."

"She'll beat you yet," the cowboy predicted out of spite. "She'll hire an army of leather slappers and put an end to you once and for all."

"Is that her plan?" Simple, but it could prove effective. Provided she lived long enough to carry it out.

"Do me a favor. I have a brother and a sister back in Ohio. Get word to them, will you? If I give you their names and where they live?"

If I had not done it for Calista, I certainly wasn't going to do it for him. "No."

"You miserable bastard." He clawed at my leg, but he was too weak to do me any harm. "Everything they say about you is true."

I was tired of his bluster, so I went after my horses. Brisco had not gone far. He was well trained. The mare took a while to collect. The cowboy's horse was behind the knoll, but I had no interest in it. When I returned, the cowboy was gulping air like a fish. "Was the promise of a thousand dollars worth your life?"

"I want . . . I want . . ." But he did not get to finish. The life was snuffed from his eyes by the cold wind of death.

I did not bury him. There had been enough delays. I pushed on until well past nightfall in an effort to make up for lost time. A cold camp sufficed. I was asleep within minutes but tossed and turned, and when I awoke an hour before daybreak, I felt as if I had not slept at all.

I wanted to overtake them before they reached Three Legs, but it was not meant to be. It was night when I got there. Only two horses were at the hitch rail in front of the saloon and neither had been ridden hard. I paused at the batwings to let my eyes adjust. In addition to a grubby barkeep, two men were playing cards. Farmers, judging by how they were dressed. The country north of Three Legs was overrun with nesters, or so I had been told. I set my rifle down and stood with my back to the bar so I could watch the door and the window. "Whiskey."

"Whiskey it is, friend." The bartender slid a bottle and a glass over. He looked me up and down. "Is that blood on your clothes? You look like you've been through hell and back."

My first impulse was to tell him to mind his own business, but I needed information. "A woman and some cowboys came through Three Legs sometime today. Did you see them?"

His eyes flicked toward the rear and then fixed on me. "Can't say as I did, no. But then, I haven't been out much."

"They might have come in here." He should remember if they had.

"Women generally stay shy of saloons unless they're doves," the bartender said. "Is the lady you're after a dove?"

The idea of Gertrude Tanner in a tight red dress cozying up to half-drunk men who hadn't bathed in a month of Sundays made me grin. "Not by a long shot." I nodded at the card players. "Are they locals?"

"Frank and Cliff? Sure are. They're in here nearly every night, but they don't usually stay this late."

I ambled to the table. The two farmers did not look up, they were so engrossed in their game. They sat rather stiffly in their chairs. "Either of you see anything of a fancy woman and some cowboys?"

"Can't say as I have, no," said the burliest. "But I've been out to my place all day. Usually I'm home by now."

"I'm home by now, too," the other farmer said. "Or my wife pins my ears back with a fork."

"That must hurt." My joke brought no response, so I shrugged and went to an empty table in the corner and sank into a chair. I put the bottle and glass in front of me. I was tired. I needed rest, the horses needed rest. Part of me was for pushing on, but the logical part was for resting until dawn and starting out fresh. I emptied the glass in one gulp

and poured more red-eye. As I was raising the glass
to my lips I noticed that the bartender and the two
farmers were watching me out of the corners of
their eyes. All three quickly looked away.

What the hell? I saw how the farmers were still
sitting much too stiffly. I saw the bartender take a
tray of dirty glasses and start toward the back, then
abruptly stop and place it on the bar and turn to
the bottles on a shelf and begin moving them
around in no certain order.

My instincts kicked in. The hints were there. I
should have caught on sooner. I slowly sipped the
rotgut and felt the liquid burn its way down my
throat and warm the pit of my stomach. Gazing
over the glass, I noticed that a door at the back
was open a few inches. A room or hall beyond was
as black as the pit.

My skin prickled. I lowered the glass and leaned
back. I figured there was only one, but then hoofs
thudded and a saddle creaked and in through the
batwings came a lean cowboy caked in dust. He
never so much as glanced my way but went to the bar
and in a loud voice asked for some coffin varnish.

I casually lowered my right hand to my lap and
held the glass in my left. I was wondering how they
would go about it when the cowboy made a show
of gazing about the room. Plastering a smile on his
thin face, he came toward my table.

"Howdy, mister. Up for a card game?"

Nodding at the farmers, I said, "There's already
one under way. You might ask to sit in with
those gents."

The cowboy broke stride and pretended to see

them for the first time. "Oh. I suppose I could. Or you and me could have our own game." He stepped to a different table and beckoned. "What do you say? Have a seat." He indicated a chair across from him.

If I did as he wanted I would have my back to the door at the rear. Shaking my head, I pushed with my boot against the chair across from me at my own table. "Right here will do."

The cowboy would not last an hour as an assassin. His face gave him away. Reluctantly coming over, he put his glass down. "Fine by me," he said.

"Don't we need cards?" I brought up.

He slid his right hand under his brown vest. "As it so happens, I have a new deck."

My own hand was on the Remington, but he did not unlimber a hideout. He did indeed place a deck on the table.

"Are you a cardsharp?" I asked mildly.

His laugh was brittle. "Where did you get a notion like that? I'm a cowpoke, not a gambler."

"Do you always carry a deck of cards around with you?"

"I got it from the barkeep." The cowboy began to shuffle, unaware of the mistake he had made.

I slid the Remington from my holster but did not raise it above the table. "When would that be?"

He froze and his forehead furrowed. "When what?"

"When did you get the cards from him? I saw

you come in and all he gave you was whiskey." I snapped the fingers of my left hand. "I know. He gave them to you earlier when you were in here with Gertrude and Bart Seton. Is that Bart in the back or a friend of yours?"

Sweat seemed to ooze from all his pores at once. "Mister, I don't know what in hell you're talking about."

"How much is she paying you? The last one was offered a thousand dollars. Not that he lived to collect."

"You make no kind of sense," the cowboy said.

I rested the Remington on the table, but I did not point it at him yet. "I don't suppose she's still in Three Legs, is she?"

"She who?" the cowboy said, glaring now.

"You better give a holler to your friend in the back," I suggested. "Who knows? Maybe he'll put windows in my skull before I put them in yours."

Panic made him reckless. He flung the cards at me and heaved up out of his chair, bawling, "Now, Clancy, now!"

I shot him in the head before he could clear leather. Shifting, I beheld another cowboy burst from the back. He had his Colt out, and fired. His shot went wide. Mine didn't.

The bartender and the farmers imitated statues until I rose, breaking the spell. Then one of the farmers exclaimed, "Thank God that's over! Mister, I want you to know we have no part in this. They made us stay so you wouldn't get suspicious that things weren't as they should be."

The other farmer nodded. "They told us they would pistol-whip us if we didn't do as they wanted."

"Frank and Cliff are telling you the truth," the bartender confirmed. "Those two cowboys were with that woman you were asking about. She and a gun shark she called Bart lit out of here not twenty minutes before you showed up."

I smiled at the news.

The hour of reckoning was at hand.

Chapter 28

So much for resting.

I rode Brisco and led the mare. The stars overhead, the yips of coyotes, the strong night wind, I barely noticed any of it. All I could think of was Gertrude Tanner and what I wanted to do to her.

The bartender had overheard the fancy woman, as I had described her, talking to the gun shark. Something about her knowing powerful people in high places, and how they should head for Austin, the state capital. Not Clementsville, as I had thought. So I took the road to the southeast, flying like the wind.

I was close to tasting my cup of revenge. I could feel it. They would stop soon, if they had not stopped already. Their mounts had to be more tired than mine. They only had one each while I had the two. Keeping the mare had paid off.

Neither the bartender nor the farmers had any idea who I was. All they gathered from what little Gertrude told them was that I was after her and must be stopped, and they would cooperate, or else.

An interesting tidbit: One of the farmers, Frank, heard the gun shark refer to the fancy woman as his "sugar." Frank said the woman did not like it and snapped at the gun shark to keep quiet.

Fury coursed through every fiber of my being. Fury so strong, so potent, I felt hot all over, inside and out, as if I were being cooked alive. Many a time in my life I had been angry or mad, but I had never experienced anything like this.

I gloried in it. I reveled in the raw vitality that pulsed in my veins. I felt as powerful as a steam engine. My fatigue evaporated. I no longer craved sleep or food for my empty belly.

An hour became two and the two hours became three, yet I saw no sign of my quarry. They might ride all night. But that was fine. I would do the same, and with two horses, I could cover the same ground much more swiftly. I was sure that by daylight the long chase would be over.

Along about midnight I reined up to switch mounts yet again. I tugged on the lead rope and Brisco came obediently up next to the mare. Without dismounting, I switched from the mare to Brisco, careful not to use my left arm more than I had to. I then switched the lead rope to the mare and was ready to go. But as I raised Brisco's reins, I spied a tiny point of flickering light perhaps a mile off across the prairie.

My breath caught in my throat. It was a campfire. It could belong to anyone, but I knew whose it was.

"They're mine!" I cried, and pricked Brisco with my spurs.

The next half a mile was a blur. I looked neither right nor left but only at the point of light, which grew slowly but steadily bigger. I came to my senses when I realized they would hear me if I went any closer on horseback. I used picket pins to ensure Brisco and the mare would not wander off.

The Winchester in the crook of my left arm so I was free to draw the Remington with my right if I had to, I crept through the tall grass. My senses were more alert than I ever remembered them being. I could not account for it and did not try.

I slowed to a turtle's pace. A stand of cotton-woods hove out of the night. The pair were camped close to the trees but not in them, which was strange given the trees offered better cover.

A black hat and vest and an ivory-handled Smith & Wesson left no doubt as to the identity of the figure seated by the fire. Nearby, a second form was curled under a blanket.

Bart Seton was having trouble staying awake. Twice he closed his eyes and his chin dipped, but each time he snapped his head up and shook it to break free. He was facing the northwest, the direction I had come from.

I circled around behind them. Their horses were too exhausted to do more than flick their ears. I fixed a bead on the center of Seton's back, but I did not shoot. He must not die quickly or easily. He must suffer, and suffer gloriously.

I glanced at the form under the blanket. It was up over Gertrude's head, probably so the firelight did not keep her awake.

If it is possible to drool with anticipation at killing someone, I did. In this instance, two someones.

Bart Seton placed his rifle on the ground and reached for the coffeepot. I waited until his fingers closed on the handle. He never heard me. So much for his reputation. I touched the Winchester's muzzle to the nape of his neck and said quietly, "So much as twitch and you're dead."

Some men would have jumped up anyway, or gone for their revolver. All Seton did was tense slightly. "Well, well, if it isn't the famous Lucius Stark. Looks like you've caught me with my britches down."

"It wasn't hard," I bragged. In fact, it had been too damn easy. Nor did I like how calm he was.

"So what's it to be?" Seton taunted. "A slug in the head?"

"You wish." I glanced at Gertrude, but she had not stirred. "Shed your revolver and hold your arms out from your sides."

"I don't believe I will."

I came within a whisker of blowing out his wick then and there. "You'll do it or I'll shoot you in the knee." That should cause enough agony to last a good long while.

Bart Seton swiveled his head to look at me with what I could describe only as contempt. "How you have lasted so long is beyond me. Did you think we would just roll over and die?"

With abrupt clarity I saw it all: that he was calm for a reason, that the bulges under the blanket were not those of a person, and that I was the world's worst jackass. I whirled, but I was not quite around when thunder boomed and leaden lightning struck me high in my left arm. The Winchester fell and so did I, to my knees. I did not draw my Remington. Not when I was staring up into the shadowy barrel of another Winchester in the hands of Gertrude Tanner.

"Finish the buzzard off!" Bart Seton urged her.

Gertrude stepped fully into the light, her harpy features aglow with wicked delight. People say I am vicious, but she was every bit as unregenerate, which made it doubly unsettling, her being female and all. Baring her teeth like a she-wolf that had caught a bobcat sniffing about her den, she paid me the supreme insult. "I didn't think it would be this easy."

Between the old wound under my collarbone and the new wound in my arm, my left side was worthless. The arm was half numb. I suspected the bone had been shattered. I flexed my fingers, or tried to, and nearly passed out.

"Why you let him spook you is beyond me." Bart Seton was beside her. Stooping, he relieved me of the Remington. "All the damn running we did, and for what? I could have taken him anytime."

"Don't use that tone with me," Gertrude said. "He's not to be taken lightly."

"Sure, sugar, sure." Sneering at me, Seton hefted my revolver. "You'll forgive me if I'm not impressed."

I was unprepared for the blow. He slammed the

barrel against my temple and the world faded to black. How long I was out I couldn't say, but I came to with water falling on my face. Sputtering, I struggled to sit up and managed to rise onto my right elbow.

"That's enough," Gertrude said.

Turning the canteen, Bart Seton scowled and said, "You keep spoiling my fun, sugar. I don't like it when you do that."

"How many times have I told you not to call me your damned sugar?" Gertrude snapped without taking her eyes off me. "Keep it up and I will be inclined to dispense with your services." She sidestepped to her saddle and perched on it with one leg bent at the knee on the pommel. "I trust you understand, Mr. Stark, why I do not end your life as quickly as my hired shootist wants."

I understood, all right. She was so much like me it was spooky. I shifted slightly so I was closer to the fire and slumped as if I was about to collapse. "What will it be? Stake me out on an ant hill?"

Gertrude chortled. "Don't be ridiculous. I'm not an Apache. I wouldn't know where to find one."

"Let me dish out what he's got coming," Bart Seton said. "I promise you, before I'm done he'll beg us to put him out of his misery."

"And deprive me of the pleasure of doing it personally?" Gertrude shook her head. "I should say not. Just because I am a woman does not mean I am squeamish."

The fire was uncomfortably hot. I shifted again,

even closer, so that the unlit end of a burning log was almost at my fingertips.

"I will enjoy this immensely," Gertrude smirked. "You have caused me no end of setbacks. With you out of the way, I am free to lay claim to the silver and live in luxury the rest of my life."

I had to goad her, so I said, "You can start by rebuilding your house. Or isn't that good enough? Maybe you want a mansion."

"Why must I rebuild?"

"Oh. That's right. You haven't heard." It was my turn to smirk at her. "I burned your house down along with the rest of the LT. The stable, the bunkhouse, there isn't a building left."

Gertrude surged to her feet. "For your sake I hope you are just trying to make me mad. My house contains everything I hold dear. Heirlooms from my mother and my grandmother. Gifts from my sister. Things I've had since I was a child. Things I can never replace."

"That's too bad. They're all ashes."

Her eyes flashed and she jerked the rifle to her shoulder, then just as quickly lowered it again. "No. I see what you are doing. You want to goad me into getting it over with. But it won't work. I want you to suffer before you die."

It was not working. I had to come up with something else. "Like your son suffered? You should have heard him scream and blubber."

Gertrude took a step toward me. "Have a care, Stark."

"Or what?" I had pricked her. "You'll kill me?

I'm dead anyway." I deliberately laughed. "You should have seen Phil when I pried one of his eyeballs out of its socket. He bawled like a baby."

That did it. Livid with rage, Gertrude advanced, raising the rifle to bash the stock against my skull. "You bastard! You miserable, rotten bastard!"

I gripped the log. As she reared above me, I levered onto my knees and thrust the flaming end in her face. I went for her eyes. She shrieked and frantically backed away, colliding with Bart Seton as he sprang to help her. Locked together, they tripped over their own legs, and fell.

I was in motion before they hit the ground. Vaulting over the fire, I plunged into the tall grass. My left side flared with torment, but I clenched my teeth and bore it. Breaking into a run, I made for Brisco and the mare. In my saddlebags was my short-barreled revolver and other tools of my trade. I might yet prevail.

Boots pounded the ground. I glanced back to find Bart Seton in swift pursuit. I ran faster, my body protesting with more spikes of pain and a fierce hammering in my temples. I had a twenty-yard lead. To him I had to be no more than an inky silhouette in the dark, yet he snapped off a shot that sizzled the air next to my ear. At least part of his reputation was deserved, after all. He would not miss a second time.

I pretended to be shot. Suddenly flinging myself down, I thrashed about, all the while hoping and praying he would not finish me off with a shot to the brain. Nothing happened, and after a minute I stopped and lay still, curled into a ball, my right hand on my right boot. Still shamming, I looked up.

Bart Seton had his Colt trained on my head and the hammer thumbed back. He wanted to squeeze the trigger. He wanted to badly. But he growled, "On your feet! I should bed you down permanent, but she would have a fit."

"Give me a moment," I gasped.

"Like hell." He kicked me in the back.

I winced and nodded. "All right. All right." Propping my right hand under me, I pushed myself up and sat with my head between my knees, sucking air deep into my lungs. "It hurts," I said.

Bart Seton laughed. "You'll hurt a lot worse before we're done."

I attempted to stand, then sank back. "I can't," I protested. "My legs won't hold me."

"You damn well better get up or you can crawl the whole way," Seton snarled, coming closer.

"I might have to," I said, and turned as if about to lower myself onto my belly. Instead, I lunged and slashed. The blade caught him right where I wanted it to, at the back of his knee, biting deep. He yelped as his right leg gave out from under him. The Colt went off, but he missed and before he could cock it I sliced him across the hand, opening his knuckles and nearly severing two of his fingers. He couldn't hold on to the Colt if he wanted to.

Cursing, Seton threw himself at me, but I rolled

aside and rose. I cut his left leg at the same spot I had cut his right, then skipped back, unfurling.

Bart Seton was nearly beside himself. He tried to stand and fell, tried to stand again and fell. Dumfounded, he glanced at his legs, then at me. "What have you done?" he bleated.

"Your hamstrings," I said.

Shock set in. Seton slid his hands under his chest and got to his knees. The instant he straightened, I was on him. My first stroke opened his right elbow to the bone. He instinctively clutched at the wound with his left hand and I opened the left elbow the same way.

Seton reached for me, but his forearms were useless. A howl tore from his throat as he realized what I had done. He couldn't stand. He couldn't walk. He couldn't hold a revolver. He was totally and completely helpless, totally and completely at my mercy. "God, no!" he breathed.

"You'll find out soon enough if there is one," I said, and turned my back on him.

"Where are you going?"

As if he had to ask.

"You can't leave me like this."

"You're not going anywhere." He would keep. I hurried, afraid Gertrude would ride off before I got there, but to my surprise she was huddled by the fire, cradling her face in her hands and rocking back and forth. She heard me and stiffened.

"Bart? Is that you?"

I saw her face, and stopped.

"Did you get him? Answer me, damn you! It's

my eyes! He burned them! I can hardly see! Everything is a blur. Take a look and tell me how bad they are."

I stepped up to her and bent and touched the cheek under her right eye and then the cheek under her left eye. "They're bad," I said.

"You!" Gertrude recoiled and groped for the Winchester, but I beat her to it. She stopped after a bit and glanced wildly about. "Where are you? What did you do to Bart?"

"He'll join us shortly."

I had to hand it to her. She was beat, and she had to have some notion of what was in store, but she squared her shoulders and said with no hint of fear, "All this because I double-crossed you and shot you in the back."

"No," I said.

"Why, then?"

"All this because of what you let him do to Daisy."

Gertrude absorbed that. "You were fond of that little tramp?" Then she did the worst thing she could have done: she laughed.

They were two days dying.

On the third day I added their horses to my string and gigged Brisco to the southeast. I was heading for Galveston. From there I could take a ship to anywhere in the world. South America, maybe. I would hide out down there for a year or so and then come back. By then the Texas Rangers were bound to have lost interest.

Cows can fly, too.